I0595329

Mrs. S. C. Hall

Midsummer Eve

A Fairy Tale of Loving and Being Loved

Mrs. S. C. Hall

Midsummer Eve
A Fairy Tale of Loving and Being Loved

ISBN/EAN: 9783337082109

Printed in Europe, USA, Canada, Australia, Japan

Cover: Foto ©Andreas Hilbeck / pixelio.de

More available books at **www.hansebooks.com**

LONDON: JOHN CAMDEN HOTTEN, 74 & 75, PICCADILLY.
1870.

LONDON :
PRINTED BY VIRTUE AND CO.,
CITY ROAD.

TO
LONG-ESTEEMED AND VALUED
FRIENDS
SIR THOMAS DUFFUS
AND
LADY HARDY
THE AUTHOR
DEDICATES THIS
BOOK.

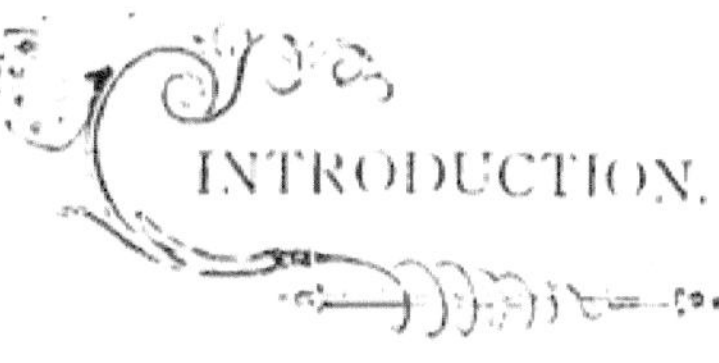

INTRODUCTION.

ow fertile of Thought are the Fairy Legends of Ireland; full of natural poetry, and seldom without a moral! That upon which this Tale is founded is, I believe, common to all parts of the Island; although I have, perhaps, committed a practical anachronism in bringing 'the Kelpies' of the North into the South.

It is believed that a child whose father has died before its birth is placed by Nature under the peculiar guardianship of the Fairies; and that, if born on Midsummer Eve, it becomes their rightful property.

This introduction will suffice to explain the machinery by which I have endeavoured to trace the progress of a young girl's mind from infancy to womanhood; the Good and Evil Influences to which it is subjected; and the Trials inseparable from a contest with the world: LOVING AND BEING LOVED.

The story was originally published in THE ART-JOURNAL— so far back as the year 1847. It was largely indebted to the aid of many accomplished artists: some of whom (my valued friend Sir Joseph Noel Paton especially) were then but commencing a career in which they have since obtained great and honourable renown. My gratitude for the valuable and beneficial assistance then rendered to me was expressed in the First Edition of this Book. The feeling has not lessened by the lapse of time.

The Book has been long "out of print:" I trust I do not err in believing it will be acceptable to a Public that has grown into existence since it was written.

A. M. H.

1869.

THE
ILLUSTRATIONS

ILLUSTRATIONS.

The Engravings by W. T. GREEN, G. and E. DALZIEL, J. BASTIN, J. WILLIAMS,
H. LINTON, G. MEASOM, W. MEASOM, A. J. MASON, &c. &c.

The Initial Letters Designed by T. R. MACQUOID.

The Cover Designed by J. MARCHANT.

Drawn by R. Huskisson.

Engraved by W. F. Green.

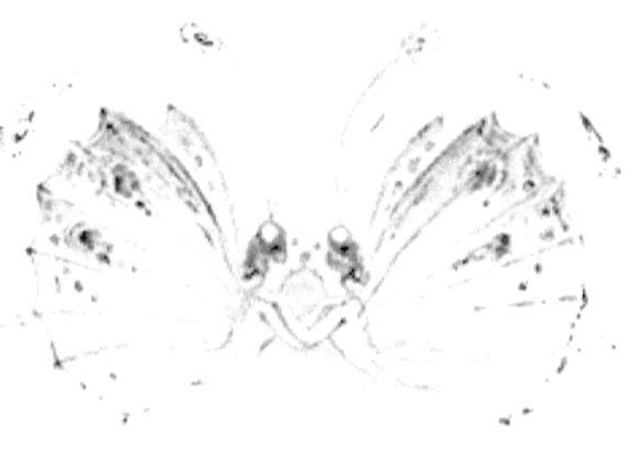

PART THE FIRST.

T was as bleak and chill a Midsummer Eve as the oldest dweller in the Lake-country of KILLARNEY could call to mind. The wind, although it did not absolutely roar through the Gap of Dunloe, or round and about the Purple Mountain, and 'lofty Mangerton of the Hoary Head,' disturbed by its harsh murmurings and audible discontent the young trees and lowly shrubs that grow beneath the shadows of the evergreen woods. All know that unearthly spirits hold their revels on Midsummer Eve; it is their fête-night: when they show to the elements there is a power mightier than theirs to direct and rule them. The Wind knew it well; yet, on this evening, it was neither entirely submissive nor absolutely rebellious. At times, it started from its dull quiet and prowled abroad; fretting everything it touched; shaking the light branches of the silver birch and drooping willow, ruffling the narrow forms of the slim laburnum, wrestling roughly with the stout holly, and scattering the delicate arbutus, whose leaves, fruit, and flowers are as fair and bright in December snow, as in the sunshine of July. The wind was not only out of season, but unnatural; it brought the chill of winter into the very midst of summer. It was, in truth, a sharp-toothed and biting wind; forcing its way into ill-built cottages—through broken windows and shrunken doors, where poverty sought warmth from peat-smoke rather than fire; piercing through every hole in the torn blanket or tattered cloak; whistling in bitter mockery of the poor man's moan; stirring the flax upon the "rock" which the feeble fingers of age were twisting into threads; causing the lamb to nestle closely into its mother's

wool, and the foolish calf to low complainingly, as it passed through the half-roofless out-house. Anon, it pelted the ivyed ruins of old Mucross, terrifying the very owls, who hooted it onwards, without stirring from their hermit-cells; and scourged the angry bats who ventured forth on their wonted errands.

The Beings who held sway over earth that night were so bent on mischief that they exerted their utmost skill to rouse the STORM KING from uneasy repose, as he pillowed his head beside the Punch-bowl—set like the eye of a cyclops in the rough brow of Mangerton; but the old fellow who was still too much wearied by exertions of the long past winter to attend their summons, grumbled his displeasure in a tone which the echoes of Glena repeated in thunder. Compelled to be content with the efforts of his bitter satellite, they sought, so aided, to accomplish great things before the last hour of midnight—scudding with it bravely and boldly through the open country: at length, growing conscious of impotence, retreating to narrow defiles and crowded inclosures—like those who, lacking power to disturb the world, revel in the minor evils of inflicting misery in their neighbourhoods and homes; but when, after ruffling the

waters of the Flesk, it sprang upon the bridge of many arches, it gave a wild howl of delight to see old Doctor MAGRATH bowed to the neck of his grey pony. "At him—at him—keep him back—keep him back," muttered a thousand voices to the wind; and surely there must have been some mysterious understanding between them, for right glad did it seem of encouragement to worry the old man, as he had never before been worried; his hat and wig flew over the bridge, and his poor bare head was buffeted as by a forest of shillelahs; but while he moaned and murmured at the rough handling of the elements, two stout fellows followed to see that he neither tarried nor turned back; and who, having neither hat nor wig to lose, cared for the wind as little as the pony, who, bending his head until his eyes were sheltered by his long shaggy mane, went steadily, though slowly, onward, as if conscious that his honoured master's services were required by no other than the fair GERALDINE RAYMOND, the young widow of a brave officer, whose premature death was about to call

into the world before its time, an infant—who was destined never to feel a father's kiss or hear a father's blessing. The cottage in which the young widow resided, was near the pretty village of Cloghreen ; it was sheltered by the deep woods of MUCROSS—the venerable ABBEY that never seems so beautiful and hallowed as by moonlight—cheered by the music of the Tore waterfall, and blessed by the view of the tiny church of Killagher, which tops the rising ground. Now, however, the woods failed to shelter her home from the assaults of the fearsome wind, that rasped against the windows, insinuated itself into every crevice, and lamented in sighs and moans—not for her struggles, but its own. Her only companion was a 'cross-grained,' but most faithful, attendant, who had been her Nurse, and looked to discharge the same office for the infant for whom she waited. Kitty Kelly was not superstitious—at least so she said; but she felt it a sort of solemn duty to provide the house with blessed salt and holy water; she had nailed a horse-shoe to the door at morning, well knowing there was a stern resolve among the 'good people' of the elements—Air, Earth, and Water—to obtain possession of any fatherless child whose existence was commenced on Midsummer Eve: such possession being the admitted right of whichever of the three Powers first entered the house where the baby was 'expected.'

She now prayed earnestly against all fairies; those of the air she knew could endow a baby with most precious gifts; while the fairies of earth—those who dwell among flowers, and partake more of our own nature—those, she thought, might do ' a good turn to a fatherless child ;' but still, 'she'd rather have nothing to do with them ;' with them—with whom ; surely Kitty knew herself better than to have any sort of fear of, or faith in, such follies—nor had she— only her grandmother, her own mother's mother, had once seen the blackest and the worst of the whole race, the real KELPIE QUEEN — the Queen of the most obnoxious class of 'good people'—they who were banished by the other

fairies from all the sports and pastimes in which the tribes are permitted to indulge; they, who are never allowed to rise from the sedges of the

Lower Lake—except on their own 'Eve,' that they may have a chance of adopting some new-born child of earth into their community—a chance which seldom becomes a reality—although it is theirs by royal charter—the charter of the Prince O'Donoghue, lord of a thousand palaces that lie fathoms deep beneath the surface of Loch Lene. Kitty's grandmother had seen the Kelpie Queen in all her magnificence arise on one of these festive occasions, from her water-palace, on the back of a huge frog, who seemed proud of his burden, and carried her with the air and bearing of a race-horse, while her dark hair streamed on either side her sallow face, and her attendant court were endeavouring to press into their service everything they could take—from a tadpole to a water-rat; she had often recounted this to Kitty, in her childhood; and Kitty, even at that early period, affected to doubt a tale, which, despite her seeming, crept through her bones, and made her very heart freeze within her bosom. She would now have given all she possessed in the world, to have had any one with her beside her sick lady; she started at every noise.

A certain wise man—known as Randy the woodcutter—had been sent off for the Doctor; and while she waited his return, she had, she thought, frequently heard him 'whisperin and cosherin at the door;' and yet he came not. At length, however, his well-known step was distinctly audible.

"Is all right, Randy?" she asked, from within.

"All *will* be right when I knock," he answered, "and then open quickly."

"Is he on the road?" inquired the Nurse, heedless of the warning; but before he could reply, a sharp blast rushed inward, and extinguished the flickering light of the lean candle she held with a trembling hand.

"The cross and a blessing about us, Kitty Kelly!" exclaimed Randy, falling on his knees. "God, he knows I couldn't help it. Why did you open the door before I knocked? I done all for the best, as the end will prove. Oh, murther! Why don't you shut the door, instead of standing there like a rock in the lake—'t was something more than the wind pass'd in now!—bless yourself, woman, dear! Oh, then, sure it's impossible to tell what would be on the wings of the wind this Midsummer Eve!"

"Nothing worse than yourself," stammered the Nurse, bravely, though she perceived, at once, that THE HORSE-SHOE was gone, and even fancied she saw 'something' flying off with it. Turning eagerly to Randy, who, pale and shivering, was gazing on the kitchen rafters — "Is the doctor coming?" she exclaimed.

"'Deed is he; and for fear he'd stop or turn back from his duty, on account of the hardness of the night, I set my two cousins to keep the road after him. He'll be here soon. Oh, sure it was only my duty I did, madam."

"Is the man mad to madam me?" exclaimed Kitty. "Stand on yer legs, and shut the door, and put the chair against it, and don't keep staring and bowing to the rafters; dear me, but it *is* a blast; and I didn't think there was more than a whisper going."

"Kitty Kelly, you're not altogether of this country," exclaimed Randy, in a low tone: "you've only been two hundred years in it—for you came in with ould Oliver Cromwell; so give way to your prayers—it's no wind that we're trembling in: of the three we're watching, one came in with me—the mistress will thank me for that; there was a second—and there will be a third. You may strive against them; I *dare* not!"

"I DARE!" replied Kitty, whose courage had in part returned—and then she started, for she fancied she heard shouts of ironical laughter; but, little daunted, she attempted to close the door violently. In this, however, she did not succeed; the wind pushed against her, and not only had the best of it, but flung her to the other end of the kitchen.

"Make the blessed sign," said Randy, yet without moving to her assistance.

"I can't," she replied; "my hand's weighed down by a ton weight." She had hardly uttered the words, when a gust of wind, freighted with most extraordinary noises—sighs, and snatches of music, atoms of laughter, and fragments of old songs, mingled with the sound of rushing waters— entered the cottage, and filled it as with an atmosphere.

"It will shut asy enough now," observed the woodcutter, rising from his knees, and wiping his brow. "Air, Earth, and Water! Oh, I'm not afraid to say my say about the good people, day or night; they never did me an ill turn, and never will; quiet, and kindly, and happy they are, and mane nothing but good to the dear lady;" and his huge head nodded, and his long limbs bent and twisted, in a peculiar sort of homage to something invisible to all eyes but his own. The Nurse thought it probable that Randy made the speech and performed his gesticulations, in the hope of propitiating the good offices of the company she now knew had come to the expected birth. It was currently believed that he could see and understand more than beseemed an honest man; and yet Randy *was* an honest man, and had the unbought happiness of

being more loved than feared. Still, the all-powerful 'they,' whispered he was a 'fairy man;' and, as such, he was consulted by many who would scruple to confess they had any faith or trust in the existence of the 'good people.' That opinion had strengthened wonderfully during the last few months; indeed, ever since the young widow had given promise that the child of a dead father was to visit a care-full world, his hours had been spent, even more than usual, beside THE FAIRIES' OAK—a withered and time hollowed tree, which hung its decayed branches over the sedges that skirted the base of the far-famed 'Eagle's Nest' (the most wonderful of the lake's many wonders); and he had been more than ever attentive to keep free from pebbles and worm-heaps, 'the ring,' which tradition and his own knowledge assigned as the favourite trysting-place of the 'good people.'

The door was now easily closed, and the candle relit at the kitchen fire; the woodcutter threw upon it an additional heap of bog-fir: the old cat's hair stood out like porcupines' quills; every now and then she opened her mouth to hiss, but closed it again without a sound; she would lift a paw, and stretch it forth, bristling with claws—then draw it back again, each claw returning to its downy sheath.

"Sit down, Randy, and don't be showldering the chimney, as if there wasn't a chair in the place," said the Nurse, through her chattering teeth.

"I know better manners than to disturb any one from their sate," he answered, bowing round, respectfully.

The Nurse crossed herself with the thumb of her right hand, and retreated to the bed-room of her mistress. The fire burned brightly—yet the cat took no pleasure in its blaze, but kept moving uneasily from one side to the other,—'wrinkling' up her coat, as if water had been thrown upon it—her tail twitching and bristling in restless discomfort.

"It's hard on you, pusheen gra!" said Randy, addressing the cat; "but you can't help yourself. They'll neither hurt nor harm you, pusheen."

"They've got possession now, and they'll keep it," he thought to himself.

"They will!" whispered a soft voice in his ear.

Randy caught hold of the fore-lock of his hair, pulled it, and jerked his head rapidly forward. "And for good," he said aloud, wishing to compliment NIGHTSTAR, THE QUEEN OF THE FAIRIES OF THE AIR, whose voice he knew, and whom he had often seen descend to earth with her train of attendants shining in the distance, like a silver halo in the moonlight.

And many a time, in the cool of a Midsummer night, when the grateful flowers drank in refreshing dews poured into their bosoms

by considerate clouds, had he seen HONEYBELL, QUEEN OF EARTH'S FAIRIES, pass on her favourite humble-bee, whose flight was guided by her page; while Nightstar descended with her train of attendant sprites, simply by the action of her own will. "And for good!" he repeated.

"Don't speak," replied the fairy, in a dignified tone; "there is no necessity; we see your thoughts as they are formed, and notice them if we please."

"The dickens a doubt I doubt ye," thought the woodcutter; for, despite his caution, thoughts would come.

"Now, don't swear, Randy; it's vulgar."

The woodcutter could not prevent himself from thinking an earnest prayer, that power might not be given them to change the child, at its birth, for one of their own.

"And why not?" was the inquiry, in a low and gentle tone—the very shadow of a sound. "Why not? Are your world's children so free from care, and the sorrows and troubles of life—that tug at your hearts, furrow your brows, weigh you down before your time—spectres leading you to graves—are they so very happy, that you do not wish them to be with us who spend our lives in enjoyment?"

"From sunset to sunrise," thought Randy: "no mortal ever knew what you do be doing when the sun shines."

"Even so," replied Nightstar, whom, on turning round, he saw seated in the very centre of a cobweb,

while HER PAGE was engaged in a combat with the dispossessed spider, who, dangling by his thread, endeavoured to defend himself against the well-poised spear of the active elf. "From sunset to sunrise," she repeated, rocking herself backward and forward on her seat; "even so; and surely that is better than spending it as you and the rest of you spend it—in heavy sleep or midnight brawling."

"You never could lay that last to me, or to any of the Kerry boys," replied Randy, speaking out boldly; for he believed Ireland the finest country in the world, and Killarney the greenest spot in the Emerald Isle. He had no sooner spoken than he heard a loud clapping of hands, and little cries of "Bravo!" and, fully aware of the compliment, he gave another pull at his head-tuft, and, to his great astonishment, found, on opening it, that he had caught A FAIRY IN HIS HAND.

"Why didn't you hold me when you had me?" exclaimed the creature, springing on a moonbeam that had just entered the window; "and then I would have told you of hidden treasure, as well as the Leprehawn you are so fond of hunting."

"Sure, it's not misdoubting your honour's generosity I'd be," replied the woodcutter. "You can give me the information, or the goold, which ever your honour plases, all the same;" and then there were shouts of merry laughter; and it seemed to the enlightened eyes of the bewildered man, that a multitude of the fairies of the three elements completely occupied the kitchen—twirling round the rafters, and filling every crevice and corner—some even clinging to the feathers of the cock's tail. The earthly good people were far more slow and heavy in their movements than those who appertained to the purer element; they ate and drank whatever they could find, and fought sham fights with each other—and real ones with the Kelpies or water fairies. The woodcutter's unsealed eyes had no difficulty in distinguishing the three distinct races, who had attended their liege ladies to be present at the birth of the fatherless, on Midsummer Eve : he knew that the change of the earthly for the unearthly child, would belong of right to whichever of the three had first entered the house, and he congratulated himself on having so managed that

Nightstar and her court had been the earliest arrivals.   Honeybell, Queen of the Earthly Spirits, would, he thought, yield honourably to the claims of her royal sister; but he had no such faith in the Queen of the Kelpies. She was a yellow, damp, distorted, little creature, who diverted herself in a huge tub, by causing the elves who make up, what may be called 'the people' of the other tribes, to be ducked whenever they were caught by her frog-like subjects.   Randy had *his* own purposes to work out, and he dreaded the Kelpies' influence: his mind filled with hope when he contemplated the gentle dignity and kindly expression of Nightstar, her attendants floating around her with ineffable grace—many of them perfectly transparent, their bosoms illumined from within, by a little spark of light like that which flashes from a diamond.   He looked upon the Queen reclining on the cobweb with as much ease as an Eastern lady in a palanquin, and having attracted her attention by what he intended to be a gentle sigh, but which shook the web, so that her majesty caught hold of the banner of her standard-bearer for support, he composed his thoughts.

"You might have conveyed to us your desire to *think*, without blowing a hurricane," said Nightstar; "but you mortals are so very boisterous. Yet I must forgive you, Randy; you are an honest fellow, and I don't think I ever yet found a black ugly thought at nurse in your mind: evil gets there, to be sure, sometimes; but it does not stay; it meets with no entertainment; you are an innocent soul, Randy, and we love you much; otherwise, we should have granted you no such royal privileges as you possess.   You have a great regard for this poor lady,

I know: she will have a daughter, I can tell you that.   And now what is to be done with the little maid who is to be with us in a few minutes?"

"She'll come to the poor mother, plase your gracious majesty, like a beautiful summer butterfly rising from her dead father's grave," thought the woodcutter.

The Queen nodded twice, and smiled. " If she is not very, *very* pretty, Randy, I think I shall give her up to my royal sister, Honeybell."

" You're a mother, yourself, I'll go bail, my lady," thought Randy, " though you are so very small and young."

" Oh, yes! I was a mother more than two hundred years ago," answered the Queen.

" What a little darling of a beauty she is," thought the woodcutter, and the fairy smiled her pleasure at the compliment. " And looks as fresh as the first drop of May-dew," so ran his thoughts. The fairy smiled again, and drew herself up with gentle pride. " She's every inch a queen," thought Randy, as her own particular court gathered about her. " If she was six feet high in her stocking vamps, she could not be more stately." Queen Nightstar had certainly much of mortal woman about her; she was lovely—witty—kind—and generous; but very, very small—even for a fairy; and yet the little creature prided herself upon her stateliness, upon her dignity, and queenly presence. She had never been so well pleased with Randy, though she had patronised him for many years; she had hitherto thought him a good-natured creature; *now*, she fancied him endowed with exceeding penetration. " You're mighty fond of the young prences and prencesses, I'll go bail," thought Randy.

" I am, of course," she replied.

" Might I make bould to ask how many your majesty has?"

" About three dozen," was the gracious reply.

" And you couldn't fix upon one you'd like to part with?"

" Part with!" she exclaimed; " I would yield my life rather than one of my children! Man—man—do you think I could have a choice!—My dear, dear children!—a mother's heart is large enough for you all. I could love ten times as many, and yet one does not rob another of a hair's breadth of love."

" Why, then, if you are so fond of the whole three dozen, won't you allow that it's hard to take an only child from its mother, and she a widow?"

" You are very provoking, Randy," said her majesty, in answer to his thoughts, " and cunning in reasoning; but we merely exchange—we leave her one of ours."

"One of the ne'er-do-wolls—that she'll see pine and die (to all appearance) before her eyes, at the end of three months: the grass isn't green yet over poor Mary Mackay, who fretted the life out of herself, after one of your changelings."

"Not one of mine—one of Honeybell's," replied Nightstar, thoughtfully.

"The baby will be all in the world left to comfort her; and sure there's plenty of children born in Killarney this holy night, by twos and threes—not wanted; where there's no house to hold, nor clothes to cover, them: wouldn't one of them do for you?"

"I don't like low-born children," answered Nightstar, with a toss of her lovely little head.

"The highest born may have the lowest bed, when all is over; any way, your majesty could make them what you plase; and it's yourself that knows that many a fine brave spirit rises from under the cabin roof; but no matter what they are; you could give them the gifts that would make them grate people—and beautiful women, like yourself—my lady!"

"I'm sure I don't want to take the mortal's only little one, if she thinks so much about it: no doubt she will be very fond of it," sighed the Queen. "Honeybell is in such a sweet temper—so well pleased with the cream and cakes, that she would, I daresay, instead of changing the child, help me to endow it. But there are the Kelpies; and you know their Queen is no friend of ours. Air has the first right of choice, Earth the second, and Water the third. She won't give it up, I am certain, even if Honeybell did."

A sudden thought crossed Randy's brain.

"I see, I see!—do it, do it," continued Nightstar, as rapidly as the thought was formed in Randy's mind; and, suddenly turning round, she addressed an observation to one of her courtiers, while the woodcutter seized a little platter of blessed salt, and tossed it into the tub where the Kelpies were sporting. It was quickly and cleverly done; instantly the hands of Randy hung as awkwardly as usual by his sides; but great was the consternation that followed; such splashing of water and whistling of wind: the Kelpies rushed out of the house in the wake of their insulted Queen, threatening revenge on the fairies of earth, by whom they imagined the trick had been played them. Randy quickly shut-to

the door, and could not help admiring the dignified self-possession of Nightstar, who called to Honeybell that the time was come. Immediately the court attendants prepared to follow their royal mistress, but Nightstar expressed a wish that they should ENTER THE CHAMBER alone; and it was a beautiful sight to see them floating onward, Honeybell holding in her hand her sceptre of fairy foxglove, and wearing a necklace of diamonds, that circled her throat with a wreath of light; eclipsed, however, by the star that glittered above the head of her sister queen. They moved, on hand-in-hand, to the birth-chamber; while poor Randy, bewildered by the perfume of dews and flowers, and the gentle music, that whispered all around him, sunk upon his knees.

"Remember, gracious Queen," he thought; "remember, every crow thinks its own bird the whitest." In a little time, a low wail and bitter cry told him that a struggle had commenced between a living spirit and a bitter world.

His entreaty, addressed to the Fairies, did not, however, content the woodcutter; the attitude he had assumed suggested another—a higher and holier petition; he prayed with all the fervency of his warm and honest heart, that the dear young lady might be saved in her hour of trial, and that her baby might be spared to her, to be the blessing and the hope of after years. Prayer gives strength to the feeble and invigorates the strong. He arose much comforted, and looked round with a smile of satisfaction upon the tiny court, who, freed from the restraint

which the august presence of their Queens imposed, unbent their spirits, and played such madcap pranks, that Randy could not but feel his freedom of sight a rare privilege ; it amused him greatly to contrast the buoyant and thoughtless energy and activity of the younger members of the two regal courts, with the bearing, impressive even to solemnity, of the high official personages who, upon occasions such as this, were always in close attendance upon their sovereigns. Randy watched them with more than common interest, for he knew they would soon be summoned to council. This man, though cast in so rough a mould, was gentle and gracious in heart and mind. He had been known for years to the good people, and they delighted to do him kindnesses. They led him to where THE RED DEER SHED THEIR HORNS, and brought him the richest and earliest of the Wood Strawberries. When the sky looked blue above, and the summer breath stirred the trees, so that all said, 'the fair weather is with us now,' they showed him where the little cloud was rising, herald of the Storm King; they taught him to dye wood, so that common fir could not be known from the arbutus or the charmed yew, so prized by strangers; they gave him knowledge of the virtues which dwell in herbs and flowers —of palmistry — of murrain stones and fairy strokes—and filled his mind with fables and old tales. Had he lived in earlier times, Randy would have suffered wizard's martyrdom. As it was, he was as often called 'Randy, the Fairy Man,' as 'Randy, the Woodcutter,'—and he had certainly imbibed some of the spirit-feeling with the spirit-repute: he was keenly alive to the beauties of Nature; heard sweet music in the murmurs of brooks, and tuneful melodies from the leaves of trees. He could tell, it was said, what the south breeze whispered to the west, and gather the birds of the air around him, be they ever so wild. He wore a

four-leaved shamrock in his bosom, and a wreath of mountain-ash circled his conical hat. The wildest deer on Glena would neither harm him nor fly from him. Whenever he passed through a village, or rested himself beneath a tree, CHILDREN WOULD CROWD ABOUT HIM; and if he gave them but the blossom of a daisy, they would think themselves happy. His only enemies were the eagles; the echo of their screams, or the shadow of their wings, were the only natural sights or sounds that damped his spirits. His haunts were the ancient hollow oak and the green grass slopes whereon grew THE FOXGLOVE—flower chiefest in favour with the Beings of whom Randy did not scruple to own himself the faithful and fond ally.

He would have enjoyed the pranks and oddities of the fairy tribes much longer, but that his attention was aroused by a smart tap on the cheek from the wand of the chancellor. "I am commanded by his lordship," said a dapper little official, his secretary, in a dark cobweb robe, and a wig composed of the down of the wild rush, "to tell you to do something rational for his amusement; we have taken much pains with your education, Randy," he added, "and would fain see its fruits."

"Would his honour like a story, grave or gay—of his own, or of our people?" Having obtained leave to use his own discretion, Randy bethought him once or twice, and then, with a low bow to the great dignitary of fairy-land, he said:—"Flowers, my lord, are very beautiful to look at, and very sweet to smell; but if you were much among the tip-tops of the family, you would be surprised at the odd ways some of them have, and the airs they give themselves. Well, those I am talking about had been used to a deal of tenderness, and were brought up under the warm shade of a fine glass-house; and the beautiful lady that tended them said, one day, 'The roses in the flower-knot last twice as long, and are much sweeter.' Well! yer Honour never heard anything like the rustling of leaves the flowers got on with, when they understood what the lady said; being brought up lonely and grand, and looking out on the world through glass windows, they thought everything in a garden must be low and common. Yer Honour, they looked down on the flowers of the garden, just as much as, or may be more, than the flowers of the garden look down on the flowers of the field—instead of *looking up* to the GREAT CAUSE of all the sweetness and beauty they possess—who knows that if fine flowers are the most admired, the flowers of the field make glad the hearts of the greatest number of innocent children, who enjoy a heaven of happiness in gathering the cowslip, the wild violet, and the star-eyed daisy: to say nothing, yer  Honour, of the favour your people show—in preference to all the flowers that ever grew in a garden—for the banks of thyme, the blue-bells, the silver cuckoo blossom, and the purple foxglove."

This procured Randy a round of applause.

"To go back, my lord, to the pampered flowers: some change of fortune coming on the lady, she was obliged to leave her palace of a house, and take shelter beneath the roof of a cottage—'There's some of my dear flowers,' said the sweet lady, 'able to bear removal as well as myself, and who knows but we may be all the stronger and better for it; I hope we are not too far gone in luxury to prevent our enjoying comfort.' So she placed them in her cottage garden; her favourite white rose folded the protecting moss closely over her bosom, lest she should catch cold, and—a—I forget the name of it—shut itself as safe up in its leaves as if it was going a journey of a thousand miles; and looked with a wave of contempt upon the manner in which the garden flowers strove, out of civility, to make room for it; while one or two grave blossoms—of the sage class—knew they should get stronger and better from being in the fresh pure air of heaven, and admitted that their new neighbour—the rose of the garden—was in every respect as much a lady as the rose of the glass-house; in the morning, the garden rose unfolded to welcome the sun, and to hear the early hymn of the birds, and to see how her buds were growing; and as the dew-drops, one by one, ascended to the clouds that had left them during night, for her refreshment, she perfumed them for their journey, and graciously thanked them for their care: but the pampered flowers bent beneath the dew, and complained of the damp and chill; and the delicate rose said that her dress was *tossicated*, and shook off the dew-drops so roughly in her pet, that the tender things broke into atoms, and the proud flower desired they should visit her no more, as she was too high-born to be treated like a common flower; and needed no help from common things; what was a refreshing blessing to others, her refined ignorance—"

"She should have learned of us," interrupted the chancellor: "we know how to bring refreshment to, and take refreshment from, every flower that grows in garden or in field: they are our drinking cups, a thousand times richer than the things made of the world's dross, which you earth-worms call 'precious gems.' Your rose should have learned of us."

"She learned of NATURE, my lord, at last," continued Randy, "for the next night not a sparkle from any cloud visited her leaves, and she saw the fleecy moisture enveloping the other flowers, and felt that the Nature she had scorned, was comforting her children, and whispering to them to be of good cheer, for that next year their blossoms should be fairer and wax stronger: and the gentle loving dews clustered upon the buds and leaflets; and at last, as morning drew near, a sharp dry air made the most impertinent inquiries concerning her quarrel with the dew-drops, and whistled spitefully in her face, and ruffled her leaves, so that, the next day, the hot sunbeams entered into her heart; and in the deepest humility she petitioned to be treated as a common flower, convinced that—"

The moral of Randy's tale was scared from his lips by a message from Queen Nightstar to the chancellor, and by the noise made by

Honeybell's page in rousing his lordship from the heavy slumber into which he had fallen.

"Keep up, mistress," said the Nurse to the widowed mother: "The jewel it is!—so like its father. A girl's born lucky that's like its father! What do you say?—'it has no father?' It has two, lady dear: one in heaven, and one over—about—around us all!—the very King of Heaven is the father of the earthly fatherless!—may He mark it to grace! Think of the comfort she'll be to you—to be your own; the weight of the world isn't half weight to the young mother who looks at her dawshy babby. 'You want to see it?' I'm sure you do; but wait till Nurse puts on its pretty cap, and makes it sit up like a lady. I tell you, dear, it's the very *moral* of its father."

"His child!—his child!—his own child! To smile like him—to speak like him! Are you sure, Nurse, nothing will happen it—nothing take it from me? I have a strange feeling, as if my child were in danger. But what danger?—there is nothing could have the heart to take my baby from its lone mother!"

Randy felt the tears gathering in his eyes, but they were quickly changed to tears of joy—for he saw the WRITHING, MISSHAPEN SHADOW, that was to have been substituted for Geraldine's infant, forced by a number of the attendants to leave the cottage. He then thought he

would peep into the interior. There was no doubt about it; Queen Honeybell looked sulky; but the lamp in Nightstar's bosom shone more brightly than ever, and her words fell on his ear more full of music than the robin's winter song.

"Let us endow her for the world, and against the world; it is some time since we have permitted the child of our choice to remain exposed to the temptations and imperfections of mortality: let us guard her, and yet leave her with her mother." What music and tenderness were in Nightstar's words, as she continued—"I am looking at this moment into that young mother's heart: I see how new feelings stimulate its pulsations: I see it expanding—welling forth its very essence into the new life which, though mysteriously parted from it, is dearer to it than ever; there is a whole universe of love—pure, unselfish, spotless love—love without limit, boundless as ocean, and deeper than its deepest caves—in that sweet mother's heart, towards the little lump of half-animated clay that is *her* child. Oh, sister! if it were given you to see the future that whirls through her brain! The great Power of all has poured into her a new nature—a stronger motive and firmer principle of life : her very heart is enlarged."

"A child deprived of its father, and born on Midsummer Eve, is by right our own," said Honeybell, pouting ; "but you have always some whimsey in your head about these creatures of earth. I do not envy you your power of seeing thoughts and hearts, believe me!"

"Let it *be* ours," persisted Nightstar ; "let us pour into its heart and mind whatever of good we can ; but let us not take it from its mother." The Queen of Earth's fairies bent her head in no very cordial acquiescence ; and the aërial troop, seeing that their queen had vanquished, were mightily pleased thereat, and played sundry fantastic tricks ; now opening the baby's sleepy eyes, to ascertain their colour, sleeking its small quantity of downy mole-like hair with their tiny hands, endeavouring to straighten its little wrinkled fingers, and sadly retarding the Nurse in its adornment, by untying the strings as fast as she tied them.

"Sister," persisted Nightstar, "help me to endow my favourite."

"We never agree on educational matters," answered Honeybell; "you are too ideal for me—better have her all to yourself."

"You do yourself injustice, sister. Let us wave our wands, and show the young mother, as in a dream, what may be the future qualities of her soul's idol : let us bestow on the fairest of earth's blossoms the most precious of all gifts that woman can receive or bestow : let us gift her with Love."

"Love! rubbish!" answered Honeybell, pettishly—"the source of woman's misery."

"And happiness!"

"I would gift her with beauty, wealth, and spirit; the world's treasures: that she may subdue the world."

"Let her mother determine," said Nightstar; "let her mother determine. Do you offer your gifts, and I will offer mine!"

The pallid mother trembled in every limb while the Queens performed their spells above her couch. At first, her vision was perplexed: she saw, floating around her, those animated atoms of the mysterious world that have so much power over our destinies—without recognising what or who they were. At length she singled out the two Queens—Nightstar, as a living thing of light—Honeybell, as only a creature, beautiful and minute. The Nurse saw that Geraldine's eyes were fixed, and that she seemed entranced; this, she fancied, was but a wile to get her to take her eyes off the child. Presently, her lady's lips moved, and she spoke softly and

slowly, as if she were replying to certain questions, which the Nurse did not hear. "Whatever will give her most happiness, and make her most beloved—no woman was ever happy who was not BELOVED," she said. There was a pause after she had spoken these disjointed words; and the Nurse observed that her soft eyes wandered first to one side, then to another. She tried to call Randy, but her tongue refused its office; she clutched the infant firmly in her arms, and kept her eye steadily upon it. Again words came faint and wearily from the mother's lips. "Thank you, thank you—if you cannot prevent the world from assailing her—it is well to teach her to endure—we must all do that—the more love, the more endurance—riches, honours, and beauty, are fine things—but LOVE IS THE PERFUME OF LIFE!" There was another pause, and the young mother's eyes were illumined by an expression of tenderness, resignation, and joy, such as had never gladdened them since her widowhood. Her lips quivered, and after a time, large tears welled forth, but disappeared before they reached her cheek—removed by some invisible agency. "There is good to be gathered from both such sponsors," she said again; "but *you* think my thoughts—to be LOVING and BELOVED. So let it be!"

A soft mild light shone through the chamber—the atmosphere was filled with most sweet fragrance, and music soft and low. The Nurse, urged by an irresistible influence, arose, and settled the infant on the weak mother's bosom. And as it drank its first draught of LOVE, it became imbued by that regenerating essence which cheers us from the cradle to the grave!

THE FAIRY RING.

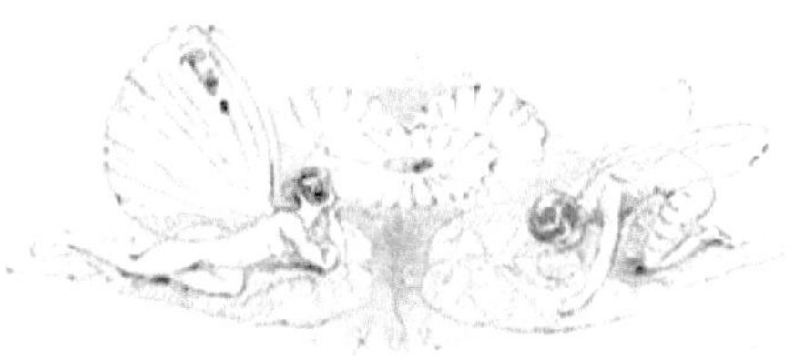

HE kitchen at 'Dovecote,' as Mrs. Raymond, in happier days, had named her cottage, was a long rambling room; dried hams and fish, intermingled with bunches of herbs, were suspended from the rafters; and in a division, 'hurdled' off for the purpose, the Nurse's favourite poultry, and, occasionally, a weakly lamb, or a brood of tender turkeys, while their red heads were progressing, found a well-warmed shelter. It was sufficiently confused and straggling to be styled 'picturesque,' and as uncomfortable as picturesque interiors generally are; it had a more than usual quantity of piggins and noggins, and

fine old chairs — some gaunt and high-backed, others both grotesque

and clumsy ; of course, it contained a dresser, garnished by more 'crockery'
and pewter than 'Nurse Kitty' cared to keep in order; a settle, a
losset, and wheels for spinning both flax and wool; and a deep
chimney—a perfect cavern of blackness, even when the fire burned
brightest—made mirthful in winter by the merriest of crickets. A door,
it will be remembered, opened from the kitchen into the chamber where
the sweet subject of Fairy contest and Fairy care had drawn her first
breath of life. In a small parlour at the opposite end of the dwelling
she received the name of 'Eva.' Before I tell how swiftly time flew—
what it created and destroyed—what it mended and tattered—I must
describe, briefly, the up-and-down, half-rustic, half-ornée habitation,
where her childhood was passing. DOVECOTE certainly did not turn

' its silver lining to the crowd ; ' the road view of the cottage was scarcely
more than a mass of white wall and brown thatch ; but those who were
admitted within, and inhaled the perfume of its delicious garden,
wondered what magic had been exercised to make so humble a place

a very paradise of beauty. There was a strange mingling of architectural
incongruities about it. The window of the sitting-room might have been
called an oriel; it was laced with stained glass, and overhung by woodbine
and clematis, where the butterfly, and that gigantic beauty of Kerry—the
great dragon-fly—sported from sunrise to sunset. Next to this, a little
square lattice peeped forth, plain and unadorned, save by the white curtain
within; and beyond that was a porch—a perfect bower of climbing roses.
At the other end was the ordinary kitchen-window, beside which Randy
was generally found seated—so much did he delight in watching the spray
of the Torc waterfall, that gleamed above the trees. Opening, as this
window did, upon the bend of the lawn, shaded by a sturdy rowan tree,
and canopied by magnolia and variegated holly, it was in itself a study
for a painter. A long grass bench, tufted with wild flowers, stretched
nearly the length of the cottage, and then terminated abruptly at the
porch, where the forest of roses rambled out and about, giving shelter
to wrens, tits, and robins, half-way to the top of the pointed gable
which rose above it. Such a magazine of animated nature as both
porch and gable had become!—the dear old gable!—which people said
had been a tower, a castle, or something of an abbey—once. It was
truly a most beautiful half-saved ruin! Its
projecting stones covered with moss a foot
deep—the green triumphant ivy trailing around
what had been a buttress—the wall-flower
and snap-dragon nodding to each other from
their several nooks; the lichens and maiden-
hair, and golden-cupped flowers, with broad
shining leaves, and the delightful tone of the
sage-green moss, that clings closely to old
stones, so lovingly anxious for their preservation, adding by contrast to the natural harmony of the whole—overgrowing the nest of
the restless martin; while, a little higher up,
the swallow — his toilsome journey over —

know that his home was ready. In a small niche-like nook an aged
owl had dwelt for more than half a century; for men as old remembered

him so long, looking out at twilight, with the same air and manner—if not wise, at least contemplative and sedate. But, after all, the glory of the old gable was the weathercock; there were old, very old, people, in Cloghreen, who remembered when the weathercock was *not* there, but none who could tell when it was put up, or by whom; in short, there was a mystery—a story about it that was growing into a legend to try faith 'hereafter.' Everybody said the weathercock was too large for the gable—too heavy for the old wall; but the wall bore up bravely; gloried in the distinction; and did not at all mind the long massive bar of iron that was passed through it, but seemed rather proud than otherwise of the curiously-wrought cross that stood out so clearly against the sky. Surmounting the whole, beneath this symbol of Faith, were crossed arrows, depending from either end of which originally hung the iron letters that designate the four points of the compass; one of these had been removed, and a hand—the forefinger only extended— occupied its place. The cross was regarded with much veneration by the peasantry, and they failed not to draw omens from the birds that rested thereon. When the winds were wild, and contended madly together, the weathercock groaned sadly, and the old gable, with generous sympathy, echoed its complaints; but, generally, it performed its duty silently—perhaps we may add—sullenly.

The garden of Dovecote had a charm, which neither pen nor pencil can convey; it was evident that the directing mind was of no common order; one that understood where every flower might not only be seen to the best advantage, but be so placed as to augment the beauty of its neighbours. Such fuchsias! such myrtles! such verbenas! as flourished there, were never seen elsewhere in the open air, even in Kerry; it was a well-arranged community of flowers and shrubs, grouped in most charming harmony — of trees bending gracefully over the green turf, where the rich-toned crocus, and the delicate snow-drop, blossomed long before they peeped forth in less sheltered parterres; everything, indeed, was trained, as though nothing had been in training; so ordered, that disorder seemed impossible.

In this happy retirement, the young widow and her child were passing their lives : the first years of infancy had vanished, as Geraldine thought, without any danger having threatened her little Eva; but Randy was by no means of her opinion: he knew full well that the Kelpie Queen—who considered herself cheated of her right—had been watching for means to taint the mind and harm the heart of the young girl; and during the week that preceded her birth-day, he took little food or repose, but wandered unceasingly about the cottage, seeking and working charms. Always on her birth-days, it had certainly been evident to her mother that her temper became fitful; there seemed a contest in her little bosom between the spirit of evil and the spirit of good. She was restless — her eyes wandered — and she had said, more than once, she heard music when her mother sung not, and a louder rush of water than the fall of the waters of the Tore. The mystery that hovered around her made her an object of the deepest and tenderest interest to all by whom she was beloved.

Abundantly was the promise of her birth fulfilled. Richly indeed was this lovely child endowed with the purest and holiest affections of our nature. Her little life had been spent in discharging the offices of kindly love to all living things that came within her sphere. Inanimate nature shared her tenderness; not a drooping flower that she would not seek to revive, nor a bruised bough that she would not bind. This, to her, was neither care nor labour; on the contrary, it was her joy— her very life. She acquired music without an effort: loving it so dearly, that the complications of the science made her pastime: and whenever she wearied of her other studies, her mother had but to say, "If you loved me, you would learn," to urge her to increased exertion. If ever child was ruled and guided by the Law of Love, it was Eva Raymond! Even when guilty of faults which, though common to most children, were uncommon in her, a word or two of tender reproach, rather than reproof, would at once cast her weeping on her mother's bosom. The purest passion sent from Heaven upon this sin-stained world is the love a mother bears her child! Enduring, faithful, and intense,—a perpetual sacrifice of self at the shrine of Nature,—a deep mystery, which, when fathomed, excites wonder at its marvellous depth and purity. And Geraldine watched over Eva with a mother's tenderness, and much of a father's wisdom. Her whole life was a mingling of hope and fear—not for herself, but for her child. Eva's appearance in the village was a jubilee; parents pointed her out to their children, and children looked upon her with delight; while her mother's friends vied with each other in returning her considerate, and yet childish, love. One she would greet with garden, another with wild, flowers; to a third she would present fruit gathered by her own hand: for, though her mother was not rich, save in the possession of such a child, she managed to have something always ready to lessen the wants of those who needed;—and surely, like the widow's cruise, the generous hand is replenished by Him who loveth a cheerful giver. Eva was liberal in giving: she was more—she was generous to forbear. She could over-come any desire of her own, by the stronger desire of gratifying another; and this in childhood is perhaps the greatest of all proofs of love; for *then* the will is strong—the reason weak. As she advanced in years, her temper, at times, became more easily excited than was seemly, and she was strongly inclined to jealousy—not envious—there was no envy in her nature—but jealous she was, if she were not loved. She would praise and caress a playfellow, and tell over to her mother all the child's good deeds, and do all she could to create in her an affection for the child; and yet if her mother manifested much tenderness towards her companion, she would shed abundant tears — tears without words or murmurs. And this often troubled the gentle widow, made her thought-ful to call some other great feeling into action, and sometimes to ponder if her choice, at the child's birth, had been the safest and wisest; for if love, the pure love of her innocent heart, brought its ecstasy of happiness, it also conveyed its poignancy of pain: and then she re-membered that none born into life can be separated from its sorrows—that the best lesson we can learn is to endure them—that the sweetest softener of our own griefs is the privilege of soothing the griefs of others.

Time was passing; year added unto year its gatherings of knowledge and affection, and also its strength of will;—another and another birth-day went by, unmarked by any obvious danger. Child though she was—a very frolic, a toy, a delight, a sunbeam, a comforter—as far as love went, a friend—still she had hours of deep thoughtfulness,

mingled with tears—unaccountable tears—and fits, not of sullenness, but
of silence. Her seventh birth-day had now arrived, and her mother
considered it as the passing away of childhood, for, in most things, the
child had wisdom beyond her years. Day broke with even more
than the loveliness of that lovely season; Randy arose with the sun
from the green bench whereon he had passed the night, and proceeded to sort the herbs he had collected in the moonlight.

They were the wild herbs that had
grown upon THE BANKS OF THE
RAPID LAUNE—where the grass is ever young and always green;
for the fairies love the moist place, and keep its verdure fresh and
sweet at all seasons: in winter the frost comes not here; in summer
no arid heat parches up the blades that are full of generous life. The
village children are happy when their plays are on this pleasant sward.

He was not long alone, for the Nurse soon joined him with a cordial greeting and a cheerful 'good morrow.' "Seven, Randy—seven
to-day! and she looked wise enough last night for double that: if
ever there was a born sunbeam, it is that little darling."

"Ay," added Randy, "whose skin is as white as the blossom of
the cuckoo sorrel; whose eyes are as blue as the flower of the flax;
her lips red as the berry of the wood-strawberry that grows on steep
Glena; her hair black as the raven's wing;—isn't that poetry, Kitty!"

"Poethry!" repeated the Nurse, contemptuously. "I'd thank you not to be drawin' comparasons of her beauty from such wild unnatural things as ravens' wings."

"True for ye," he answered; "and I wonder any mortal has the daring to lift up his voice when such as that is looking at him!" and Randy reverendly uncovered his head to the sun, which had just risen from behind the mountains—a huge eye of glowing fire, whose rays penetrated the deepest and darkest forests of the beautiful glen.

"The birds don't mind it," said Kitty; "you hear them singing."

"Hymns!" replied the woodcutter. "Hymns, and bits of praise and thankfulness: the flowers, poor things, open their leaves to the same tune; every blade of grass lifts itself up in gratitude at sunrise. Sure, I heard the unfledged birds learning their matins from their parents an hour ago in the old gable. Such a twittering!—and now, hark how they sing out!"

"I think," continued the Nurse, after a pause, more in compliment to Randy's feelings than to her own: "I think I never saw so round a ring as that down yonder on the grass; there's twice as much dew on it as on any other part of the lawn. What made it, Randy?"

"Agh!" was the only answer to this leading question.

"Well," she continued, "I never thought you a bit like yourself since the night she was born. Seven years this blessed Midsummer night —and what a night that was!"

"It's yourself and the ould pusheen cat that's alive still—'tis you both might say that, if you had any knowledge," replied the woodcutter.

"I and the cat! the ould grey pusheen that sleeps the four quarters round, barring Midsummer?"

"That's it!" explained Randy: "that cat will never sleep another Midsummer night after what she went through: she always looks ould at Midsummer. A dale that ould pusheen might tell the world of what she sees and thinks; but she's wise and—silent. There's more than one might learn a lesson from a silent cat."

"You know all about herbs and cats, Randy; but you never say how I look," said the nurse.

"Indeed, then," he replied, mingling his observations with comments

upon his herb-gatherings: " I think you always look the same: the elder's
a fine thing, and so is the ash; and the hazel, and liverwort, and ragweed,
so are they—fine things;—I don't see any change for the better on ye these
twenty years. Camomile, it's bitter but true—the herb for you; and
the sweet of the violet—the colour of her own eyes. There's an ould
rhyme that was ould when my grandfather was young: something about

> ' The rose is red, the violet's blue,
> Carnation's sweet, and so are you:'

but there's no flower of the garden sweet enough or beautiful enough to go
alone upon her birth-day. But what's here," he exclaimed, hastily ; " I
never could have gathered the wild rue, nor the wet dogweed, nor the
water nettle ! Was I mad, or are they put here for a warning ?"

"He *is* mad, and he always was mad," said poor Kitty, "and knows
more, I fear, than a Christian man should ; and yet sees nothing hardly
worth seeing around him ! Lord help us! Why
doesn't he catch the ould CLURICAUN, that does
be mending his brogues, night and day, under
the shadow of the cow-thistle ? Why doesn't he
lay hould of him and make him give up the purse
o' goold he carries, ever and always, in his pocket.
A fairy man ! enagh ! and can't catch the only
fairy worth catching—the ould cobbler that would
make the little mistress as rich as she is beautiful! a fairy man!" and the Nurse retired to
her own territory to prepare the several ' treats '

her best skill could devise, in the forms of Sally-Lun and Slim-cake, for
her darling. But Kitty was not allowed to remain long at her occupation.
She had enough to do to answer the taps at the door, and receive the
various little tokens by which high and low, rich and poor, sought to testify
their affection for Eva Raymond. Long before she unclosed her eyes, her
mother was praying by her bedside—praying earnestly to the Author of all
good to protect her child through time and for eternity. The mother, so
fair and young, seemed like a sister bending over a sister's couch; but no
sister ever framed such prayers—no sister ever felt such love ! It increased

the more for that she saw the child's face grow troubled, while slowly, from
between her closed lids, large tears came forth, flooding her glowing
cheeks, and her head moved so restlessly on her pillow, that Geraldine

awoke her, and while folding her to her bosom, murmured forth blessings
and caressing words, such as have their source only in a mother's heart.

"I think I have dreamed such dreams before, mamma.   I think I
have, but I am not sure ; now that I see you and the sun, I am again quite
happy ; but it was so damp and cold."

"What, my child ?"

"The water, mother ! but now it is all gone !"   And then the Nurse
came in, bearing a full basket of gifts; presently the shadow of Randy was
outside her window ; and in the happy elasticity of childhood, forgetting all
troubles, she bounded forth upon the lawn in the fresh air and bright sun
of morning, as a young roe from a thicket on the wild-wood sward.
"Hark, mamma ! how sweetly the birds sing ! and listen ! there is the

wood-quest. I do so love the coo of that dear bird: and here is Randy. Am I to wear that nosegay of curious herbs all day, Randy? Oh! I will; you gave me the same last year. I am quite, quite happy now—quite happy, and thankful, and will be so good. Look, look, how brightly plays the waterfall! Look! I never saw the spray so high above the trees." Her gaze was again turned towards the waterfall, and again she expressed a wish to watch the play of its gems in the sunlight, exclaiming, with more than her usual eagerness, "Oh, mamma! how I do long to bathe in it: to feel it fall among my hair, and grasp its jewels in my hands."

"Not fresh and fasting—go not near water at all, this day," replied the woodcutter; "oh! darling, be led and said by me, the whole of this blessed day. Listen, avourneen:—A pair of thrushes, dear, built their nest in a beautiful bower, and an ould wood-quest had a grate love for them, and used to sit and watch, and think how happy they were, and pray that they might be always so: but the male bird said to his mate, 'it's a poor country, and I must go into another, and gather food against the young ones come out in the nest we have made, and cry for food; and we have none to give them.' And the poor mate said, 'Don't go, avourneen deelish, for when the time comes we shall not want food; there has been a hard winter, and the sunbeam always comes out when the cloud is gone; so you see, there will be plenty of red-worms in spring, and ripe berries in summer; and He who sends both will take good care that we want neither: go not from me, for life as it is, is all too short to enjoy your song;' but he would go; and the fowler spied the brave free bird as he winged his way, his heart full of the memory of his own nest: and his eyes full of the image of the patient loving mate, who would have stayed his going; and the cruel fowler aimed at his true heart, and his aim was steady, and the bird returned no more."

"Hush," whispered Eva; "hush, Randy! look at mamma!" and then in a loud voice she added, "I do not want to hear any more about the old thrush-birds, Master Woodcutter; but I do want to hear about the young thrush-bird and the old quest; that's yourself and me, Master Randy. Ah! I've found you out, and I'll finish your fable:—the young thrush-bird was a wild, wilful, naughty, little bird, that would fly hither and thither, no matter how the old wood-quest croaked."

"Wood-quests don't croak, Miss Eva."

"Well, cooed!" she said, laughing; "though the coo of an old wood-quest is almost a croak; is it not?"

"It's anything you like, avourneen deelish! and you may laugh as much as you like, if you mind me."

"Well, I will, indeed I will; but, Randy, whisper," and she drew down his rugged head; "make fables about anything but mamma and poor papa; it kills me to see mamma's tears. What were you thinking of, you stupid Randy?"

"Of you, darling—the powers forgive me! of nothing else do I ever think! but I'll mind, dear, and not fret the mistress again."

Eva held up her finger as she turned away, saying, with a playful pout: "Every other little girl has her own way on her birth-day; while I dare not move but in your shadow, Randy. May I gather you some flowers, mamma, and some to give to those who so remembered me? I will sit by your side and bind them up, and after that we will go to the cottages, and then—but I will first gather the flowers." While her mother watched her movements, Randy stood by the mother's side.

"I learned a dale," he said, "last night; some I may tell, some, indeed, I don't quite understand my-self; those *you know* watch and wait upon her, and pour right thoughts into her mind, and love her, and think her as worthy love, as she will be of honour; their power will be with her for good, till she is herself a mo-ther; but danger is over her still, and she must beware water; she must

beware water," he continued, trembling from head to foot, so intense was his earnestness; "by night and by day—at Midsummer more particu-larly—the whole of this blessed day and night, until to-morrow's sunrise, lady, she must beware water."

"Well, so she shall, Randy; I promise you," replied Geraldine, "she can meet no harm among our own flowers; and see," she added, "she is moving her favourite plants within your fairy ring."

"They danced on it all last night," said the woodcutter: "it was a great sight; a sight you could never forget, lady; a lovely night too, and the small stars dreaming their way through the heavens; and they all dressed so beautiful; but I am sure things are not going on in all parts as they like: for many of them had bows and arrows, and long spears, and that's a sign of warfare; but you'll watch her, lady, you'll let me watch her all day, and don't let her go near water. They throw that spray ten times higher than ever, just to dazzle her," he said, pointing to the boiling waters of the Tore; "they swarm about it like bees. I wish the waters were chained in the bowels of the earth. I had a father and two brothers drowned at sea!"

Mrs. Raymond never contradicted the woodcutter! she promised that Eva should only move in his shadow, and invited him to enter the cottage with them; but Randy said she was safe beneath the shelter of her own roof, and while she was with her mother he would rather watch the waterfall. He rambled over the lawn and among the flowers, gazing every moment upon the bounding river, that, through a passage of jagged rocks, finds a peaceful path in the valley. At last, wearied by watching and the excitement of his own thoughts, he sat down beneath the shade of an evergreen oak, where not a movement of the half-sportive, half-angry waters could escape his observation. He began to think of himself, and how much more knowledge he had than other people; his confidence in his own powers increased, and a boastful spirit warred with his better nature; he said: "I am of myself strong; I am brave; I care not who helps me; I can save her! Ay! dance away, imps of the dark waters. I, Randy, the woodcutter, defy ye all!" Eva's silvery laugh fell upon his ear, and he would, if he could, have recalled the presumptuous words, "I care not who helps me;" but his gaze was fascinated by the spray; and he lolled lazily upon the sward, questioning almost if he was quite himself; he might be O'Donoghue of the Lakes—so uplifted did he feel —and why? In a little time longer he ceased to ask why; once he caught the stony eyes of a large yellow frog fixed upon him with a sort of cunning inquiry; but what cared he for either the Kelpie Queen or her steed! How the foam and spatter of the waters dazzled and made him wink! and then he felt hot and thirsty, and, at the moment, a grotesque

and distorted dwarf, carrying in both hands a huge china bowl, stood
by his side, and on tip-toe offered him to drink : at first Randy motioned

him away; but there arose from the
bowl a very fragrant steam; and the
dwarf asked if he feared to drink to his
young lady's health, of the mountain dew,
sweetened with the richest honey of the
wild bee—'mountain dew'—name which
libels the purest and holiest draught that
Nature sends to Earth from Heaven!
And as the woodcutter's good spirit
had been half vanquished by the spirit
of evil that taught him to overvalue
his own strength, and the enemy had
power over him—he drank—and slept.

The day was passing rapidly, and though Geraldine missed the woodcutter, she never doubted that he was active in his self-imposed duty. She had many cares to think of, and when Eva, after bestowing the flowers she had gathered in the morning, asked permission to go into the garden, she gave it, adding, " Remember, Eva, you are not to go near water. Nay, my child, I am quite serious; if there were no other cause, you must not give pain to our old friend Randy. You must promise."

" I do, mamma, I do; I shall find the woodcutter in the garden, and keep with him; he said he would to-day tell me the tale of the weather-cock." And away she went, full of life, singing along the alleys, and

bounding over the lawn, calling loudly on him who heard not: and whom, at last, she found sleeping soundly. The child turned away not to disturb him, and as she did so, she caught sight of the Tore waterfall. Never, she thought, till that moment, had aught so beautiful appeared before her; she clapped her hands and sprang onward with joy. Resting on the very crest of the waterfall was a perfect and en-tire rainbow; myriads of tinted stars dropped from its arch, without in-juring its brilliancy or form—mingling with, and yet apart from, the snow-white foam. If all the jewels of the east had been flung into the mist, they could not have produced a more dazzling effect, than did those which Nature lavished upon the sportive waters. The fascinated and bewildered child, though she had stolen away on tiptoe from where Randy slept, now called impatiently to him to accompany her; once, twice, thrice—each time she was farther from him; but he, the true and faithful hearted, when not under the influence of the evil-spirit spell—he heard her not. Her promise to her mother was forgotten. Oh! wayward, unthinking child! the sin of the Garden of Eden was with you while the sun shone, soft music sought to win you to the banks of the wildest thyme ; huge humble bees invited you to their cells, and offered you the rich banquet of their honey ; voices whispered from out the virgin lilies, and rustled the leaves

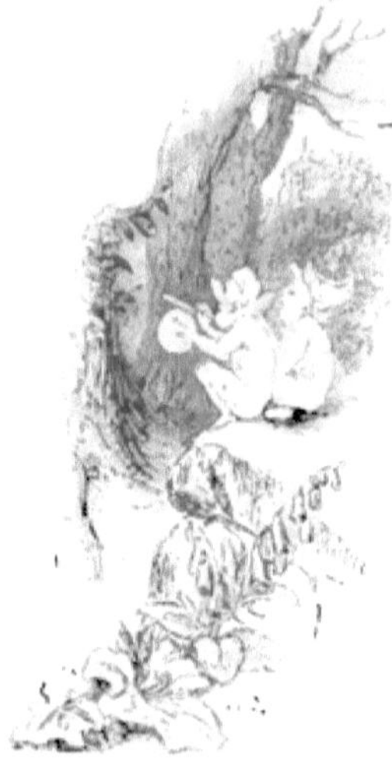

of the bright rose ; if the Kelpie Queen had spread snares and painted shows to lure you to her waters, the votaries of the spirits of earth and air were watching, like true subjects, in the absence of their Queens, to frustrate her evil courses.

But in her green and slimy palace the Kelpie worked, and sent forth her people to do her bidding. She could weave spells in her dark cell beneath the waters the length of a Midsummer day. Nightstar trusted to a mortal; the Kelpie discovered that mortal's weakness. Alas! the child heard the warnings but heeded them not ; their *unaided* power was too weak—Nightstar was above, waiting to descend on the gray vapour which succeeds the last beam of the setting sun. On went the child, and as she passed, she heard behind her sighs and sobs of sorrow; her favourite flowers drooped their heads—they could not look upon her—they would have warned her, had they the power; the lark hovered above her head—his delicious song gushing forth at intervals, as he rose and fell, but the child heard not—heeded not; the robin crossed her path, and looked with his large lustrous eyes into her face; but her eyes were dazzled—her better self was overpowered. On she went; the precincts of her own garden were overstepped; and the mocking fiend that had tempted him, now roused the woodcutter with snarling laughter. He awoke, and his permitted eyes saw at once the danger.

" Rouse up, proud Randy, and save her now !"

The bewildered man, who had quaffed the poison, arose ; he staggered from side to side ; he had deprived himself of power over the members of his own body. He would have called, but his swollen tongue refused obedience to his will ; conscious of his own impotence—he saw the peril he could not avert.

She stood below the second fall, her arms extended towards the magic rainbow; the water was welling up to kiss her feet; beneath it the face and form of the Kelpie Queen, veiled by her flowing hair,

was dimly visible. If he had been himself, a few bounds of Randy's active limbs could have placed him by her side; but self-betrayed—self-abandoned —he gazed without a move. The waters were rising around her—another minute and she would be lost to earth and sky for ever. He knew—he understood— but he could neither cry out nor press forward! but he heard the sneer of the fiend, "Great Randy, save her!" His blood

whirled madly through his veins, and then came a shriek—a woman's shriek of warning and of agony. The child looked back—and saw her mother! She sprang from the fatal bank into her arms.

"Why did you scream, mamma," said Eva. "The waters were so calm, and you frightened away the rainbow."

"There was no rainbow," answered her mother. "The Fall has been more than usually dark to-day; but you broke your word, Eva; you have made me unhappy."

The child had forgotten her pledge until that moment, and shame and sorrow came to her young bosom. She would have knelt for forgiveness, but it was sweeter to hang about her mother's neck, hear the pardon uttered before it was asked, and have her tears kissed away.

The day seemed to have fleeted strangely and rapidly; the long, long twilight of Midsummer was approaching—when the evening and morning meet together upon the hills, and rejoice that no cold and shivering night divides them from each other. Though unconscious of the danger she had escaped—shame at her broken promise, and sorrow at her mother's displeasure, kept Eva silent and sad. But she soon regained her elasticity, and pointed with earnest delight to a tall tree whereon a wood-pigeon sat cooing to her young on the topmost bough: the bird bent downward its loving eyes, and the child gazed upward with a gesture of delight. Her little heart bounded with affection towards the

bird; but, as she looked, suddenly a hawk darted upon it. The next moment, Eva was pressing the dove to her bosom, to which it had flown for shelter, while the fierce bird, disappointed of its prey, wheeled above her head, evidently pondering whether he might not strike the child and come off victor. Although her cheeks were flushed, her little foot stood firmly forward; her arm was stretched in an attitude of defiance towards the pirate of the air; her lips were open, and her head was thrown back, while her mother stood astounded at the boldness of the hawk, and the courage of a timid and tender girl, who would tremble at the falling of a leaf, and shrink from a shadow—now strengthened by Love to brave the anger of the feathered assassin, whose scream sounded like a curse from his purple beak, while his distended talons were drawn closely upon his mottled breast; and yet she quailed not; her little hand continued uplifted to save the thing that trusted her; and then came a flash—a report—the murderer in his turn reeled, and a cloud of feathers floated to the sward; the hawk wheeled in a broken circle once round, then, with wavering motion, disappeared among the trees.

"I'm enough myself to do *that*, anyhow," quoth the woodcutter; "praise be to the author of the strength, as well as the will, for such a service," and then he crouched forward like an animal that deserved and expected chastisement; while Eva exclaimed—"It is saved! it is saved! —but I will not let it go yet: look how still it is: it shall soon return to its young; it will coo in its own woods; but it will still be *my own* darling wood-quest, *that I saved*. Oh what a happy birthday, to have found something that trusted me!—something new to love!" The child stood at her mother's knee; she held the wood-quest to her heart, and, though smiles were playing on her face, her eyes were brimming over with tears. "I am not crying, dear mamma; I hear its young calling it! I hope I am not selfish, but I do not want it to fly away *too* soon."

"My own sweet Eva," replied her mother, with a troubled countenance; "that bird will never fly away."

"Oh yes, it will," answered the child, in full confidence of the power of affection; "it would not leave its young—it would not of its own self remain with me for ever."

"Nothing," answered her mother; "nothing, however much we love it, Eva, remains with us, for ever. My dear — *dear* child, the poor bird is dead!"

"Oh, no!" she replied, in a tone of anguish. "Oh, no! it cannot be; I felt its heart beat against mine when it came first; and then it laid its head just there. It cannot be; I do not think the hawk touched it; death cannot come so soon. If you take it from me, mamma, take care it does not fly away too quickly."

"I will take it as tenderly as you can, dearest. See how its head hangs; and though its young call it in such plaintive tones it heeds them not; its tender eyes are already dim; your own bosom, Eva, is stained by its blood. My poor child, this sudden and violent death is new to you;

the cruel hawk struck too surely—although it escaped to die at peace upon your innocent heart."

Eva enveloped herself in the folds of her mother's dress, and her sobs were loud and bitter.

"May all springs and sweet waters dry around them!" exclaimed Randy; "and neither thorn, nor rush, nor the sting of the poisonous nettle move in their defence, but leave them unarmed to the sharp bill of the merciless heron and the vengeance of the king-fisher. May the broad-backed frog refuse to do their bidding, and the great Lake King forbid them his hunting-grounds! I know their dark den by the old WEIR BRIDGE: I know it well; the water under its one arch is as black as their own hearts, and rushes along like the fury of their own wicked wishes. May the sunlight never come there; — may no moonlight shine on  the path or brighten the way of those that put this sorrow on her, this blessed day." The woodcutter paused for breath. "Fool that I was—fool—fool; and now to strike her through her feelings. Oh! won't there be murder when the moon rises? and how will I ever face Nightstar? Oh, fool! The viper—the toad—the black-water sarpint! She worked me cruel usage, and my heart will tremble with the torture it went through to the day of my death. If that had been a right bird, it would have been lying upon the grass. Augh! I know her better than ever now; in league with hawks and eagles, is she! and wanting such as that blessed angel to sit in the slime, and twine her hair with the shells of the stripy snail and the rattling pearls of fishes' eyes!—her face to be the lamp and her voice the music of the dark and dripping palace." And so the woodcutter vented his anger both on himself and the Kelpie, in words not loud but deep; yet neither mother nor child heard him; the child continued weeping bitterly, and her mother would have carried the bird away, but Eva entreated her to leave it a little longer.

"Let me keep it a little longer, mamma—just half an hour; I will give it up in half an hour. Do, mamma—dear mamma! I will not idle nor play with it; I will only keep it until I understand what death is."

"My child, it is a bitter knowledge; I felt its bitterness long since," sighed her mother.

"I know—I know," she said quickly; "that was when papa died; but do let me keep it. It was so alive when it flew to me such a little time ago, and seemed so happy. I loved it in a moment, and could have died to save it!" and then her tears flowed afresh. "You tell me to pray when I want good gifts from heaven: is to understand death a good gift? May I pray for it, mamma?"

"It is, indeed, right to pray for understanding," she replied. "You now see that the life which moved its wings, and gave it power to go hither and thither, taught it to rear its young, and caused its pretty cooing to sound in the woods—is gone!"

"Where?" inquired the child. "And did it go out of this deep red wound?"

"It is not given us to know *where* it is gone; but it *is* gone: and wise as we think ourselves, we have no power to call it back. But you must remember, that if it will have no more pleasure here, it will have no more pain."

The child shook her head, and, taking the bird in her hand, passed into her chamber, laid it down on her little bed, and then knelt by its side. She uttered no sound, though her lips moved, and ever and anon, tears fell silently on her clasped hands, and she would fondle the bird, and resume her thoughts and prayer. Who can tell what feelings were shadowed forth at that solemn moment to that deep-hearted child! More than once she pushed back the hair that clustered over her brow, and pressed her hands upon its rounded surface; her eyes, so blue, so expressive, radiated with new emotions—beaming with elevated sensations; her mind expanded, and palpitated with increased knowledge; she seemed entering on a new existence; she prayed earnestly, not taught words, but framing her simple petition in her own language. How earnestly she desired goodness and patience; that sudden death might be kept away from all she loved; that she might become wise, and that many might love her, and that she might love all the world and comfort the poor; she felt both resigned and elevated by this humble sacrifice; more than once her mother entered, unperceived, and unwilling to disturb her, silently withdrew.

A bright light, as of the glory of the setting sun, entered; and knowing that the sun had set long before, and the grey clouds were descending over earth, the child was astonished; and at the same moment she started, for she thought she heard the rustling of wings, and flushed with the hope that the bird had revived, she touched it, but it had grown so stiff and cold that her fingers were involuntarily drawn back; and she forgot she had learned nothing of the mighty mystery concerning which she would have inquired; but an increase of hope, and faith, and love, seemed infused into her nature. She had become tranquil, and returned to her mother with a quiet smile; then placing the bird in her hands, she said, "Let us bury it: it will not be naughty to love it in its grave." And as they carried the dead bird to the foot of a hawthorn bush, where the grass was greenest, and the earliest beams of the sun shed their light and warmth, they heard the bereaved birds lamenting their loss, and they saw the wood-pigeon's mate comforting and feeding them—calling on her he should never see again, with a loud and peculiarly sorrowful cry.

Randy dug the grave and covered it over, and walked silently back to the cottage; there, casting himself along the green bench, he waited the summons he knew he should receive from Nightstar.

Bonfires blazed from every hill, and the happy children of the village raised a tremendous one, in honour both of Midsummer and the birth-night of Eva Raymond. They looked well through the trees, and recalled to those who mingle the past with the present the Baal fires of old. The woodcutter never moved from his post; it would be difficult to record his thankfulness for the child's preservation, or his contempt for his own unworthiness. He resolved humbly to submit to any punishment his royal mistress might inflict. He saw the distant fires die away, one by one, upon the hills—the voices of the children ceased altogether—then from

the cottage he heard the night hymns of praise and prayer arise—the dog took his last round in the garden, and licked the woodcutter's hand as he passed—and the lights that threw such shadows on the lawn were extinguished—a discontented grasshopper once or twice moved its restless wings beneath a broad dock-leaf, and the corn-crake in the distance seemed at last to have the world to herself—so silent had everything become.

Suddenly there appeared glimmering lights among the trees, and the soft low note of the fairy bagpipe struck upon Randy's ear. "I had nothing to be ashamed of this time last year," he said ; " but surely my repentance, and the bullet I shot, will plead in my favour :—and there is no harm done," whispered self-justification ; yet Randy courageously put aside so dangerous an ally, and resolved to say nothing for himself. But the woodcutter could not see them distinctly, as he had done in former times: there seemed a mist—a veil—between them and him: he heard the music and the booming hum of Queen Honeybell's great bee; while the lights of Nightstar's fairy host glittered brightly, and the twanging of her minstrel harps sounded clearly enough ; but he could hardly trace the outline of the fairy Queens, as they took their seats upon the 'hillock,' in the very midst of the ring. Instead of dancing, as usual, the Queens continued in grave consultation, attended by their ministers of state. Randy could see them come and go—pass and repass ; and suddenly there arose a great tumult, and the music (to which they had paid no attention) ceased ; and Randy himself was called forth and confronted with the distorted sprite that had tempted him to neglect of duty. Nightstar addressed the huge and trembling mortal in a voice of tender displeasure, that wounded him more severely than if she had reproved him in an angry tone. She told him that all was known to her : but now she only asked if that *thing* which some of her people had secured, while he was seeking to escape from her dominions, was the spirit that had tampered with her sentinel. Randy identified him at once, and, without further question, she

decreed that he should be given over, within five minutes, to the bees of Honeybell's court, whose honey he had so often plundered — to work their pleasure with him until sunrise. It would seem that this was considered a hard sentence, though it afforded infinite delight to the great bee, who advanced at once to take the imp into custody. He was a bee of most savage aspect, and the cowardly cup-bearer shrunk before the sword-like sting, and rough, hairy arms he extended towards THE SLIMY FACE of the Kelpie Queen. Randy felt that his turn must come next, for both Queens regarded him silently for some moments ; but, as they did, his eyes became clearer, and he saw more distinctly—and they whispered together. That was a good sign. The woodcutter knew his thoughts were penitent, and his sorrow sincere ; but Honeybell looked sulky, and Nightstar sad—and tears gathered in the poor fellow's eyes. But as he stood, there arose a tumult among the outposts of the ring, which suddenly gave way, and the Kelpie Queen, her dark hair streaming like a death-pennon behind her, her eyes glittering like rubies, cantered into the assembly ; and then, springing on the grass, demanded her place by the side of her royal sisters. The Queens arose, and descending, hand in hand, into the arena, declared they would rather resign their throne than share it with her, and dared her to mount it alone. Dark faces showed more dark amid the troops of light, and there was a breathless silence, broken only once by a shriek from the Kelpie page.

"Who dares to punish my subject?" demanded the fierce Queen.

"I dare," answered Nightstar, with dignity; "how dared *you* send him to tamper with my people?"

"He gave the oaf to drink when he was athirst; and, like all mortals, he knew not when to stop."

"This double dealing is unworthy of royalty—even royalty such as yours," replied Nightstar. "You gave him (for yonder imp is your familiar) of the poisoned drink, heated at your own furnace. You gave it him that you might lure my charge into your power to be your slave ; and not content with that, what you could not vanquish, you persecuted, and mingled so many tears with her young cup of life, that the hardness of premature wisdom has chilled her interest in existence. Shame upon you, there is nothing lovely that you would not either enslave or destroy!"

"The child is mine," said the Kelpie, daringly. "The child is mine : your jugglery cheated me of my right. Did not you refuse her?" she continued, addressing Honeybell.

"I gave her to Nightstar," replied the heavy-lidded Queen.

"Hear this, lords and ladies of all courts," exclaimed the subtle Kelpie. "*She* having no right but to choose, does not choose, but gives what of right was mine—the infant rejected by Nightstar and by herself."

"She was *not* rejected by me," interrupted Nightstar.

"Then why is she not here?   I see changelings in both your courts, but not the prize—the orphan Raymond," rejoined the Kelpie.

"Because I choose her to remain with her earthly mother.   She being mine I leave her where I will.   I appeal to no lords and ladies ; such is my will ; and I maintain it, as befits my state," quoth Nightstar.   "I say this to you, dark reveller of the lake."

The Kelpie started, awed by the brightness and boldness that animated the fragile form of the Air Queen, and the dark faces of her troop drew back.   "Give me my page," she said.

"Go ask him of the Bees," replied the haughty Nightstar.   "You have made our revels dark by your presence.   We would be rid of both : at the crow of cock you can send for your base satellite."

"The craythur only did his duty in obeying his Queen," thought Randy.

Nightstar applauded with a smile.   "Nay, release him," she continued, "the victim of his treachery suggests to us, that he only did his duty in obeying his Queen."

At that moment the cock crew, and the woodcutter, rubbing his eyes, looked into the soft haze of a Midsummer Morning.

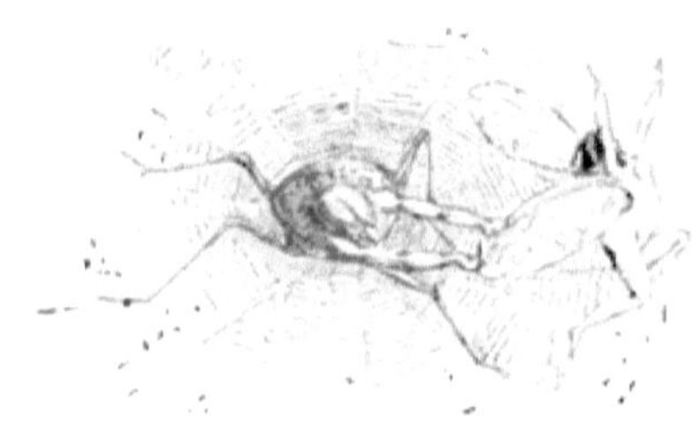

Drawn by Wehnert.
Engraved by E. Dalziel.

PART THE THIRD.

N the spacious and lofty hall of an ancient castle near Killarney, adorned after the fashion of old, rather than of modern, times, two youths, apparently about the same age, were occupied—each according to his taste; it was evident that, however close their connection, their pursuits were opposite; one was seated in the deep recess of a window, that overhung a clear and rapid river; beside him were scattered various implements of the chase; a long fowling-piece rested against the seat, and he was eagerly engaged in fitting a string to a good yew bow; his brown hair clustered around his head so thickly, that it was difficult to ascertain its form; the brow full, the eyes grey and sparkling; the nose straight and delicate; the mouth large, but the mould was so perfect, and the lips were so sharply chiseled and rich in colour—so fertile of smiles—that Cormac's admirers called it beautiful; yet, even when in repose, its expression was unpleasing and often painful. The other youth was seated also, but at another window. It would have been difficult to guess which was the elder and which the younger of the two: brothers they might be—relatives they certainly were; their hair

and eyes were of the same colour; the brow of Sidney was more full,
his eyebrows were better arched; but the great distinction was in the
lower portion of the face; whether in action or repose, Sidney's mouth
expressed the firmness and decision of character that usually determine
a man's fortune; the chin was finely modeled, sufficiently large, but free
from every taint of sensuality; when he smiled, it was with the eyes
rather than the lips; sometimes, indeed, they parted, and then his
eloquent countenance was lit up by the sunshine of an elevated and

most happy nature. He had been drawing—for an open sketch-book
lay upon a table that stood in front of the richly-carved chair whereon
he sat; nor was that the only indication of his taste—a half-finished
map was kept open by a box of water-colours, and a French horn and
a fishing-rod rested on the deep stone sill of the open window. Everything in the room appeared in keeping with its ancient state: even the
youths had that aristocratic bearing which indicates the consciousness
of rank.

"What are you thinking of, Sidney?" inquired Cormac, having, after many efforts, tightened the cord to his pleasure. "What *are* you thinking of? that shake of the head is no reply. *I* was thinking how opposite we are in habits, and yet how united in affection; you are so contemplative; so fond of books; your heart is so tender, and yet you are so firm; so deep a lover of music; so cautious; so serious! a MAN at eighteen; *I* am thoughtless, changeable, impetuous." He waited, as people, young and old, often do, when they enumerate their faults, in the hope of contradiction; but Sidney made no attempt to stay his words. "I have a bitter will, and a hard heart," he added, at length.

"You have not a hard heart, Cormac," said Sidney; "I know not what you mean by a 'bitter will,' but you have the impetuous will of a Talbot." Cormac smiled, and looked rather pleased than otherwise. "How are you going to spend the remainder of the day?" added Sidney, while arranging his sketches, so as to leave all things in order.

"I hardly know; my mother is so unreasonable. Women never judge rightly about their sons. If I take up a gun, she thinks I must be shot; if I go on the lake or river, she trembles lest I should be drowned; if I ride, she fears I shall break my neck;—I wish my father had lived."

"How unfortunate! to have a mother who loves you, an old inheritance, and an ancient name; to be *the* person in your own home considered above all others!"

"You should not say that, Sidney," replied his cousin, "for I think my mother loves you quite as much as she loves me—and no wonder!"

"She has indeed proved how she loved her husband by being a child to his parents, and a parent to his brother's children. My father said his children had two mothers," replied Sidney, in a voice trembling with emotion—an emotion proceeding from the knowledge that his aunt considered him necessary to his cousin, but had never loved him.

"And there it is again," said Cormac; "I never had a brother; though to be sure you are the same thing, Sidney. But, if I had half a score of brothers and sisters, like other fellows, I might do as I like. My mother could not have watched them all as she watches me."

"We have been at Eton so long, Cormac; and she is so delighted to have you home," suggested his cousin; "and so proud of you."

"And yet, Sidney, I am not as much beloved as you are," said Cormac, in a discontented tone. "Wherever we are, dogs and children find you out; when we returned home together only last week, many of the old men in the crowd who welcomed me back, kept saying, 'That is the young master in the blue cap; we should know him anywhere, by his smiling eyes and sweet face;' *my* cap was scarlet; and yet I bowed and smiled twice as much as you."

"That was but a mistake made by half-blind age."

"Not at all; you have the luck! Your shilling always does as much good as my guinea. But let us think of something else. You deserve the popularity and have it—I deserve—but no matter. I wonder would the arrow carry this strip of crimson to the top bough of yonder ash. Come, take your bugle, and when you sound, I shoot."

The youths stood together at the window; the one with the bow drawn to its full extent; the other, his head a little thrown back, and the bugle ready to sound its ti-ri-la in honour of the shot. Born within the same week, they were nearly the same height: but Cormac was more athletic than his cousin, Sidney more lithe and graceful than Cormac. The arrow, bearing its thread of crimson, sped its way, and the echoes of the narrow pass over which the castle hung took up the blast of the horn; now whispering, now ringing forth the long-drawn note in many varied tones —tones, so varied, that both youths held their breath, less they should miss the slightest sound.

"Well blown! well shot!" said Cormac, after the first intonation had died upon the air. By my word, it leads me to believe the strange stories of our Lake Region, when such a note is repeated in so many modulations. My arrow may have struck some Dryad to a tree; it passed the ash."

"It would be sure to do so," said Sidney; "the ash is a charmed tree."

"And you to tell me that with a grave face!" answered Cormac. "You, so wise! you to have faith in old wives' tales! I remember the pleasure you took, long ago, in hearing about Lake horses and

Phookas, and 'Our Cousin O'Donoghue,' as my stately mother calls him—O'Donoghue, who, every May morning, rises from his palace, a thousand fathoms deep, and rides over the Lake, attended by bevies of sylphs and fairies. I never could listen with patience to such legends, much less believe them."

"Nor I, exactly; but we hear much we do not believe, that, nevertheless, has for us a strange interest."

"Well, that is true. I am sure I remember the wild story that went through the country about little Eva Raymond. Was she not the child of one of your father's brother-officers, Sidney?"

"She was."

"I dare say," continued the loquacious Cormac, "she is not as pretty a child as she was."

"Child!" echoed Sidney; "she is fourteen this very Midsummer Eve."

"Well, that *is* a child, I am sure. Is the old story kept up ?"

" Yes."

"And is she as closely guarded by the old woodcutter as she used to be ?"

" I believe so."

"And do the people make as great a fuss about her as they did at first ?"

"She has grown so lovely," exclaimed Sidney, in a sudden burst of enthusiasm, "that strangers watch outside her cottage to see her shadow as it crosses the window ; but, after all, beauty, mere beauty, is the least of her attractions. You should hear her sing, or even speak ; and then you would know what music is !"

"And so, Master Sidney, you have been to Dovecote without my mother's knowledge."

"My father was her father's friend ; it was only civil to call," was the reply as he turned away ; but not before Cormac saw that he blushed like a girl at the mention of her lover's name.

"Luck, again !" he muttered.

"Luck ! what luck ! You forget that when we were here five years ago I used to go to the cottage frequently. I never thought you cared about her, and Lady Elizabeth does not visit Mrs Raymond."

"After all, if my mother will not permit me to shoot, hunt, or boat, while we remain here, I shall be very glad, Sidney, to go with you to Dovecote."

" You know how particular your mother is, and how much she likes to maintain etiquette ; you had better ask her sanction, Cormac."

Of course the high-spirited youth laughed at the suggestion. He thought of beauty less than most youths of his age, he had acquired conventional ideas at Eton, and believed rusticity and vulgarity synony-mous terms. His English mother, Lady Elizabeth Talbot, considered she performed her duty to her tenants by visiting Ard-Flesk at intervals of five or six years, for two or three months at a time, 'to keep up,' as she pompously expressed it, 'her son's knowledge of his people and inheritance.' Sidney overrated, as all generous minds do, the kindness shown to him and to his kindred. He had been from childhood necessary to his cousin's happiness, and Lady Elizabeth permitted no one but herself to thwart Cormac. The beauty of Eva Raymond was rendered still more dangerous by the mystery believed to hover round her; but Lady Elizabeth held herself and all hers above such influences, and in the centre of the Lake country, while rowing upon its waters, beneath the very shadow of Ross Castle, on the lonely shore of Innisfallen, or passing through the deepest defiles of the savagely wild GAP OF DUNLOE, she

delighted to express her disbelief in fairy lore and legend—to say, what even I, in my Saxon dwelling, as an ally of the 'good people,' should not care to repeat. The effect of this imprudence was manifest in the nightly disturbance of her household; strange noises rattled through Ard-Flesk; sleep became a stranger to the inhabitants of certain portions of the castle; the dairymaid complained that the cream was 'broken,' and not a tithe of the butter yielded; the coachman, that his horses fell lame; the henwife, that the eggs were sucked; the butler vowed that 'something' not only drank the wine, but left it running, as through a pin-hole; and once he staggered from the dim and vaulted cellar, pale as a ghost, and said that his candle had been blown out as he unlocked the door, but that he had seen a number of quaint little creatures

no longer than his thumb, dressed in the strangest fashion; some wearing cocked hats and square-cut coats, running along the moonbeams that slanted upon a huge pipe of claret—some with flagons, others with outlandish bottles, others bearing vessels full of wine on their heads —all detected in the very act of robbing the cellar; the lady's maid, whose little malignant person was so stiffened out that she suggested the idea of having been dipped in a bowl of starch and hung in the sun to

dry, complained most bitterly that whenever she was going to sleep something tickled the sharp point of her nose with a nettle, and that, consequently, she had not closed her eyes for a fortnight; and what made this fact the more extraordinary was, that a simple country girl who slept with her, and whom she unmercifully fagged during the day, rested soundly and sweetly, despite the efforts to awaken her. Cormac's favourite hunter had been nearly ridden to death by the Phooka the night before he wanted it for the field, and more than once the powder in his flask had been found wet when he knew he had left it dry. Sidney had nothing to complain of; on the contrary, his pony, from having been a vicious, ill-tempered beast, had become gentle as a lamb, and endowed with the affection and intelligence of a dog; his fly was sure to hook the finest salmon in lake or river, and the tenderest echoes repeated every note of his bugle. But Cormac and his mother, instead of endeavouring to propitiate the good people, who were justly offended with much, both said and done to their annoyance, accounted for everything in a mode so matter-of-fact, that they irritated the Fairies, as much by their obstinacy as by their contempt.

Lady Elizabeth was very particular and formal in all things connected with her toilet; draperies of the finest muslin, starred with gold, descended from her inlaid looking-glass; a cheval-glass stood at the right angle of her dressing-table to give effect to the profile and the figure, and cosmetics were carefully enshrined in boxes of filigree silver. She always dismissed her maid when her lappets were pinned on, and completed her adornments in solitude;—I should write 'repairs,' rather than ' adornments ;'—the tint for the cheek, the pencil for the eyebrow, the pearl powder for the throat, were used in secret; but, of late, the stately lady had been so bewildered, that more than once she had applied the rouge to her

eyebrows, and the black pomade of Ispahan to her cheeks! Yes: she had done this more than once, and yet she knew it not, until the faithful mirror of the drawing-room undeceived her.

Lady Elizabeth felt that her dignity was invaded by some malign influence she could neither account for nor control. Fairies of air and earth form an estimate of human beings very different from that which human beings form of each other; their good opinions, and consequent services, are not to be bought by wealth or station; they love to succour the oppressed, and to clothe virtuous russet in shining light; they are a

high-minded, independent race; for ever whispering good counsels into listening ears; and even if Lady Elizabeth had treated them with common courtesy— had permitted the bit of butter to be left on the lintel of the dairy — the first cup of wine drawn from the new pipe to be poured on the floor of the buttery—the heifer's first pail of milk to be thrown inside the fairy-ring —I doubt if they in return would have permitted one who was 'hard to the poor,' and unfriendly to the widow, to remain unannoyed at Ard-Flesk.

Cormac's curiosity had been roused by his cousin's few words of praise, so warmly given to Eva Raymond; and though he knew that Sidney's ideas of beauty did not correspond with his, he was seized with a desire to visit the young Lady of Dovecote; suddenly he remembered that his arrow had flown in the direction of the cottage, and felt a wish to recover it; but at the moment the dressing-bell rang, and knowing how particular was his lady-mother, that a fit appearance should be made at the formal and prolonged meal, he postponed his search until the evening After dinner, the Lady's steward craved audience, and the cousins were desired to remain until it was over. He told her that a man was lying under a tree in her Ladyship's wood, ill of 'the fever,' with which he had been stricken; and he wished to know what her Ladyship would please to have done for him. Lady Elizabeth became angry, and desired he should go away; and the steward said he was not able to go; but that it was the custom of the gentry, when poor creatures was fever-stricken, to order a hut or shed to be placed over them, and he wished to know, as the man was in her wood, would she permit him to erect a little shed for his shelter; and Lady Elizabeth declared "No!" that he ought to be punished, not protected, and was sorely displeased with the steward; but he was an old servant, and feared not to speak his mind. He said the man had been seized in the night by 'the sickness,' and repeated that, even if he could, he would not, move, lest others might suffer by his visitation. Lady Elizabeth said she supposed he was a poacher, or some fellow of bad character, to be in her wood at night, but that he must go home, or to prison. The youths looked at each other, and Cormac did say it was hard to send a poor fellow to jail for having a fever. "He is no poacher, my Lady," added the steward; "and, indeed, I may say he *is* at home; for his life is spent, innocent-like, among the woods and hills; he has winter shelter in a summer-house, a kind lady gave him to live in, but the creature's prayer is that she may not hear he is sick, for fear she should come and see him; and so, maybe, get 'the sickness' herself: oh! but his moans are woful. I hope your honour's Ladyship will not go against the custom of the country, but give him shelter, for the love of God."

"I am sure it is Randy, the woodcutter!" exclaimed Sidney; "do, dear aunt, let me entreat, with old Matthew, that he may be sheltered; he saved my life once from a red-deer on Glena—a brave old fellow: the deer followed me furiously, but when Randy appeared, went away as gentle as a lamb. We both remember him, Cormac." The young men united their entreaties, but Lady Elizabeth continued inexorable; she talked a great deal, declared her belief that illness, particularly fever, and more particularly than all, Irish fever, was sent as a punishment to the poor for being idle; consequently only the idle got the fever. She showed, to her own satisfaction, that industrious folk were always healthy; she had examined the state of the country, during her visits of a month at a time, every five or six years, and taken great pains to point out to them what they ought to do to improve their minds and clothe their bodies; and their declaring they had no means to do as she bade them was the consequence of laziness; she considered, indeed, as do other people, equally wise, that sickness was a shame and poverty a sin, while doctors were abundant and food was plentiful.

"What a fool I was to tell her anything about it," said old Matthew, after he left the room; "I'd as soon lose my life as try to move him

against his will; and he'll perish where he is. Oh, then, what business
at all have those in Ireland who have no heart for the sick and poor!"

In less than half-an-hour after this little scene, the cousins left the hall,
Cormac carrying his gun, and, warm as the weather was, Sidney threw his
cloak over his arm. It was as fragrant, as glowing, and as balmy an
evening as ever Midsummer brought upon its wings; every bird, and
bee, and flower, rejoiced; the refreshing dews still hovered over the earth
they would bless with a long draught of love before the morning came.
At times, the lads encountered a current of air so laden with heat, that they
said it might rain and thunder ere the next day's noon; and then they
hurried on, with lightsome steps, and, after a time, with lighter hearts, for
Lady Elizabeth's harshness was painful to think upon, and Sidney esteemed
her so much, that he could not bear to believe her guilty of unworthy
actions; and continually repeated to himself, "She is afraid of fever
on our accounts—that is all—that must be all; she has been so very kind
to me;" and as he thought this grateful thought, all things around him,
all things he looked upon, increased sevenfold in beauty. Away they
went, and soon their jests and merry laughter set the echoes dancing
above them; the shadows of the trees crossed into a most fantastic
pavement the grass upon which they trod; and once, as Cormac raised
his gun to bring down a golden-billed blackbird, that was seated just

above his brown mate in a hawthorn bush, the bird broke into such a gush
of music, that he let his piece fall, and met Sidney's earnest look with a
smile as bright as the blackbird's whistle was loud. "It would," he
exclaimed, "it would have been downright murder—it was so like saying,
'could you do it!'" On they went; how the rabbits scudded before
them; the hare started from her form; the burly cockchafer struck
against their hats, and their faces were netted by the tracery of the
gossamer spider; while at intervals the belling of the red-deer sounded
far, far away.

"Are you sure we have got on the right track?" he said, at last.

"Yes," replied Sidney, "I have noted every tree and turn as the
steward told me. I really think, Cormac, you had better come no farther,
for here is what they call the
'Weary Well,' and this turn to
the right will bring us to the
river — look — there is the
bridge. With me it is a part
of duty to see the poor fellow;
he never did for you what
he did for me." They pro-
ceeded onwards, however, and
at the next turn, before either
spoke again, they stopped involuntarily, for two overhanging trees formed a framework,
into which a most exquisite
bit of lake and mountain was
set as in a picture-frame. The
most luxuriant foliage dipped
into the water: fold upon fold
of trees of various hues, of

which they saw but the topmast branches, made the mountain base appear
a continuation of gigantic garlands, while towards the summit, one pile
of rocks against another stood out against the sky. The youths knew
the islands underneath by name, and whispered them to each other; for

the scene was so still and lovely that they did not dare disturb it by the sound of even low voices. At length they turned away.

"How can my aunt leave a scene like this, for the pent-up life of a crowded city?" asked Sidney.

"It is certainly beautiful," replied Cormac; "but the misery of the people is its blight!"

"It would vanish as it does elsewhere, if you were always at home," said Sidney; "but look—here is the tree. Now, Cormac, go no farther. If you were to take this fever I should never forgive myself: back, dear Cormac."

"I will not go back," replied Cormac. "If my mother will not do so, it is my duty to protect him." And, despite his cousin's entreaties, he continued to walk by his side, until their progress was arrested by the sound of voices in conversation. "Hush!" exclaimed Sidney, and his countenance changed from its usually calm expression to one of trembling eagerness and joy. "Hush! she is here—she has found him!" Cormac followed silently, until Sidney paused.

The woodcutter supported himself on his elbow, beneath the shade of one of those gigantic laurels that grow only in the Lake country, and mingled the most earnest entreaties that Eva would leave him, with prophetic warnings as to the care she ought to take of herself, while, little heeding his words, having drawn a large branch to the ground, and secured it by a long sash, she draped a shawl so as to protect him from the night-dew. No description could convey an idea of the ease and buoyancy of her movements, or the gracious and tender expressions by which she entreated the poor sufferer to lie down upon the pillow of heather she had heaped for his relief. Exercise and anxiety had imparted a glow to her usually pale complexion; and, though her words were full of cheerfulness and hope, her eyes frequently overflowed with tears, and her voice was broken like that of a nightingale when it laments the passing away of spring.

"I'm safe enough, darling of your mother's heart! jewel of the mountains! and the only fear I have—mavourneen deelish!—is that you'll come to harm through the sickness that is over me. Oh, then, how did you hear it at all?"

"I missed you in the morning, and my mother thought you were long coming. I asked of all I met if they had seen you; and when I heard

where you were, I came at once. Do not fear for me. I have been, from night till morn, watching poor fever-stricken people, and never felt an ache; never has weariness been upon my eyelids. Now I will go; but will return ere the moon rises."

"Stop!" exclaimed the woodcutter; "stop! as you value my everlasting rest—as you value your mother's love—as you value your own life—come not back to me to-night! Don't you remember this time seven years—don't you mind since! But you don't—you don't! The knowledge and the trials are on *me;* you can't see them—so best. They hunted me with the fever-hound — the fleshless yellow dog with the open mouth—swift of foot, with hot blighting breath—that preys ou fresh graves, and carries the pestilence through sleeping towns into the mountains! I was gathering herbs by the Weary Well when he got up with me, and I ran; but he ran me down here—your poor Randy, jewel! Ay!—I see ye—midges you seem to her!" he continued, looking upwards; "I see ye, capering and face-making: I know and serve your masters! Hurt but a hair of her head, and how long will ye get leave to sow toadstools on the woodpaths, and dance your lanterns over shaking bogs! Oh, you're all of the same family. Don't go near water, avourneen—don't. There's plenty of kind Christians will build a shelter over the woodcutter! Go home, Miss Eva: to think, this blessed day, of your coming to look after a poor wandering crature! See, I'll lie down like a lamb, as you tell me; but do not come back: I'll be spared, a lanna—I'll be spared! There's some will work good for me this blessed night; but, if not, Miss Eva—well, I won't say it—only don't cry—don't —or the Kelpie will be gathering your tears, and setting them for jewels in her crown."

"Let us offer to assist them," whispered Cormac to Sidney.

"No, no," murmured his cousin. "No: wait till she goes, and then I will give him the medicine, and cover him with my cloak."

"But why? I want to speak to her," persisted Cormac impatiently.

"You may catch the fever; besides, would you not rather look at than speak to her?" answered the trembling Sidney; and then he seized Cormac's arm to prevent his discovering himself; while, so great was his emotion, that his cousin for a moment believed he had caught the distemper that already shattered the woodcutter's wits.

Eva had vanished like a vision; and Sidney stood by Randy's heather couch: the poor fellow knew him at once: but, instead of thanking him for his kindness and charity, he implored him to follow and protect Eva Raymond. "There was as good as a thousand dancing here while she was in it," he said, rapidly, "and now they're gone. It's after her, they are! Keep her from water, and the Plank-bridge—see her by the wood-road safe to her mother's side: tell her I sent *you*—not him—not him," he continued, pointing with seeming abhorrence to where Cormac stood at a little distance: "NOT HIM!—I see things—evil things—whispering him—now, as he stands—I see!—Oh, my grief!—to be so tortured with the knowledge of what I can't hinder;" and he covered his face with his hands. "Away," he added, "and at once ;—I don't want cloak or cover;—faith in her safety will be my saving:—away!" Well the wood-cutter knew that he was not left without protection: one of the most skilful

herbalists of Fairy-land was left to guard him ; and, lest he should grow sleepy with long watching, a gentle and loving fay was ordered to attend and keep him to his duty. Sidney, who, when Eva was in sight, lacked the courage to address her, the moment she was gone, felt the most intense desire to follow. He had not confided to his cousin that many times since their return he had watched and waited to see her curtain withdrawn at daybreak by her small white hand—to

hear her voice answer the sweet birds' matin song—to gather the rose-leaves that fell from the flowers she had touched—to feel the ecstasy of breathing the air she breathed—to teach his pen her name, until, if it did not obstinately refuse to write aught else, it would run on with such wild words, harmonising so together, and expressing thoughts, and hopes, and fears he never dared to frame upon his lips, that, at last, the silent, feeble instrument — the poor feather of a bird !—became his confidant, his cherished friend. He needed no second bidding from the woodcutter. Cormac thought he was wild, and called to him for explanation, but received no reply; and, half annoyed, he followed along the path, musing on the vision of beauty he had seen,—as he had never mused before ; a sharp and bitter pang shot through his frame, when he remembered that Sidney had the privilege of looking upon Eva whenever he wished : and had enjoyed such privilege without communicating it to him : he felt offended ; angry and harsh thoughts arose in his mind against his cousin : in all the endowments bestowed by Nature upon her favourites, he knew

Sidney was his superior; and until then his easy nature had been content to admit such superiority; but now—even already—he valued his own position and wealth as nothing worth compared with the advantages possessed by his cousin. His ears, unaccustomed to the tones and dialect of his native country, had not caught the meaning of the wood-cutter's half-muttered words; yet, suddenly, the idea flashed upon him that Sidney had followed Eva, and he hastened his footsteps, hoping to overtake him. Urged by mysterious whisperings, his rapidity increased, until he rushed forward, careless of huge drops of rain that struck upon his brow, and the sudden gathering of a storm, which in the Lake country descends almost before its darkly spreading pall enshrouds the heavens. In a mere span of time, Nature had so completely changed her aspect, that the scene could only be recognised by its mighty landmarks; the lakes were a mass of heaving and leaden-coloured waters; fierce gusts of wind dashed down the ravines, like wild horses, admitting no master; the forest moaned heavily as their crowned heads bowed to *their* King of Terrors; the sharp pinnacles of the mountains speared the clouds, which hung in fantastic forms around brows that would not be capped by a perishing vapour; the sheet-lightning, at one moment descended as a broad and shining pennon upon the waters, the next the sublimely awful instrument of Almighty vengeance darted from the seething clouds, ere the deep and heavy thunder lumbered forth the slow announcement that it was about to run its course. There was something so startling in the sudden outbreak that Cormac paused, and viewed the scene in wonder at its singular magnificence; the pent-up rain had not yet mingled with the lightning; its violence was suspended over earth, upon which the surcharged clouds prepared to fall in overwhelming force. Suddenly he heard a scream—a shriek—so sharp as to seem supernatural; and, looking up, he saw an eagle floating amid the storm, as if its delight was in the elemental war that filled all other created things with terror. Beneath where the bird now rose—now descended—Cormac perceived that a gully, half-river, half-lake, was crossed by a fragile plank, rendered almost unnecessary in dry weather, by the huge stepping-stones which broke the water into a thousand dimpling eddies; the recent summer rains had filled the channel to overflowing, and as it was within a few yards of the Lake, it tumbled violently over every obstacle, and uplifted its waters against the little bridge, that showed like a thread over the whirling caldron.   An artist

would have deemed its white foam a graceful foreground to the purple hue of the mountain that rose beyond the dark lake to which the narrow but impetuous torrent was hastening; and while something of the same idea passed through Cormac's mind, he saw Eva Raymond move from the shelter of the overhanging bank, and step with modest fearlessness upon the plank,—intending to reach Dovecote by the pass of the Plank-bridge,—the very bridge of which the woodcutter had warned Sidney. To his unspeakable horror, Cormac distinctly saw the plank raised, by the force of the waters; yet still she moved as calmly on, as if walking on her mother's lawn. He was a long way above her, yet he shouted to her of peril;—in reply, he heard again the scream of the eagle: and felt that no voice could reach her ear. At once, he dashed down the path that commanded a view of the perilous pass; suddenly, he saw Sidney risking his life on the fragile plank; and, though convinced that the maiden's chance of safety was increased tenfold, it was like a blast of the lightning on his brow, to note him there. Sidney stretched his arms imploringly towards her, and she, half turning, waved her hand to him, as regardless of danger as if unconscious of its existence: one huge swell, yellow and frothy, curled around the plank ;—the fragile bridge heaved in the air, and in an instant—almost as rapidly as thought—both, both so full of life, had disappeared! How the elements warred above them, and how the cruel waters hurried them towards the lake; but Sidney struggled bravely, for he struggled for more than his own life! He gained a rock!—he stood upon it in safety—he was saved! but it was only to gaze into the waters, and then dive into their depths for the treasure they held back. Cormac remained powerless upon the bank that overhung the fatal spot where both had disappeared :—there was no vestige of the plank, no indication even of where it had rested; but the river boiled over at his feet. Suddenly, he heard his name called; it was Sidney's voice! he sprang in half-delirious ecstasy to the place from whence it came; and there, battling the strong and angry current, he saw his cousin, one arm wreathed round Eva, while, with the other, he clutched the strong bough of a tree which overhung the stream. It seemed from the moment Sidney grasped it, that the torrent played less fiercely round them ; or it might be that his strength had returned, for, almost without Cormac's assistance, he drew the delicate form of the fair girl upon the bank.

"Your old luck, Sidney," whispered Cormac, as he bent over her. "She recovers."

Eva Raymond was restored to consciousness much more rapidly than they could have expected ; the cousins seemed unable to render her any assistance, though both were filled with the deepest anxiety ; so intense was their watching, that the tempest subsided without their observing how rapidly it ceased in the valleys and how swiftly it passed from the mountain tops. As she returned, in her dripping garments, to Dovecote, the trees were laden with rain-drops, and the fragrant thyme sent up its

perfume as incense to her footsteps ; night forbore to perplex her with its shadows ; and the very air vibrated as if with joy at her preservation ; the lakes had resumed their tranquillity ; and Nature seemed again at peace. Cormac endeavoured to entertain her with Eton jests, and the pleasures of a city life : and talked lightly, as youths of small sympathies often do. Sidney spoke little ; his care being to remove every burr and bramble from her path. She replied to Cormac, but thanked Sidney by looks rather than words, until after a few minutes' shelter in her fond mother's arms, amid tears and blushes, she presented him as her preserver.

Meanwhile, Randy remained on his heather couch, incapable of rendering assistance to himself or others.   The rain did not penetrate the shelter which the forest leaves afforded ; he muttered to himself fables and scraps of old songs, until at last he slept.   As the night waned, the woodcutter was shown the murkiness and despair that reigned in the Kelpie's palace beneath the waters of the Upper Lake.   He saw the Queen cast herself upon the steps of her throne, and, for a time, none of the dwellers of that dark region dared to offer her consolation ; at last her favourite lizard presumed to lick her hand, and the most musical of her frogs croaked forth a song of solace on his reedy harp.   But this, instead of soothing, seemed to drive her to desperation ; she vowed never again to meet the Queens in amity—she entreated all bad spirits to join her in luring the Child of Earth to her destruction.   The distorted

creatures of her court trembled as her fiery eyes rested upon them, for well they knew she would soon devote them to the vengeance that demanded sacrifice.   The turmoil was terrible ; a fierce war between THE IMPS, HER PAGES, AND THE FROGS, HER STEEDS, restored her to partial self-command ; and after having bathed her swollen eyes in a decoction of the poisonous mandrake, she gave ear to the counsels of her Nurse, who had rare experience in all wicked mysteries, having been created of the slime of the waters of the Nile, as it lay upon the land of Egypt ; she blamed her darling for periling her liberty against a whim. But while she grimaced and gesticulated the vision became confused ; the woodcutter's sight was disturbed by the flapping of the wings of monstrous bats, and the spectre dance of marrowless bones that had lain beneath the old Weir Bridge, and in the charnels of Mucross and Aghadoe for centuries ; the roar of cataracts was in his ears, and he felt himself hurled forward into the depths of O'Sullivan's cascade ; and then he called on Nightstar, and asked why she had deserted him ?   And the sound of the oozing waters melted away, and the forms of the Kelpies became dim and pale, until a vapour, formed of fading rainbows, where all the hues were blended into one another, in most delicate harmony, shut out the evil sights of evil spirits: and a strain of melancholy music encircled him on every side, so unlike the usual music of Fairy-land, that he hardly recognised its source, until—not commanding the revels, as in past times— not bandying repartee with Honeybell, nor enjoying the frolics of Puck,

nor leading the mystic dance of Midsummer, nor excited to laughter or mirth—he saw the QUEEN DESCENDING ON THE WINGS OF A BAT, and when they had stepped upon earth, he recognised Nightstar absolutely weeping, as she reproached Honeybell for her carelessness of Eva at that eventful time. Honeybell seemed intent on extracting the one drop of sweetness from the trumpet-like tube of the woodbine, and then cast the half-crushed blossom to the great bee, who turned it over with his trunk, and thought how very wasteful great ladies were of the good things that fell to them. She listened with more than her usual pout to the remonstrances of Nightstar, whose words fell as sadly as softly from her lips. " I do not think," she said, " of the misery yonder fiend of the waters has cost me. I know her enmity, and can meet and overcome it. She has cast my trusty servant upon a bed of sickness; it shall be the renewal of his youth. She endangered the liberty and life of my well-beloved; it will end in her own banishment and slavery; but you, Honeybell, to tamper with Eva—you to thwart me thus! What should the child know of the love that frivolous mortals dally with—the very scum of the passion of noble souls ? "

" You live so much in the upper air, sister," replied Honeybell, peevishly, " that you lose all sympathies with the beings of earth."

" Not so; I seek their elevation. I honour LOVE from its first dawning upon the world to the very last, when it triumphs over all perishable things. Had I not deemed it the worthiest of all boons, would

I have endowed her with it? But the bud must not be forced to blossom before its time: the hearts as well as the heads of these poor mortals need ripening. Troubled as I am with many cares for the good of others——"

"That makes you so excitable, my dear Queen," interrupted Honeybell. "I remember when you enjoyed your existence as much as I do mine."

"I enjoy it more than ever now," replied Nightstar; "we, my royal sister, have higher motives than sipping sweets from flowers, or passing time in mere idle frolics in the moonlight. I comment on my anxieties only to excuse my frequent absence from Eva's pillow. I have been passing from one country to another, but would not have consigned to your care either my adopted child or my faithful partisan, had I thought you would have deserted the one, or played with the feelings of the other; not only have you whispered follies into Eva's ears, but you have perverted, by your worldliness, her mother's nature. See I not at this very moment, when her child is sleeping under the influence of my surest spells, that she is weighing the merits of the brave, the true, the earnest, the faithful youth, who, poor though she believes him, has *that* within him which never failed to achieve the highest honours your earthly world can give; yet she—a mother—a good and tender one—with the face of her precious child lighting up her darkness—even she rates these high qualities at scarce a feather's weight, and absolutely though unconsciously, regrets that her child's life was not saved by the sensual Cormac, rather than the high-hearted Sidney!—Now, mark you, Honeybell, it is not because the red fluid runs in unequal currents through their young veins, for Sidney has as many far-off ancestors as Cormac; but this usually wise and good, and always devoted, mother envies the worn out coronet that may glitter on the cramped and narrow brow of an earl's daughter! This is your teaching, Honeybell."

"I respect the aristocracy," she exclaimed.

"And so do I," replied Nightstar; "many of my greatest favourites are numbered among its daughters—I have scores under my protection who have never heard my name, whom I shield from worldly influences and their contaminations—and who are pure as they are beautiful."

Honeybell felt inclined to sneer; but the earnestness of her royal sister was so lofty and true, that she turned away her face.

"But Nature," continued Nightstar, "has its nobles as well as antiquity and rank. I honour the self-created glories of mind: I venerate those who achieve greatness by labour—endurance—patience—and the high purposes that exist only with high souls."

"I know all that, my dear sister," again interposed Honeybell; "and so do we all—at least it has become the fashion of late to *say* so; but instead of finding fault with me, as you have done, I expected a public vote of thanks for my good management. Two lovers secured to a little village damsel—and two such lovers! either sufficient, in four or five of our hours—which they call years—to set a palace in a ferment!—What do you want for your adopted? A young girl's heart vibrating between lovers is pretty sport to me; but if you look angry and come to *that*, I think I have as good a *right* as you have to suggest what I please to Eva. Disturbances seem rife in Fairy-land about this young mortal! She is mine as well as yours."

"Honeybell!" exclaimed Nightstar, reproachfully, "do you not remember you generously gave her up to me?"

"Well, perhaps I did," replied the vacillating Queen; "and a troublesome gift she is likely to prove—particularly when in love."

"IN LOVE!" repeated Nightstar. "Really, Queen, I did not think you could have used a phrase so vulgar. Oh, sister, sister! see you not the difference between loving and being (as gross mortals call it) in love?"

"You are too refined for me!" exclaimed her sister, impatiently; "and I am so weary, and the night is so fine, that really all I can do is to consign her at once to your superior management! Cannot you render her and hers oblivious of the past? and my elves shall unite with yours in driving the Talbots out of the country."

"The high-born and wealthy are far too ready to leave it," replied Nightstar; "and you know we have no power to erase a blot from the living heart—to render an immortal mind oblivious! But my poor woodcutter is at this moment thinking a fable that may teach even me——how dark buds become bright blossoms—and—"

Randy was so delighted to think that the Queen should have commended his invention, that he started wildly up, and saw Sidney Talbot bending over him.

"How long and how soundly you have slept, and how refreshed you look!" was the youth's salutation, as he stood in the full glory of the rising sun.

"Slept! Master Sidney!" repeated the woodcutter; "never a wink was over my eyes since I parted you.—You're lucky born, sir. I told you *that* many a long day ago, and I tell it you again—lucky! There's high fortune before you—far off to be sure, but still there. Well, it's often I've seen it; the dark bud opens into the brightest blossom; 'sleeping!' it's little sleep the woodcutter ever gets between them all; but it's all for good; and you'll have grate luck, Master Sidney!"

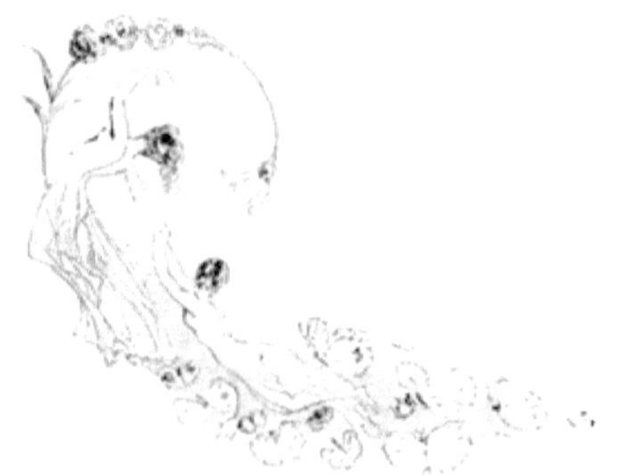

Drawn by F. W. Hulme.

Engraved by Joseph Williams.

THE VISIT TO THE SICK.

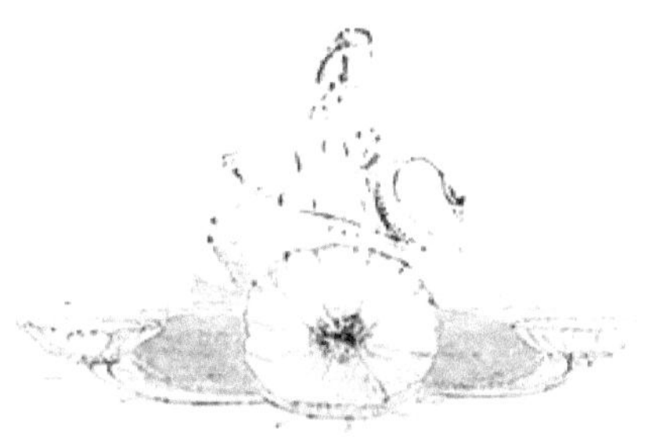

PART THE FOURTH.

LONG and dangerous illness, of many months' duration, confined Lady Elizabeth Talbot to the solitude of Ard-Flesk; and, much to her delight, Cormac, her beloved, but most wayward, son (instead of going abroad, as she had, after much entreaty, consented he should), declared his desire to remain with her; the opinion of Sidney was not asked: in all things he was assumed to be the shadow of his cousin. A marked change had come over these youths; each had grown distrustful of the other; their companion-ship had been of the closest kind; alike in person, connected by blood, brought up together from earliest childhood—still, they never had been friends; there was neither the bond nor the influence of sympathy between them—nothing, at least, of that vital sympathy which not only creates, but continues to invigorate, true friendship. Tastes may differ—pursuits may be widely opposite—a thousand minor sensations, or even sentiments, may divide without separating—differences may even be many and oppositions not unfrequent—but FRIENDS must think and feel alike upon all great subjects; there must be mutual faith; mutual respect: each uplooking to the other's immaculate honour and truth; there must be no hope-lagging—no cowardly mistrust: neither closed hearts, nor sealed lips; there must be a generous forbearance, and a pliant, if not a gentle, humour in all whom God ordains to act the glorious part of 'friend.' From necessity, or circumstances, companionship often creeps through years of human life; and so these youths might have proceeded in good tune one with the other, had not a sudden jar destroyed the harmony which had grown of habit rather than of choice. Yet Sidney cherished a deep and earnest regard for Cormac; he was of an affectionate nature; he had loved Cormac, and thought that gratitude commanded he should continue to do so. At times, Cormac's better angel triumphed, and he pondered what he had discovered that forced him to consider Sidney with estranged feelings. It is true they went and came together; in society they seemed almost as before, except that perhaps a harshly expressed opinion would escape from the one, and a look of reproach from the other; and once a bitter taunt broke from Cormac's lips, which roused Sidney to a reply so firmly brave, that the colour faded from the young heir's cheek until it became white and livid: Lady Elizabeth looked up from the sofa, and demanded what it meant? She heard the answer but not the provocation, and as Cormac had immediately quitted the room, Sidney was too generous to exonerate himself by explanation; thus the mother thought her son had been wounded by the one who ought to shield him from all unkindness; and when, afterwards, she questioned Cormac, she heard, much to her pain, that Sidney was hourly proving himself unworthy the consideration they had both lavished upon him. She heard this, and though not quite as quick to believe, as Cormac imagined she ought to have been—still it dwelt upon her mind, and moved her greatly to her nephew's disadvantage. Cormac did not tell his mother that the same night the harsh words had passed between them, Sidney followed him to his room, wept true and earnest tears of sorrow at the falling away of their affection; and was met by indifference so chilling—indifference so closely bordering upon insolence— that he occupied the remainder of the night in questioning himself, and resolving as to what his future course must be. But for one besetting memory he would have bounded from the window to which he pressed a brow so heated, that neither the gentle moonlight nor the midnight air could relieve its throbbings—and have rushed upon the world, strong in the strength of an independent and manly nature. Nothing could be more soothing than the calmness and stillness which prevailed over the sleeping world—yet he was insensible to its influence—his young mind was a chaos —his brain refused its office to calm the beatings of his heart; and at length his head sunk upon his arm, and he entreated aid and direction from the Power that is never appealed to in vain: supplicating Him who listeneth in darkness as well as in light, and whose ear is never deaf when sorrow and trouble speak rightly. Comforted in spirit, his thoughts arranged themselves harmoniously; hope, with its train of blessings, re-entered his mind, and, looking upwards, he wondered if one he loved watched the stars as he did—at that hour—when Nature was most tranquil and most pure. Suddenly the wood-cutter laid his hand upon the window at which Sidney stood: but the youth had grown so accustomed to his appearance at all times and places, that he had ceased to be surprised—meet him where he would.

"I heard every word you said, Master Sidney, dear," said the poor fellow; "and much good has it done us both, sir. It's a fine thing to open the heart and let out all the bad and take in the good that's sure to come at our bidding. A shut heart is neither for God nor man! But wicked things are always busy about, sir: only they may be overcome; and I'll tell you a story about that. I saw a mighty purty sight once, Master Sidney. You know I can't abide the eagles in the air: thieving robbers they ever and always were, and cruel; if people knew as much about them as I do, they'd change their mind, and not call them royal birds

—for no reason that I know of, except that they're high above themselves ;
nor I can't bear spiders, sir ; they're the very moral of attorneys, spinning
all that's in them out, to catch fools ; grabbing everything they can into
their own nets, and if they've nothing else to do, devouring each other ;
though the old mother spider will take care of her eggs, if she's very
hungry, she'll eat her young ones. Now, Master Sidney, there was one
of them, with a speckled body as big as a thrush's egg, and long hairy
legs, and goggle eyes—a grate deceiver intirely ; his net so fine, that the
midges couldn't see it, and so strong, that it would hold a cockchafer ; he
was the terror of all the butterflies and bees in the neighbourhood, and
though in his den were heaps of bones, he kept his net so clean and
beautiful, that it looked like a rainbow in a ring. The 'good people'
themselves were bothered with him intirely, for though he had no power
over *them*, he was always trapping some of their favourites ; the soft
young bees—out, for the first time, to try their strength—or the innocent
moths, and the dancing flies, and scarlet ladybirds ; no matter what,
he never cared ; and when one I know, sent her lord chancellor to call
him to order, he said he'd desire no better company than his lordship
in his den ; he was as grate a robber, and more unnatural, than the
wildest fox on the Toomies mountain ; well, sir, the lord chancellor
brought back such a report of his strength, and his poison fangs, and
I don't know what, that no one cared to go near him ; until a wise butterfly, that has carried *some one* I know, in the shelter of her beautiful wings,
many and many a sunny hour, so that not even a sunbeam saw her, said,
'I'll away to punish this evil spider.' And the butterfly set a trap-cage,
and baited it with a delicacy the spider loved ; and the lord chancellor
said, 'It is useless, behold he is already bloated with too much ; his
appetite is palled ; you could tempt the hungry with food, but not such
a spider as that.' And the butterfly bent her great horns in respect
to the law lord, but for all that she kept her own opinion. 'Greediness,'
she said, 'never has enough ; even as the rich men of earth seek to
heap one guinea on another, so will this greedy spider distend his
spotted skin to add one morsel to another ; it is only the wise and
good who understand *enough*.' And she set her trap-cage, and the
spider felt the vibration of his net, and he waggled from one side to

the other, and at last clasped the cage with his long legs; but could not move it; so he went to the other side, and found two bars open. 'Oh, oh!' he said; 'oh, oh! now I can get in and feast,' and in he went, and when he was safe, down went the bars, AND THE BUTTER-FLY BORE HIM AWAY IN TRIUMPH, to wait the judgment which all impure doers must meet sooner or later.

"I think more about such things since the last sickness I had; only the cares of the good people that depend so much on me, and Miss Eva, and yourself, come across me—and that bothered and bothering ould creature, Kitty Kelly, she sets me foaming — she's so worldly-minded! Oh, then, isn't a worldly-minded woman a woful thing! You remember the flowers you gave Miss Eva? The darling settled them in her own *chancy* bowl, and I watched her looking at and trimming them with her heart in her eye. 'Is there any new kind of flower among them, miss darling?' I said to her, pretending innocence, as she kept taking them in and out of the water. 'No, Randy,' she answers, 'none.' 'Because you're such a while giving them the last touch,' I said again. She never turned round to smile at me, as she often does, but carried them away, and I couldn't help thinking how much fairer the living flowers of the Almighty's garden are than all the flowers of the field. Now, sir, would you believe it, but the minute Kitty Kelly got Miss Eva's back turned, she threw them all out, and filled the bowl full of the fruit Master Cormac had brought her!"

"And what did she?" inquired the almost breathless Sidney.

"She cast *them* out, sir—flung them over the lawn. I wish you had only seen what I saw," continued the woodcutter, as, seized by one of his fits of sudden wildness, he clapped his hands; "there they went! hurroo! rolling past Kitty's window. *She* could not see what I saw; and thinking they kept going on of themselves, cried out to know ' what ailed them, hopping in the grass?' Well they might hop!—well they might roll! three little fellows kicking one apple! Hurroo!—two at a strawberry! How pleased they were to see the rich fruit scorned

because of the rich giver—that was sport! How they danced!—you'll hardly believe it; but it's as true as that the moon is shining. I've seen the Queen herself sitting like a star on Miss Eva's forehead, and she never a bit the wiser! but," he added, sorrowfully, "there must have been talk about it; for an hour after I heard the jewel sobbing in her little chamber, and the mistress had a troubled look: but keep a good heart, Master Sidney — it's grate fortune is before you, sir— grate luck! Sure there isn't one about the place this minute that doesn't love you before any other—"

"That's not ' luck,' either to them or to me," interrupted Sidney—

" And only wishes you were in it, instead of them that are—."

"God forbid," said the youth; "and you must not say this — nor think it. My cousin will be a blessing to you all hereafter, when I shall be far—far away,—perhaps to return to you no more."

" Whist! whist!" exclaimed the woodcutter, "and don't be doubting that way! I've seen all about it, as if it was in a book; but they'd be angry if I told you, dear, and, maybe, let me see no more—but it's grate, sir—grate; there's a thrifle of crossings, and deaths—but they're as nothing to the grateness that's far off!'"

"My poor fellow!" exclaimed Sidney, laying his hand kindly and fondly on the shaggy head that rested on the stone-sill, as though it had been a pillow of down — "My poor fellow! I am sure you wish me well!"

"Wish you well! enagh! Wish you well! I wish the red-deer that salutes me in the glen; the innocent hare—the shy thing that never winks as I pass; the robin, that gathers my crumbs; the corn-crake, that keeps me nightly company; and the singing grasshopper that turns into the cricket, and tells about summer to the winter fire on the warm hearthstone;—I wish everyone of them well; and don't I wish something more than *that* to you!—*you* who saved HER, when the little light of sense I have was taken, and my arms had no strength, and my feet no swiftness. Oh, Master Sidney, you've been nursed away from your own land, or you'd know that a *cowld* word is as bad as a stab to an Irish heart: wish you well—avourneen!" He turned his honest face upwards as he spoke, as if desiring the stars to bear witness to his truth, and Sidney saw that his eyes were full of tears. "She," he added, pointing to the moon, and speaking rapidly—"she knows me better than you; and often when I'm alone with her through the night, I think of the time when, maybe, I shall look down from her mountains upon the mountains I love so well; is that a sin, Master Sidney? I'd rather it wasn't; for though I'd be sorry to stay ever and always in this world, when the things I love would be going from me; still, if it was only in shadows, or the same as the clouds above there, I'd like to think that when I'm gone from Glena, and never to hear the echoes of the Gap again, or gather the heath on the Purple Mountain, or arrowheads off the Reeks—that I could look on the cabin where I was born, and the beautiful lakes I've lived among ever since; is it a sin, dear, to think of looking down on one's own grave, and watching to see who comes near it!" Sidney was himself so much affected, that he found it difficult to dry the tears to which the poor woodcutter had yielded. "Midsummer will soon be with us again," he continued.

"I can see THE MIDGES DANCING TO THE MUSIC you cannot hear. But the Queen's to the fore, herself, this year!

"Do you hear that, my young Master," he added, as the echo of the cock's earliest matin crow died away in the distance. "There's something awful in the way them birds hear the march of morning sounding down from the sky, and tell of it to the world; there's no streak of light in the heavens; the stars are not winking; the Lady Moon looks quiet enough: the very tops of the highest mountains don't know it yet; but *he* does; he knows what o'clock it is, as well as if he had a Dublin repeater under his wing. It's as thrue as you're there, Master Sidney, with your eyes fixed on me, and your mind wandering about Dovecote; the very Kelpie, I've told you so much about, was often inconvanienced by rising to the top of the lake, when she should have remained at the bottom; and she thought if she could coax a grey cock to come with her, she'd have a good time-teller always at hand and know more than her neighbours; Kelpies were ever and always fond of playing at horses, and so she turned herself into one, and came streeling, and looking mighty asy-going, about the yard, where the early cock used to be scraping up a living for his wives and families. 'Are you ever hungry?' she says. 'Often,' says he, 'for in coorse, I must do for them craythurs before I think of myself.' 'Come with me,' she says, 'I'll carry you on my back to where you'll have full and plenty, and no trouble, and jewels to hang about your neck, and nothing to do, only tell the hours' 'I'm grately obleeged to your honour, and I'll serve you gaily,' says the cock, 'and faithfully, to the hour of my death!' 'When he's too old to crow,' thinks the Kelpie, 'he'll give grate sport to my coort, hunting him. Are you coming?' she says. 'In a minute,' says he; 'I'm only gathering my wives and children to put them up first.' 'But they can't crow,' says the Kelpie, 'and I don't want them; I have not enough to feed all your wives and children.'

'Then I'll stay where I am,' says the gallant cock; 'I'm not going to lave all my little chickens and their mothers, and my hatching hens, to the mercy of a cowld starving world, with no one to take care of them or purtect them. I should be ashamed to crow if I was guilty of such maneness.' 'Well, bring 'em,' said the Kelpie, spitefully. The cock looked

up at the horse, where it was snorting and blowing, and clapt his wings. 'No,' he answered, 'we'll stay were we are; no good comes from those who tempt us to forget the duties we are all hatched to perform. I'm grately obleeged; but I'll have nothing to do with you; so the sooner you are off the better.' "

" Can you read the planets ?" inquired Sidney, abstractedly.

" Not as well as I do palms; but there's grate reading in Nature, Master Sidney: what do you think of the story I told you?"

" Truly, Randy, I did not hear it."

" I thought as much," replied the woodcutter; " it's wonderful, when the heart talks aloud, how deaf the ears grow to every thing else!"

The woodcutter wended his way towards the cottage, and Sidney threw himself on his bed, to dream what dreams he could.

After the events of that day, Cormac and Sidney avoided each other, by unspoken, but mutual, consent; and the Lady Elizabeth grew towards her nephew first cold, and then bitter; it was hard to bear, and harder still, when Sidney implored her to tell him in what he had offended;

to hear words drop like icicles from her lips—words which carried con-
viction that the affection she had once borne him had departed. He
wrote to his father: the reply attributed blame, and advised concilia-
tion. It was only when wandering around Dovecote, when hearing Eva's
voice, when assisting in her missions of charity, when singing the same
song, or READING THE SAME BOOK WITH HER, that he was happy; and

yet 'happy' is but a cold word to express his emotions—the emotions of
his deep, earnest, engrossing love. It was his life—more, far more than
his life; a ministering angel she was of all the holy offices that create
blessings here and hereafter. Cormac, too, often brought to the Dovecote
the passions of his ardent and stormy nature; he was Sidney's cousin,
and, therefore, was for a time welcomed by Eva; he was Lady Elizabeth's
son—the heir of Ard-Flesk—that secured a welcome from her mother.

It had chanced that on the Midsummer Eve which followed the rescue
of Eva from the waters, Lady Elizabeth arose in an angry humour; it was
true her little starched maid had been with her the previous night, until
the matin crow of the early cock; it is true that her ladyship had been
tart and snappish to Cormac during the previous week; that she had
hinted 'that sons had their own purposes to serve when they remained
with mothers;' that she had read a homily to both young men on the
evils of low connections; that she had spent half a day in studying

Rochefoucault, and the other half in repeating his maxims; that her mind was filled with an extraordinary 'something' that would not be content quietly to subside into nothing, as was the case usually; both the youths felt that some event must happen, but there was between them no confidence as of old, and they could but resolve their own thoughts; Cormac glared fiercely upon Sidney, who met the glare with the calm light of eyes so full of truth and power, that his cousin for an instant turned inquiry into himself—rapidly, but not satisfactorily.

"It's little use I'm to Miss Eva," mused the woodcutter, as he traced the progress of Sidney through the dew of the meadow that led to Dovecote: "it's little use I'm to Miss Eva now; and that brave young heart afoot before the sun at Midsummer: and Master Cormac will be here, before noon, only he comes a visiting on a high-trotting horse, decked with whip and spur, and a gay green riding-coat; and the children salute him, and stand still as he rides by, and say to each other, 'that's the young lord of Ard-Flesk;' but they bless Master Sidney when he goes along, and they dance before him in his path. How Nightstar scorns the gay youth on the fine horse, who brings gifts to the mother—and distress to the child!" Thus Randy thought, before Lady Elizabeth had arisen from her bed, and commanded that four horses should be harnessed to the family coach, and the new liveries which had never been worn since a royal duchess looked at the 'fittings' of her London drawing-rooms, and deigned to observe that they were very well—'for her!' Her ladyship ordered forth the new liveries, and commanded her little maid to array her in the costly folds of a scarlet cashmere, while a plume of white feathers descended over her left shoulder; and as she stood on the stone steps of the ancient house, the butler and porter bowed behind her, and the footmen, with dress bouquets, bowed before,

and waited her ladyship's ascent to her carriage; yet none of them had the smallest idea as to where her ladyship was going; if the little lady's-maid knew, she kept her secret well.

"Where to, my lady?" inquired the head footman, while the coachman bent down his head to listen; and the porter and butler extended their necks, and the other footman, although he looked indifferent, opened his ears, and Cormac's bloodhound, Keeldar, rose up from his lair, and after peering from beneath his eyes, and shaking, growled; and her ladyship's own old spaniel wheezed to be taken up; and the footman, after a long pause, repeated the question, "Where to, my lady?"

"Drive on!" replied Lady Elizabeth; "and drive fast, particularly through the village: I cannot endure the sight of misery."

"She can't abide the sight of misery," repeated the porter to the butler; "I wonder she doesn't put them out of it!"

"It's against law to make a fire and burn the poor," said the butler, as he kicked the spaniel his mistress had committed to his tender care.

"A little would do it!" continued the porter, musingly; "a little goes a great way in charity; anyhow, the people who give are of that opinion; but a little *would* do it here; and sure she'd not be troubled with such pains about her heart, or such meagrims and things in her head —if she'd try: just relieve one or two families as an experiment. Randy has a fable about that—of how a fine sick lady grew better as her purse grew lighter; and whenever she gave a guinea she lost an ache! Well, it's

a curious world, and I will always say so," he continued, as he sunk gradually into his chair: "a very curious world, and of all places I was ever in, this is the strangest and most unnatural. I never get through a quiet night's rest, and I don't know one that does."

When the carriage and horses of Lady Elizabeth Talbot stood at the road entrance to Dovecote, it was nearly as long as the cottage itself. Numbers gazed upon it, in the distance, speculating upon the visit, and fearing that, having heard of her beauty, the 'proud lady' was going to take Eva away—just as beautiful damsels of old were 'lifted' by enchantment. The old weather-cock turned and creaked so audibly, that the coachman directed his eyes upward, while the startled inhabitants of the old tower, in their turn, fixed theirs on him, until every leaf seemed instinct with life. The horses reared and snorted, and in one of the ruined windows of the tower, Randy's head was set as in a frame-work of knotted ivy.

It was in vain the coachman shook his whip, and the footmen extended their gold-headed canes towards him; he continued muttering and gesticulating, until, as some of his expressions reached their ears, they were awed into silence by the 'Fairy Man.'

The majestic lady entered as Eva, more in sadness than in joy, was drawing up the strings of her harp. Lady Elizabeth had a keen perception of the beautiful, and her taste had been rendered fastidious by a long acquaintance with the best models of classic beauty; she brought all living creatures to the test of the Grecian statue; and, consequently, refused to be satisfied with much that less fastidious critics called 'perfection.' But when she passed within the sanctuary of that humble cottage, and met the beaming eyes of the young girl, who received her with a heightened colour, but with no more confusion of manner than youth and modesty rendered graceful, the lady forgot for a few brief moments the object of her mission—completely overpowered by the loveliness she could scarcely believe was real; after gazing on her silently, until Eva turned from her high-bred stare, " I wished," she said, " to see your mother, young lady. I do not desire to give you pain."

" Nor her !" exclaimed Eva—the expression of her face changing to one of deep anxiety. " You cannot surely wish to give my mother pain ? If it must be—let me suffer instead: lady, we are one in heart and soul—we have no secrets from each other. Oh, do not give her pain !"

Lady Elizabeth gazed upon that form, trembling with emotion; many thoughts crowded her mind, jostling each other with fearful rapidity; but one prevailed above the rest: all her arts, all her indulgence—her wealth, her rank—all she had in the emptiness of her hollow soul, most coveted—all she had lavishly bestowed—all had failed to procure *her* a tithe of such love ! " Do you then love your mother so very dearly ?" she inquired, taking her hand, and looking earnestly and inquiringly into Eva's faultless face.

" Love my mother !" repeated Eva, almost unconsciously; " surely every child loves its mother."

" Yes," replied Lady Elizabeth, " in a degree; but you look so much love. Love such as *I* have met with, has its own purposes to work out; have *you* no purpose in this love ?"

"Oh, yes, lady! a great—great—purpose; the purpose of deserving and keeping hers."

"Now tell me truly, young lady, have you no secret hid away from your mother in some dark corner of your heart?"

"None!" she said, and the light of truth shone in her eyes; "none!"

"You are born to be believed," answered Lady Elizabeth, unconsciously dropping the hand, "do you not know me?"

"I know to what house this noble dog belongs!" answered Eva, laying her hand on the bloodhound, who had preceded his mistress; the dog turned, and placed his head under the hand that offered the caress.

"You must know Keeldar well: he would hardly do so much to me; and they say his race never caress those who are not of gentle blood."

"He does not lose caste by caressing a Raymond!" was Eva's reply—proud in words, but not in tone; it sounded a truth—not a boast; "I know him well, Lady Elizabeth; he always accompanies his master."

"Then you admit that Mr. Talbot is a visitor here?" inquired the lady, unable to repress her astonishment at finding Eva so self-possessed on a subject upon which her own anxiety made it difficult to enter.

"We see him occasionally, and I am always pleased when he brings Keeldar; the dog is so noble and so true."

"Do you then prefer the dog to the master?"

"I am fond of Keeldar," said Eva, smiling brightly.

A few hours past, and Lady Elizabeth would have rejoiced; now she felt offended—offended that anything belonging to herself, but to her son especially, should be regarded with indifference. Her senses were captivated by the beauty and gentle frankness of the lovely girl who stood before her, in all the purity of innocence and youth. She had heard that poets had such themes, and painters such models—not to be found in Nature. She was one of the many who go through life disbelieving in Nature, considering it the indication of shepherds and milkmaids, and assimilating it so closely with vulgarity, that at length the two seem to be inseparable.

"Good Keeldar!" continued Eva, caressing him; "he is so generous!

He shows his high descent by gentleness to the little dogs that bark in his path; he would not catch a leveret, or harm a nestling; he protects even the wild birds that gather in our mimic lakes: dear Keeldar!"

"And you like him better than his master," repeated Lady Elizabeth, fixing her penetrating eyes upon the fair face which beamed upon her.

"Mr. Talbot is your son, Lady Elizabeth," replied Eva, "and intends us all kindness; but—I am very, very fond of Keeldar."

"Mr. Talbot would appreciate the compliment," said the lady, proudly; "yet," she added, thinking as worldlings do, that truth is but seeming, and finding it impossible to believe that Eva could be really indifferent to her son and heir; "yet, by your own admission, he has been here without my knowledge. Is it not so?"

A hue of deep indignant crimson flushed Eva's cheek. "Without your knowledge, lady! Why without your knowledge?" The girl looked timidly, and yet, frankly, towards the imperious woman.

"I will not talk with her," she murmured; "there is a spell about her : I pray you," she said aloud, "send your mother hither."

"Lady Elizabeth, I entreat!" exclaimed Eva, advancing.

"I will not speak with you again!" she said, hastily turning away from the eloquence of her beseeching look. "I seek audience of your mother." "She would honour the choice of an emperor," was the thought that rushed through her mind, as Eva disappeared; nor had she arranged her plans when Mrs. Raymond entered the room. The greeting was brief; and the lady-mother, in a few short, hard, hurried words, reproached Geraldine with laying a snare in her daughter's beauty to entrap the heir of a noble house. Geraldine's nature revolted at the idea of her child's name being so used. It is not to be questioned that she had built, as mothers often will, a lofty palace, wherein her soul's idol might reign a triple queen—of riches, love, and beauty; but Eva herself had overthrown the structure; and the mother was roused into forgetfulness of all save that she had a child to justify and protect.

"I do not think," she said, and her voice rang upon the lady's ear, like an echo of the one she had heard a few minutes before; "I do not think your ladyship's rank or wealth entitles you to enter a house, however humble, and insult its mistress. I do not deny that your son has spoken to me of his affection for my child; but, as it was not returned, there was no need to trumpet to his mother the fact of his rejection. I confess I should have rejoiced had he been older, and had it been otherwise; but not now! I would not suffer her to wed the best prince in broad Europe without a welcome from his kindred."

"Refuse my son!" murmured Lady Elizabeth, and she clutched in her hand the stick whereon her weakness leaned, and all the grandeur of her ancestry and state rushed through her brain in wild confusion. "Refuse the son of Lady Elizabeth and General Talbot! the sister and daughter of an earl of seven descents! the hero of eleven battles and two forlorn hopes! Married three times into ducal families in less than fifty years! Received eight times the thanks of the commander-in-chief, and once the thanks of Parliament! Never had even a younger son in any profession, saving that of arms, for three hundred and thirty years! Cousin to half the peerage, and O'Donoghue of the lakes! Fifteen thousand a-year, and forty-five thousand pounds in diamonds, that have been heir-looms twenty times! Madam," she continued, aloud, "I'll not believe that your daughter dared to refuse my son!"

"As you please," replied Mrs. Raymond, with a dignity which at once compelled Lady Elizabeth to feel that she had forgotten herself; "will you permit me to ring for your ladyship's carriage."

"No, madam; will you do me the favour to let me once more speak to your daughter?" inquired Lady Elizabeth, trembling with unchecked rage, which carried her beyond all self-control. When Eva entered, she took her hands, and, compressing them between her own, gazed steadily upon her. As she did so, she regained her composure, and by degrees all traces of anger faded from her face, even as the densest and most ob-noxious vapours pass away before the brightness of the morn. "Is it true that you have refused the love of my son—refused it earnestly?"

"Most true," replied Eva.

"And you have done this of yourself?"

"Yes, lady."

"Do you not know that he is rich?"

"I have heard so," she answered, carelessly.

"And of noble descent?"

"Truly!"

"One, whom once seen in the world, all high-born and most lovely maidens will labour to allure!"

" You wrong all high-born maidens, lady, in supposing them guilty of
so mean a craft ; if they loved him indeed!" she continued, blushing as
she spoke ; " but, even then, they would surely wait to be wooed, and not
permit wooing either, unless a true love could be given in return."

" And did *you* thus ?"

"Truly, lady, I hardly know. I hope I did—I think I did ; for,
from the first evening, when—when his cousin saved my life—he complained of my coldness."

" Who? Sidney !"

The tell-tale blood, summoned by the sound that was music in her ears
—a name that nestled in her pure young heart—rushed in a glowing
current from its citadel, and steeped brow, cheek, and bosom, in the deep
roseate hue of love. " He saved my life," she murmured : " poor as it is,
it is my mother's world. He saved my life."

If any of the harsh thoughts, which had been her counsellors during
the pompous progress of Lady Elizabeth to the Dovecote, had time to
whisper her who often gave them scope and entertainment, they would
have recalled to her memory, much that Eva's few simple words and
maidenly emotion had obliterated. She stood mortified and abashed
in the presence of a girl, blushing and trembling, on the threshold of a
new sensation, which, according to her destiny, was to guide her from her
cradle to her grave. Lady Elizabeth would have gloried in her power
to tear asunder two young loving hearts, casting the tenderest to perish—
a trophy of the power of her house ; but now that Eva had put away
Cormac's love, as a thing of no value—and, as she saw, cherished another
affection in its stead, she would have sacrificed many of her diamond heir-
looms to have been her arbiter of fate. She expected a triumph—she
experienced a defeat ; and, angered but not humbled—she still clasped
Eva's hands in hers, while the girl again murmured, " he saved my life!"
Strange to say, no rejoicing came over the spirit of Lady Elizabeth that
her son was safe from the snare she considered to have been spread for
him ; but every feeling merged into one of indignation, that a Talbot—
and her son—should have subjected himself to rejection by a simple
cottage girl — "and the growth of her charity (as her heart in its
contraction designated her nephew) substituted in his place." As she

withdrew from the most unsatisfactory visit she had ever made—was it her irritated nerves that conjured up the sound, or did peal after peal of low musical and yet ironical laughter ring amid the leaves that tangled on the walls of the old tower? And why did the swallow stoop so low in its wheeling flight that the ruffle of its wings agitated the feathers which drooped upon the proud lady's shoulders; and Eva's robins rush into the martins' nests that clustered beneath the thatch; and the two old fleshy-faced bats, who were never seen but after sunset, peer down from their grey stones, and scream, and squeak like monkeys; while the white-eared owl who had followed the weather-cock from whence it came, and mused beneath its sheltered base, in half-sleepy silence on atmospheric changes, why did he brave the sun, and, with winking eyes, hoot like a maniac? The very atmosphere became uncomfortable to Lady Elizabeth, for she could hardly breathe. Little knew the proud lady that her discomfiture at the Dovecote had

been reported—long before she had passed its threshold — to Eva's guardian. Randy had descended from the tower, and taken his seat on the centre of a mound, underneath the

old gable, beside which the lady must pass ere she issued from the gate; while, peering from a broken window, Kitty Kelly also watched —with different feelings and opposite conclusions. The countenance of the woodcutter was expressive of sly triumph; there was a volume of quaint joy in his rough face, as the news was brought to him by a troop of tiny beings, invisible to all but him; who, though they spoke no word, indicated by a thousand merry antics, that a great victory had been achieved. They vanished as they came; and the next moment Randy stood beside the garish footman, hat in hand.

"Glad to see your ladyship abroad to hear the blessings of the poor, and to thank you myself for the fine shelter your honour put over me when I was down in the sickness in your ladyship's wood," and he bowed with uncouth solemnity.

"He speaks of sickness!" said the lady to the footmen: "I never remember relieving him."

"Maybe your ladyship hasn't the best of memories—I *have*," observed the woodcutter, still with seeming respect. "Do you ever think of Dives and Lazarus?" he questioned; and in an instant his manner changed, his eyes rolled and sparkled, and the terrified lady shrunk into a corner of the carriage. "Stand back," he continued, addressing the servants who would have removed him—"and let the coachman get his horses to stir if he can!—My lady, the brightness of your diamonds will not light you to glory—nor gold, that never brought sunshine to a poor man's house, make soft your bed in heaven! There isn't a poor half-starved *colleen* that gathers wild strawberries on Glena would take your place and your trouble along with it. Whisper— you wanted a daughter as well as a son, but she's not for you," he said, pointing his finger derisively; "she's for your betters"

"Take me home!" exclaimed Lady Elizabeth.

"Take her," said the woodcutter, with increasing wildness of manner, "to where the body we pamper must go to, whatever becomes of the rest—to the little cold wet grave, that all the violets in the world can't sweeten! Go to Mucross, my lady, and learn your lesson there. The thigh-bones of strong men, that carried them through the wars of life—now white and powdery; the bare empty skulls of proud and beautiful ladies, with hairy worms for ringlets—are there. Drive her to Mucross!—Hurroo!"

The horses, frightened by the yell, set off at full gallop; but when the carriage arrived at Ard-Flesk, Lady Elizabeth was so overcome by terror, that she was carried by her servants to her dressing-room.

"And, mother," questioned Eva, on the evening of that day, as she sat on a low stool at her mother's feet, in the depth of their oriel window, "were the ladies of rank whom you met before you married, and of whom you tell me so little, were they like that proud unhappy lady who grieved us so much this morning?"

"Not many like her, dearest; but some, whose heads were not sufficiently strong for the giddy height on which they stand,—certainly a little like her."

"Poor thing!" she exclaimed; "now it is all over, and I look back upon her and her words, I am so thankful that my lot is not cast in the noisy world. I feel as if I never could be happy there: it must be so like struggling in a torrent," and she shuddered at the remembrance.

" You cannot live always here, my child! you must not."

" Why, mother?"

" Your education will need perfecting."

" Nay, mother! are you not my teacher?"

" There is much I do not know—much that you must learn; besides women have a destiny of usefulness to fulfil; a part to act, not in the torrent of life, but in its under current: they must not live only for birds, and flowers, and trees."

" The poor!—my mother!"

" One great duty, but not the only one; you must learn, Eva, to live in the world, to love the world, to serve the world, yet to withstand the world; a time may come—must come—when I shall not be with you, when you must think and act for yourself; when ——"

" Mother you are not ill!" interrupted Eva, starting in sudden apprehension at the thought of separation.

" Thank God, no, dearest; but well or ill, a mother must prepare her child for the future; you must, despite yourself, bear in mind, that the practical wisdom of manhood is often oblivious of youth's first love."

" Nay, mother!"

" You must hear me; there are few things more brittle than man's love; few things which the world so speedily makes shipwreck. Man must enter that world; and necessity compels woman to enter it also, though by a narrower path, or she can never be a help-meet for him. Alas, my child! if his father remembered our old friendship; if his aunt forgot her pride; if he were of a proper age; even if the love that shares your love for me in your young heart, should hold its faith, and Sidney hold his with you, you will have to endure——"

Eva did not now look up; she hid her face in her mother's lap, and replied—" Nothing."

" Nothing!" repeated Geraldine.

" Nothing, dearest mother, with you and with him."

" One little word—Poverty."

" We are not poor," replied Eva.

And thus it is, thought Geraldine, that young hearts feel, and think, and love, and hope! What a vision is their life! Sleeping in faith and trustfulness, and dreaming dreams that make an earthly heaven! then waking to the chill and cold of universal and particular change! *She* has slept and dreamed too long!—yet let me wake her tenderly, if wake she must; is not such a dream better than to be learned in the tricks and petty toils of a single day (for such *is* life); bearing onward bravely to attain the perfecting which leads to immortality? "My darling child!" she said, as she covered her brow with kisses, "I have been vain and foolish. I thought you could have loved Cormac, and I knew his mother's leave would follow his desire if she once saw you; there would have been wealth, position, power,——"

"Stay mother," interrupted Eva, "was it for these you wed my father's fortunes, saying, as I have heard, when his cousin, the great judge, would have wooed you from him, that you would rather carry a knapsack for Edward, than sit on the woolsack with Horace. Ah, mother!" she continued, half rising, and flinging her arms round her neck, "I have found you out!"

"And would you, Eva, do as I did?" replied Geraldine, struggling with her tears—"would you be the millstone round the neck of a brave spirit, which, but for you, could run its course, untrammelled, to all the honourable distinctions that men so largely covet?"

"No," she answered; "I would run it with him, run it at his feet, run it through poverty, through sorrow, sickness, misery, shame!—no not through shame—shame could never mate with him—and at the last, guided by him, would find strength to mount with him—bright in his glory. Oh, mother!" and Eva sank at her mother's feet, "teach me how to do this; take me anywhere to make me worthy a destiny so high; strengthen my exertions, elevate my mind, and I will be to you the truest, dearest child, that ever knelt for blessings at a mother's knee!"

What a sweet time it was! and how sweetly mother and child mingled together their tears and blessings; they were FRIENDS—friends in the highest and holiest meaning of that sacred word—each full of love and admiration of the other; and how the mother advised, and the child listened with meek ears; still thinking that worldly wisdom was hard,

and wondering why it should be needed; but yielding in the fulness of
love and duty to one who must know better than herself; relieved, too,
by the certainty that in future she should hear no more of Cormac.
Geraldine spoke of leaving Dovecote for a time; and that Eva heard
with tears, listening for words that promised their return; and then she
thought of the woodcutter, Randy! What would become of him while they
were gone! and so the evening passed in smiles, and tears, and counsel,
and sweet confidence; the evening of a day that added years to Eva's
store of knowledge of herself and of the world; and though no further
mention was made of Sidney, yet Eva saw that her mother, however

indistinctly, kept him
in view; at last,
calmly and sweetly
her arm hung round
her mother's neck, her head resting
on her mother's shoulder, she slept
half-dreamily, for the bright spirit
of her birth was with her then, soothing her with sweetest music, until
the various passages of her destiny were faintly shadowed forth by sound.
First, the spirits of childhood's favourite flowers raised their small voices;
they came from the shady nooks of DEEP VALLEYS AND OVERHANGING

woods; they came from daisies, and harebells, and violets, and cuckoo-sorrel, from the tangled vetch, the mellow clover, the purple columbine, the tender forget-me-not, and the tiny trumpeting honeysuckle ; and, having played their parts, under the command of Nightstar, who led the minstrelsy with a silver wand tipped by a sapphire she had borrowed from the rainbow, they melted into the dewy atmosphere and vanished; to be succeeded by the cultivated spirits of the garden—achieving bolder strains, and what would be considered finer music—louder it was—voices from the deep-mouthed aram plant, the gentle gum-cystus, the perfumed heliotrope, the heaven-hued salvia, the gorgeous tiger-lily ; and, above all the rest, the half-fledged spirit of a rose warbled so, that Eva would have caged it for ever in her bosom; for she had known and loved that strain from infancy, though she had never before recognised its source. These fragile and transparent things did not pass willingly from her sight, as the spirits of the flowers of childhood did, to make way for those of youth, but were somewhat rudely jostled by a multitude who rushed forward with all the eagerness of full and anxious life—each striving to be heard, rather than contributing to the general gush of melody. All was novelty and excitement. At first, Eva felt confused; she listened to one and then to another, and her brain whirled ; but, after a while, she again heard that beloved strain, clearly and distinctly above the rest—above the grating voice of the grumbling scutch-grass, that would exalt itself beyond its station—above the wail of the multitudes of atoms singing the requiem of ' Love lies bleeding,' to the genii of hard-bosomed camillas and expiring tuberoses, too intent on the excellence of their own strains to heed the wailing. Much did she delight in the spirit of a sturdy acorn, who told forth the glories of his race in measured rhythm, and even sympathised with those who would have succeeded in climbing highly, had their aim been holy ; but the elves of the nightshade and the spirits of the gaudy poppy, however soothing their melodies, like the syrens, only tempted to destruction. Gradually as these elements mingled together they became confused ; each subsiding into the other, and losing its own individuality in that with which it became mixed. Eva would have recalled the flowers of her childhood, but Nightstar, inclining towards her, whispered that though their essence would be always with her, *they* could return no more.

At times, sighs mingled with hymns of praise ; and as the rout passed on, the shriek of the murderous mandrake rose above the voice of the spirit of the rose; and though gloomy forms appeared in the distance, half-shrouded by the branches of the yew and the cypress, moaning forth such strains as

are heard only echoing from tombs, still the chant, the happy chant, that had accompanied her life gained strength; and as the shadows of noisome trees and heavy-leaved flowers became so dark and mournful that Eva felt her strength exhausted, her mind obscured, and life struggling through the last pulses of existence, she was suddenly revived by a burst of purest harmony, and a light softer than the setting sun, and free from the coldness which the silent and mysterious moon casts with her beams upon the earth; and looking upwards, she saw THE SPIRIT OF THE ROSE beaming with a glory all its own; and then she knew it for the spirit of UNIVERSAL LOVE, and in an ecstasy of renewed existence, she held forth her arms towards it; and as she did so, a voice called "Eva!" and she knew the voice of Sidney.　On the instant all around her became confused, the beauty of the season faded, heavy clouds, stained and murky, gathered around her, and shut out Nightstar from her sight.　Again the voice called "Eva!" and starting from her troubled slumbers she awoke, not knowing which was the real, and which the world of dreams.

PART THE FIFTH.

ONEYBELL was enjoying to the full the luxury of a Midsummer Night, couching upon roses, while her husband (husbands are always lovers in Fairy-land) poured the richest gifts into her lap, and the sweetest flattery into her ear; troops of her attendants were disporting around her; some engaged in hunting the gossamer spider; others in extracting nectar from the flowers; others, again, blowing bubbles and debating whether the dew gathered from the rose produced a colour different from that shaken off the petals of the lily. Honeybell smiled at the somewhat angry discussion of her courtiers, and, with half-shut eyes, indulged her mood of most luxurious laziness, from which the voice of Nightstar hardly aroused her, as, swifter and brighter than lightning, she stood before her sister Queen—the wand with which she had wrought out Eva's vision still trembling in her hand.

"Uprouse ye!" she said—"uprouse ye, and come with me! ere the flowers we both love are polluted by human blood;—up, fair Honeybell!—there is only time to act—none to think;—but now, as I passed the bank whereon my subjects were sporting, I saw a hideous

Banshee glide over earth.   I know that it bodes evil to those we
love and protect.   Uprouse ye, then, and come with me!"

"Eva is always in some fresh trouble," said Honeybell—"I thought
you told me I should have nothing more to do with her; yet, methinks
my counsel would serve her better far than yours; your gifts are always
leading her into a maze of anxieties; while mine would give her freedom,
joy, and love—if you would but let them work."

"It is for Sidney I most fear," answered the Queen.

Honeybell was roused in a moment. "He is worthy a throne in
Fairy-land!" she replied; "evil to him! up, spirits mine, up, and
arm ye!"

"With all good thoughts and honest spells," interposed Nightstar.

"With weapons of all kinds," interrupted Honeybell; "a victory
prepared for, is half gained before a battle is fought."

"Follow in the best order you can, only follow!" exclaimed Nightstar; and as she spoke she rose into the air, glittering like a meteor.
Quicker than thought could travel through mortal brain did the benevolent
Fairy speed to avert mischief: and, alighting on a dove, that surmounted
a half-ruined pavilion, which terminated the south end of the terrace at
Ard-Flesk, she paused to arrange her plans. It was not without dismay
she beheld troops of dark spirits congregated below, crowding, and crushing, and exulting: her arrival had not been noted by the ill-favoured
crew, and upon looking back, she beheld with pleasure the most gallant

Knight of Fairy-land, followed, high in the air, by the glittering
banners and troops of the united kingdoms.   Loud words came from out

the pavilion ; words loud and harsh from those whose union had been that
of closest brotherhood.

"Tell me not," said Cormac, "that you have acted in all fairness!
Who poisoned my mother's mind against her only son?—Who told her
of my stolen visits to the Dovecote?—Who sent her there to hear that,
tutored by you, Sidney, she I loved had learned to spurn me?"

"Will you hear me?" inquired Sidney, and the sweet music of his
voice was tuned by truth to perfect harmony, while Cormac's passion
choked his utterance ; "you must have seen how coldly your mother,
of late, has looked upon me : your name has never even been mentioned
by me to her."

"Hints can be given without the mention of names," said Cormac.

"Not by honest minds," replied Sidney.

"Honest!" sneered Cormac—how the fiends exulted at the sneer—and how they deepened its effect!

"Heed it not!" whispered Nightstar to Sidney—"high souls care not for taunts unmerited."

"Are you a man to bear it!" croaked the counsellors of Evil.

"Honest!" echoed Sidney. "Cormac, you know I am honest; though you scowl on me, you know in your secret heart that I am honest; that, even in this course of love, I have never worked darkly to win—"

"What you cannot, dare not, wear!" interrupted Cormac, fiercely,—"even you would hardly tempt Eva forth upon the world to share a beggar's portion."

In the very torrent and whirlwind of strong passion, which tempted Cormac to utter these words, he felt his heart stung by sudden pain, and he would gladly have recalled them.

"Be calm and triumph!" whispered Nightstar, on one side.

"Are you a man to bear it?" suggested a fiend, on the other.

"I am no beggar, Cormac," replied Sidney; "and ere our lives draw to a close, my name may fill as full, as bright, as honoured a page as yours. I feel it HERE! my heart tells me that none ever felt the power of self-reliance, pure from its divine source, refining and elevating what nature has bestowed, without assured triumph. I mean not to speak boastingly; but the time *shall* come when you will recall this, our last meeting, with sorrow for the injury and insult you have wrought upon me, both by word and deed."

The crawling fiends that served the Kelpie shrunk backward as he spoke, and the Fairy hosts waved their banners in exultation.

"Why need he go forth?" suggested Honeybell to Nightstar: "why should he leave this certainty of love?"

Nightstar could hardly repress the indignant smile that rose to her lips at the worldly-mindedness of her sister.

"I have written my farewell to Lady Elizabeth," continued Sidney; "after what passed to-day, I could not again meet her. Are we to part thus, Cormac?—we, whose heads rested on the same pillow; whose breathings mingled in the same prayers; who learned out of the same book?"

"Never to be forgotten by me," broke in Cormac. "*You learned*— often had I to suffer that reproach. Why am I cursed with wealth and station? In all things you pass me in the race of life!"

"It is hardly yet begun," said Sidney.

"It may be soon ended for one or both of us," muttered Cormac, darkly;—and the very air seemed breathless.

Sidney held out his hand. "Will you not say good-bye?"

Cormac gathered himself back, as a fierce dog before it springs. "Where go you from this?" he questioned.

"You need not ask," replied Sidney.

"I need, and will, sir; you pass not beneath the shadow of this porch, unless you promise that you go not *there*—not to the Dovecote."

"I shall make no such promise," replied Sidney, roused, but by no bad passion; "and yet I will pass it for ever!"—he advanced.

"Now, strike!—be not baffled. The steel is sure—he sees it not— be not conquered. Conquered by whom? Strike! Who sees? Strike, and at once!" suggested the fiends, who had too long been Cormac's counsellors.

"Stand back!" said Sidney; "this is child's play."

"It's man's vengeance," exclaimed Cormac, striking, with sudden fury, at his cousin; but a power stronger than his own hung upon his arm, and, missing his aim, he stumbled forward. As Sidney passed the threshold, Cormac raised his voice in a curse of such deadly import, that it was echoed by a shriek which trembled amid the trees; and then he called his cousin the name that brands a man's brow, and sinks into his heart—he called him 'Coward!' The youth turned; and, as he paused beneath the full beams of the queenly moon, he looked more noble than the finest Apollo that ever endowed creative sculptor with immortality.

"I go hence," he said, "wronged and insulted in many ways; but I will not go until you retract that last dark word. This scar upon my arm, won in defending you, now three years past, proves me no coward; other things recalled might be my witnesses. I am neither coward in act nor word; had you not been filled with sudden passion, you had not dared to lift your finger against me. Am I a coward, Cormac?" Both now stood in the open air, both in the beauty of manhood's youth; Sidney, with folded arms, remained firm and motionless: "Am I a coward, Cormac?" he repeated; and his cousin shunned the light of his clear, well-opened eyes.

"No!" was the brief reply; "I wronged you there: for *that*—that only—I ask forgiveness."

Eagerly the frank and generous heart threw wide its portals at the words; before another could be spoken, he grasped Cormac's hand in his; then casting it from him as suddenly as if it had been a serpent-sting, he exclaimed, "You struck at me with *that*, Cormac!"—and he pointed to where a tell-tale beam of light showed the blade of a foreign dagger, which Sidney had withdrawn from his grasp, and cast upon the ground. "You struck at me with the dagger my father gave us when we acted plays together! It is indeed time I left this house!"

"Sidney, Sidney!" shouted Cormac, when many minutes had dropped into the passing hour, and the woods loomed between him and the moon, so that he thought he was alone with darkness; "Sidney!—but it is better he should go. Always the advantage," he muttered; "no wonder that I hate him!—and yet, when I hate him most, the knowledge of his virtue shines around me, so that I dare not look into myself. Of late I quailed before those eyes whose light was once *my* light—a guide in all things. For that I hated him the more;—why should *he* guide *me?* Had I been quite myself," continued the unhappy youth, "I never could have struck him with that *thing* that crept into my sleeve! It is the thought of Eva that drives me to this," he continued, bursting into tears —and wilder, madder thoughts than he had known before whirled through a brain that was really fevered by the effects of disappointment, and the strong, contending passions of an indulged and pampered nature. He cast himself upon the grass, and pillowed his burning brow upon the wet moss; then he would have risen, and followed Sidney whither he knew he had gone: but his limbs refused their office.

"Tarry one moment," said Nightstar to Honeybell, when the evil whisperers had crept into slime and darkness to hide after defeat, and the Fairy troops, their duty well performed, took to the air and vanished. "Tarry one moment ere you return to your revels, and give me your attention. The time is fast approaching when the love and duty I owe Eva will call me forth in whatever shape best suits my purpose; I go with her into the world, leaving you and others of my own people to take charge, not only of my dominions, but of the thoughts and actions of the poor children of clay, who are more frequently beguiled by weakness than by sin. Look at that creature, so tortured by evil influences, that nature, outraged by their violence and torn by their results, has given way; and see, I have appointed a watcher, to calm, to soothe, to enlighten, to seize upon the body's weakness, and become its strength. You say he may turn from the monitress. True; but her silent words will have been heard; and who can tell when they may be recalled? Never, my sister, abandon one of those erring mortals; beset as they are by temptations: we should seek to comprehend only to conquer; never resign one of them, however low or lost, to what their blinded fellow-creatures call 'their fate.'"

"You preach a fairy crusade, my fair sister, only suited for the spheres," said Honeybell.

"We must not be content with being the fable of a child," replied

Nightstar, seriously, "when we can be the monitors of men—the guardians of women."

"As you please," answered the blooming Queen, as she stepped gracefully between the wings of her attendant bat. "We will not forget your injunctions, and for all our lightness, will fulfil them to the best of our ability."

Nightstar hung for a little about the pavilion, and seeing that none awoke to convey Cormac in his state of utter helplessness to the shelter of the house, she aroused his mother; nor did the gentle-hearted Queen speed away from Ard-Flesk until its heir rested on his own bed, over which Lady Elizabeth hung in most eloquent sorrow, while the Fairy's invisible agent soothed the ravings of his fever.

The night was nearly spent when Sidney paused at the garden gate of the Dovecote, where Randy waited his arrival.

"You are surely not going away, Master Sidney," said the poor fellow; "all the things you told me about are up yonder—all but this great book. Oh, Master Sidney, don't lave us for the wicked world beyond these mountains!—don't lave us!—trouble is everywhere. I can't tell what ails Miss Eva, but she has been sitting all night at the window, and sits there still. Oh! to think of sorrow coming here, when there's so much of it due to those who never felt its chill about their hearts. Shall I tap at the window and tell Miss Eva you are here, Master Sidney?"

"Not for the world, Randy. What I have to say to her must be said in the bright light of morning. Hope comes with its breezes and its beams! We must think and speak now as man and woman, not as girl and boy."

"Why, then, the Lord look down on the both of ye, Master Sidney, dear! Sure it's wonderful how you've grown up from babbies under my very eyes, jewel!—I thought you said you'd wait till morning, sir, to speak to her."

" And so I will, Randy ; but I may sit near her window."

" You can see her reading that great book, sir. She reads in it every night and morning.— Whenever anything troubles her she goes to *that*. Isn't she very young, Master Sidney, to be drawing comfort out of printed books ?"

" That book, Randy," replied Sidney, " comforts young and old, rich and poor ; and if you could understand it——"

" I did, Master Sidney ; only, when I was her age, I used to think books were only fit for those that couldn't get out among the fields and flowers— the pleasantest of all things for reading: but people grow wiser

every year, dear. I wish, agra! they grew happier at the same time."

Sidney was indisposed for conversation, and when he had seated himself on the grass bench, Randy sank down at his feet. " I'll tell you a lagend, Master Sidney, to divart you," he said. " There's a lagend here, sir—how—but first, sir, you mind there's an island in the Lake they call O'Donoghue's Library ?"

" Is there ?" said Sidney.

" Now, you know there is, sir ; sure you pictured it twenty times when you've been putting things down on paper ; and the rocks are like books— I mean, the books were turned into rocks. Well, a very handsome young lady was thinking to herself one day, and she rowing in a boat, what a dale of larning must be in them rocky books, and how much she'd like to have the reading of them ; and she turned her little cot's silken sail to the wind, which kept going round and round O'Donoghue's Library, in compliment to her ; thinking, at first, only how pretty the grey moss and the green moss, and the herbs and creeping things looked coating the

books—that's the rocks; and then the thought came into her head that
the green moss, with its little blossoms of white pearl, told her a dale of

the vanities as well as the freshness of youth; and the grey old moss
preached her a regular sermon of wisdom, telling her tales of what it
had seen, and how God's sunshine mingled with the billows of the lake,
even in the stormiest weather; and how, bare as the rock was, it gave
the old moss enough to live on, which the grass of the beautiful meadows
would hardly believe possible; and, by'n-by, the little starry-eyed snails
—tiny striped things—said how pleasantly they lived within them grate
books: many a time, by the same token, have I seen them snails when
they wern't altogether so comfortable; when the good people would be
teasing them out of their life, of a moonshiney morning, keeping them
from their drop of dew. And little wriggling worms, with tasselled horns,
spoke to the lady in praise of the barren rocks; and the little fishes, and
curious crawling things, boasted of the shelter and purtection they afforded
them; and while all this knowledge, and a dale more that I can't think
of, was coming to her as sweet as music on the wind, who should rise up

on the head of the waters but O'Donoghue himself, and putting a quiet smile on his grand ould face,—'And what are you going to pay me.'

he says, 'for reading my books,' he says. 'Oh, grate king!' makes answer the lady, 'I have never read a line in them, but I should like to, very much.'—'Nonsense,' he says, 'begging your beauty's pardon, but you have been reading them these two hours. Haven't you been larning of the grey and green moss, and of the starry-eyed snail, and the tasselled-horned worm, and of all the small and great creeping things, what you never knew before; turning over page after page of the book of Nature, the finest, grandest, ancientest book that ever was shut or opened,' says the king; and the lady bowed her head and thanked the king and owned the pleasantest reading ever she had was in O'Donoghue's Library! He minds me," murmured Randy, when his tale was ended, "no more than a plover's whistle,"—and the poor fellow laid down at his feet, and fell asleep.

The prospect of exerting mind and energy roused the best feelings in the heart of the noble and enterprising youth. He must, he knew, consult his father, and though he feared he had neither money nor influence to push his fortunes, yet he could reckon upon his wisdom and affection; and, above all—what sons do not always meet from fathers—sympathy. He well knew he would approve his leaving a home to which he was no longer welcome. Sidney loved his aunt better than she was ever loved before, and panted for the time—which, with the hopefulness of the young, he believed could not be far distant—when he should revive her affection for him. He had abundant plans for the future. His drawings had been frequently termed "masterpieces of art;" and he certainly cultivated such enthusiastic acquaintance with Nature, that it added freshness and truth to his vigorous pencil, which might win him fame and gold hereafter. Love had taught him poetry; and could he doubt the excellence of his verses, when Eva wept at their pathos and exulted in their heroism? What most boys encountered as difficulties he had considered enjoyments; his mind, like an alembic, distilled perfumes from that which others thought sapless leaves; and few men at five-and-twenty had minds more fully stored than Sidney at nineteen. These varied and enviable acquirements gave him self-reliance rather than self-confidence; and—as all do, before experience teaches knowledge—he fancied the world would receive him with open arms, and help him to independence and fame. His thoughts and ambitions—exalted and purified by the love which exalts and purifies all the aspirations of man—rose far above the lofty mountains that shut in the fair valley; and, confused as they were, still certain hopes and feelings were clearly defined, though arising out of a chaos of the future. How proud he should be of Eva! no puny-freckled jealousy suggested that he should shut her within the casket of selfish love. How he should glory in the admiration she excited, knowing that the high treasure of her heart was all his own! If dark thoughts of Cormac crossed this vision, he set them aside in the belief that some sudden madness had stirred within him; and then he longed for morning to tell her how bright (poor youth!) his future was!—how they should write each other brief chronicles of each day's love and labour. And at last the morning broke — it did not come tardily — what Midsummer morning ever did? — but he thought so, and chided its delay, as the vapours climbed the hills, resting like loitering travellers on the way—now hanging on a pinnacle, and then creeping into some damp cave, until driven forth by those arrows of light, which the sun casts forth at his first rising. At last, from within Eva's chamber, he heard her voice warbling Handel's hymn—

"How cheerful along the gay mead."

The voice was feeble: it came forth like a sigh—as if her heart went not with it. Strange, that at the sound of that subdued tone his sensitive spirit fainted—it brought to him a sense of unworthiness—a lack of strength to work out the lofty purposes wherein, but a few minutes before, he had triumphed; and he longed for her to come forth, as was her custom, to meet the morning when it descended from the mountain tops.

"Eva! Eva!" he exclaimed at length, impatiently; "Eva! all night I have watched here. I would not disturb you, though I have much to say, and little time to tarry, Eva!"

She came to the summons, not blushingly, but with a sober step and heavy anxious eyes; yet her chill and trembling hand met his with as fond a pressure as it had ever done. "I slept last evening," she said, "on my mother's shoulder, and saw such Midsummer visions! And then I heard your voice through the burley that succeeded;—it called 'Eva,' Sidney—just as you called me now. I have read and prayed, and read again: but I have never slept or slumbered since. I know that something has happened. What of Lady Elizabeth?"

"I have left her for ever."

"And that!" exclaimed Eva, bursting into tears; "*that* is my fault."

"No, Eva; nor mine. The links dropped away one by one, and at the last a single shudder set the poor captive free. I must leave you now for a brief time," he continued, speaking rapidly; "first go to my father, and counsel with him; then, out into the world. A Talbot cannot lack station! And I will *make* the wealth I covet—but for you; and then, oh, Eva, we shall be so happy!"

"When you have made the wealth?" she inquired—her woman's clear-sightedness seeing beyond the extended boundary of his hopes.

"Yes, when I have made the wealth! And have we not read together of many brave adventurers on whom it poured in golden showers —of some, lacking even the advantages I possess — of name and education?"

"Yes," she said; "we have read of its being achieved, when the head, prematurely whitened, was seeking a cold green pillow for its rest. And we have seen pictures—you yourself drew one—of Fame blowing its trump above the tombs."

"Eva, this is not like you; you are not yourself this morning.

Look out into the light, dearest! Look on the fair earth—the fairer
sky; listen to the music of your own birds; they are giving you welcome.
The old surly weathercock—our iron sentinel—has not creaked once!
look ——"

"At your bright hopeful face, Sidney, better than all my premature
wisdom, as my mother sometimes calls it," she continued, smiling her
own sweet smile; "it is going fast; it is seldom more than a shadow,
except," she added, turning away her face, "when you talk of leaving
this!"

"And yet it must be," he replied; and then he spoke without reserve,
as men speak to those they love and trust; and Eva, recovered from her
dreams, suppressed her own regrets, and strengthened his right resolves;
not, however, heightening his hopes—for her mother had told her many
tales of blight and sorrow, so that, even hoping with him, she feared to
hope too much; until after some gentle reasoning, in which the timidity
of the girl blended with the forethought of the woman, warmed by his
enthusiasm, and believing in him so truly that, yielding to the delightful
thought that the world must do so too, their young hearts beat in unison,
and spoke out in the sunny air, as though the future was eager to do
their bidding.

Sidney opened the great book Randy had carried, and enjoyed Eva's
delight, as she turned over the sketches and finished drawings which had
tempted him to think the world of art almost at his control.

"How glorious it will be," she said, smiling amid the tears that
would flow at intervals, "if your father sanctions your choice, and you
really become like the great painter, to whom princes and kings rendered
homage! I wonder if his early drawings were as beautiful as these!—
and never to tell me, Sidney, how hard you worked, and how many
you had done."

"At first," he said, "it was only my amusement; but of late I have
looked to Art as a means of life and fame! And now what think you
of this?" he added, drawing forth a portrait.

Eva bent over it in astonishment. "As like," she said, "as what my
mirror gives—but far more lovely; is it for me?"

"No, Eva, I cannot part with both—but this is for you. I meant to

have left it by your harp, to remind you when I am gone of one who
goes forth to win what he thinks will be granted more to your prayers
than to his deserts."

She took the sketch he had made of himself.

"Do you not like it?" he said, seeing she looked upon it doubtingly.

"How kind—how good of you to do it for me! but it is hardly like
you, dear Sidney—it has not your bright, happy, animated, yet sensitive
expression; the eyes are not so full of light."

"Exactly what I think of yours, beloved Eva; it is so spiritless
when you are by—so quite unworthy of you; and yet—why it is but
canvas after all!—the shadow of the substance—the memory of the
reality; something to recall the words that passed between these lips; the
dove-like sweetness of those eyes. Let us put them both away now."

"Nay, give me mine!" she exclaimed. "I can speak to *it* when *you*
are gone—tell it my thoughts, bid it good-night, and then again good-

morning. I shall lock it up, Sidney, and only let my mother look at it sometimes. There, stand away; ah! now it is more like—oh, yes!— your lofty brow and richly curling hair. But it will not smile upon me! I wish you had painted the smile! You leave others to do you justice!"

"I shall be jealous of my own canvas," said the young lover; "and yet joy to think it your companion when I am gone."

Sidney tarried at the Dovecote till the day was nearly done, hearing much of what Eva's mother considered worldly wisdom; though it may be doubtful whether Geraldine had ever practised one of the sage maxims she so zealously endeavoured to impress upon his mind. Anxious as she had been to secure Cormac the rich jewel of her daughter's love, the conduct of Lady Elizabeth, her stern bearing and determined pride, had roused her; and during that day she felt a secret pleasure in her child's love for one who had the courage to preserve his own dignity by quitting his rich and powerful relatives and looking fortune boldly in the face. The very fact that such a course received her approbation proved how little she had in common with the worldly wise. She entertained a high opinion of Sidney's talents; and her ductile nature—to the full as loving and gentle as was that of Eva, but without the higher qualities which her child inherited from her father—was not calculated to withstand the influence which their hopes and aspirations exercised, while full of youth and loveliness, they sat side by side, thinking hours minutes, and wondering how time could pass so swiftly. At length, farewells were taken; and even after the very last, Eva accompanied Sidney down the garden path, to the little gate leading to the meadows, beyond which sported the waters of the Tore.

"I ask yer pardons, darlings of my heart," said Randy, advancing to where they lingered, finding it almost impossible to separate; "I ask yer pardons; but you don't mind the ould woodcutter any more than you would a sod o' turf—or anything dead, or senseless at yer feet—only, I want ye to part here, just in this gap, where the swallows meet when they're gathered from the four winds of heaven, to build their nests and rear their young in our own land; there's a rowan tree over yer heads to keep ye from harm; and that little stream at yer feet—small as it is— is constant in its track; it's a fine thing to see the constancy of them wonderful little things—going alone, singing, through the world, and yet keeping in the path the Almighty let them take from the first.   See how

thick the cuckoo sorrel grows here; the rale original shamrock it is; and the forget-me-not, that, I know, is more the flower of love than the rose; and the bog myrtle—and every sweet flower; and even a tuft of the hare's-foot fern; no weed or evil plants come near the Whitestone Well; every plague and every curse stops at the other side of that little strame! if you must part, jewels of my heart!—part here — cross yer hands, darlings, left and right; then, right and left

over the stone —the stone the White Doe rests at, once in every year,
when she visits the WHITESTONE WELL—and God go with the one,
and God be with the other!"

Prompted by a delicacy, which all the conventionalities of the world can never teach, the poor fellow wiped the tears from his eyes with his rough hand, and walked on.

The fragile girl, all trembling as she was, had more command over words than had her young lover. "Go," she said, "go, Sidney: I will not say do not think of me — for I hope that would be impossible! but I say, do think of me! and thus—to press forward in all things that will tend to your own honour: for in that only can I rejoice. Yet do not;" and here her voice, but not her purpose, faltered—"do not waste time in writing much—a line will do, to say you are well; but let me have that line; and do not work too hard, whatever it may be you work at; we are both young, and years hence will be time enough—" she would have said "to be united;" but the words would not come—she hung her head, repeating, "time enough; and so, the blessing of God be upon all your labours!"

"We part in perfect faith, and truth, and love, one to the other," murmured Sidney—"I full of hope—" but his voice sounded so like its knell, that she said, "Not in that tone—yet full of hope—of certainty!" As she spoke—it was a trifle, a thing of nought; but when the feelings are excited, straws, shreds, perfumes, a sound, a fancy even, sweeping through the brain so rapidly that its course cannot be noted, will be read as an omen, either for good or evil—and so it chanced, that a

single feather from the wing of an eagle, which silently and unperceived
had floated above their heads, dropped at Sidney's feet.

"There," she exclaimed, pointing to the royal bird, which for the
first time in her life, she looked upon with pleasure. "There, at your
feet, is an omen of success; and see, he pilots the path you are going!
follow, Sidney, and so high and so glorious will be your destiny, even in
the full light of a glowing world!"

When Eva returned to the Dovecote, she found the bloodhound,
who had so often accompanied both Cormac and Sidney, seated
at the door, with that grave sad expression of countenance which so
peculiarly distinguishes the race. He rose silently, followed her into
her chamber, and half-curled round her feet, casting stealthy glances
towards her weeping face.

"Poor Keeldar!" she said, patting his head, "you never did this
before: poor Keeldar!" and the noble fellow shook his flapping ears,
and replied with a low whine—then curled himself up again, seeming
determined not to be driven away. At night, he was turned into the
lawn; but the next morning found him on the grass-bench beneath Eva's
window—her self-elected guardian.

Four days had passed—and the interest Eva evinced in the movements
of the little ragged Killarney post-boy, 'who travelled,' as he called it,
into 'the town'—and then back to the village with 'the news'—at whatever hour suited him best—was something new and extraordinary; and
many turns, upside down, did he give the letter, which, on the afternoon
of the fourth day, he presented to her. "I'm sure I'd ha' brought it
yesterday, miss, if I'd thought you cared about it; for I forgot it on the
counter of Bill Henesy's shop – an' I half-way home; and minded to turn
back; but I didn't."

The emotions excited by a first love-letter are better either imagined
or recalled, than described. Into the deepest shadow of the deepest
arbour of the garden, did Eva rush to read—what for the truth, the
earnestness, the heroism, and, withal, the delicacy, of its passion
might have been proclaimed from the house-top, without bringing the
faintest increase of colour to her cheek. No fairer lady's bower could
be imagined than that she had chosen; the shadows of the trees crossing

each other fantastically around her; the music of the wild bird lending melody to the scene, and her thoughts, half - real, half - romance,

deepening into the enchantment which belongs to the dreams of early love,— when she was abruptly summoned by Kitty to the cottage, to meet Lady Elizabeth Talbot.

The great lady came not in the pomp of equipage and dress, as before; her toilet was suited to the chamber of sick-ness, rather than her gilded state; her looks, haggard even to wildness; her natural energies stretched to their utmost tension; and when Eva entered, timidly, her mother seemed almost as much dis-tressed as their visitor. "I cannot expect sympathy from either!" were the proud lady's first words—"and yet you are both women—you, a mother! and you so young! how stern and cold you look!"

"I!" exclaimed Eva, "I, lady?"

"Ay—you! and no great wonder; I suppose Sidney has told you something which causes you to regard my son as little short of a——" she shuddered, and examined Eva's countenance with more than her usual scrutiny, adding, "is it not so?"

"Whatever may have passed between your nephew and your son to still more determine Sidney to seek his own fortune, lady, we know not. We saw he had been deeply wounded," said Geraldine, "but he would not speak of it; it was among the past and painful things of which even his young life has had so many: he has set his heart and strength against the future—and so best."

Lady Elizabeth breathed more freely; there was in Eva the same open, frank look that accompanied her mother's words. She read human nature with a keen, clear eye; and it was but the effect of the excitement and anxiety she had undergone, and the half-ravings of her son, which had made her a false interpreter of both looks and words. "Let all such things be past," she said; "I come to you as a suppliant. You little know the depth and strength of the love you have cast from you. My son is writhing in all the agony of fever ; night and day he calls upon your name; entreats me to bring you to him, that he may see you once more. The physicians tell me that his very life depends on his seeing you—on hearing your voice. Young lady, I am told that you have frequently braved the pestilence whose very name I shrink from ; that you are often found in cabins, by the pallet of disease and death! Is this so ?"

"Lady, it is! I fear no sickness, and think of death only as the uprising of life. Why should I fear?"

"How strange!" murmured the lady ; "such faith and firmness dwelling in a form so fragile! I hardly know how to frame such a request," she continued, turning to Geraldine ; "but if you will permit your daughter to see Cormac — to speak a few words to him — the physicians say the effect may be so tranquillising, that the only child will be spared to the widowed mother !"

How strange are the contradictions of the human mind! No matter what a mother's own experience may have been ; no matter how clear are her views of happiness, of love, of duty,—still she is seldom, if ever, proof against the glittering chance of a wealthy union for her daughter. Geraldine would not have sanctioned a dishonourable word or thought in Eva; and yet *she thought*, "How sad it was that she could not love Cormac!—but who knows, who knows ?"

Lady Elizabeth interpreted the silence of both mother and child disadvantageously to her entreaty. "I pledge myself," she said, "that no tie shall bind you ; that if he is happily soothed by the interview, you shall return with blessings—blessings such as mothers only can give—blessings on the goodness that permitted you to yield to my earnest prayer. I, an aged, widowed mother, could kneel at your feet— could implore for him what I would not do to save my own life! My only child is struggling against death; the light that is *my* light is even now flickering; mysterious forms contend over his wasting and sinking form. It may be, that the little reason left will be gone before I return ; that you may come when it is too late to recall him to himself:

but make the trial, I implore you!—and may you "—and she turned to Geraldine—"may you never know the terror of being a childless parent!"

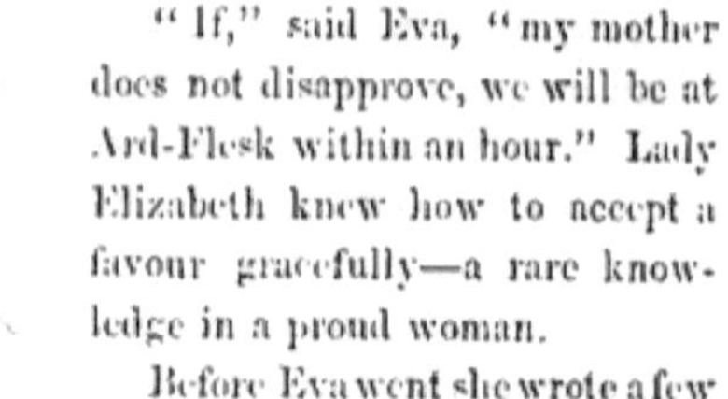

"If," said Eva, "my mother does not disapprove, we will be at Ard-Flesk within an hour." Lady Elizabeth knew how to accept a favour gracefully—a rare knowledge in a proud woman.

Before Eva went she wrote a few hurried lines to Sidney. "Have you told him where we are going?" inquired her mother.

"Certainly, dearest mother," was the reply.

"Will it not make him anxious and unhappy?" suggested Geraldine.

Her daughter's bright face beamed upon her. "Oh, no!" she answered, "he will be glad; it is what he would have wished. Surely, we can trust each other!"

Theirs were the mutual confidence and trust that are as force-full in absence as in the daily watching of suspicious care; feelings that keep even a stricter guard in solitude than amid a crowd; which no cankering jealousy can ever taint; and, as they have their source in truth, their aim and end are virtue!

How still and dark looked the old house at Ard-Flesk!—while, as if aware of the necessity for silence, Keeldar lifted his feet stealthily, as he followed his adopted mistress through the hall, and up the carved stairs, into the dimly-lighted drawing-room. How magnificent it seemed to both its visitors! Eva had never seen anything so grand. The servant advanced, and drew up the blind of the centre window. Geraldine glanced upon the velvet hangings and the richly-gilded furniture, and thought how perfectly her daughter's figure was reflected in the various mirrors.

"All this could have been yours!" she whispered in her ear. Eva started indignantly; but, self-reproved, she pointed to the window, where the eye wandered over a tract of country, the birthrights of many proprietors,—a rich and glorious landscape, unrivalled in the world.

"That is mine!" she said: "it is mine to look at, to wander through,
and to enjoy. Fie, dearest mother! to wish to stint my inheritance to
a few yards of old hangings and gilded cornice that a fly can sully."

"She is a strange girl," thought Geraldine, unable quite to comprehend
the change that had given such firmness of mind and originality of thought
to her character; "strange and great!"'

"Oh, mother!" she continued, "why is it that we bound our enjoyments by the consideration of 'mine' and 'yours?' the world is full of
beauty; there is no wall set round its valleys, no darkness shrouds its hills;
it is the Almighty's! and we his people have an inheritance of enjoyment;
the peasant who walks the mountain path can revel in the same light,
and air, and glory, that we do now, and yet this Creator's bounty is
unthought of—so freely given to all." Again she turned, and, looking

through another window that commanded a view of the distant town, skirted by the bountiful river Flesk, she pointed to the human habitations, containing inmates to whom Nature had given the high privilege of enjoying her works as freely as to the young lord of the domain, who shared, in common with the lowliest kerne, the evils incident to humanity.

It was a fair scene—a scene of surpassing beauty—outspread before them ; the river flowing through a most fertile valley, and rushing into the Lake—to which even liberal Fame has been a niggard, when compared with the lavish bounty it derives from Nature.   Beautiful Killarney ! Large is thy endowment of loveliness!   Great is thy store of hallowed memories !   Glorious are thy associations with the past !   What a world of wealth art thou to Poet and to Painter !

Before Geraldine had time to reply, Lady Elizabeth was in the room. Fixing her eyes, as before, upon Eva, she said, "You are a glorious creature! and may God bless you for the sacrifice!"   She understood her at that moment better than her own mother.

How awfully through the deep hangings, the silence and darkness of that chamber, came the ravings, and strained, unnatural murmurs, of the youth, whose burning brow could find no rest upon its pillow ! Lady Elizabeth's fantastic airs were overwhelmed by a mother's agony. Sometimes she would press her hands to her ears, to shut out his incoherent words; at others, she would bend down her head, that none might be lost. When he called on Eva (which he did frequently), she replied, addressing some soothing epithet to the sufferer; but he neither recognised her nor her voice,—muttering that she would hate him still the more for what had passed. Of all the fearful things that youth can look upon, is the sudden striking down of one of its own age: when hours seem numbered; passing, at once, from the sunshine of the world, into the solemn mysteries of the chamber of death. The ear becomes fearfully alive to the pulsations of the heart—the veins throb—the once familiar and cherished objects of our love are mingled with strange unnatural creations that mock our vision—the impossible being the reality of over-excited fancy; all things grow distorted, yet still retain their grasp on humanity.

Never had Eva felt any atmosphere half so oppressive; she who had been so often by the couch of want, as well as disease, had never heard such fearful and incoherent ravings as shrieked throughout that lofty chamber.

"You are very pale—and you tremble," said the physician, kindly taking her hand.

"But I will remain, sir, if I can be of use to your patient," was the maiden's reply.

"God bless you, young lady; I am sure you would; but the time is past."

"He will recover, sir, I hope."

"We are all right to cherish hope; and I think in this case we have a peculiar right to do so; I am sorry you have been so tried."

Lady Elizabeth passed from the room with Eva.

"I shall never forget this!" said the lady; "and you must not forget me! wear this for my sake." Her anxiety, deep and earnest as it was, did not prevent her wishing to relieve her pride by discharging an obligation—a feeling too frequently mistaken for generosity—and she pressed a jewel of large value upon Eva.

"Forgive me!" said the young girl; "forgive me the plainness of my words, lady! I intend no discourtesy; but I cannot be paid for an act of mere humanity."

Again Lady Elizabeth would have forced her to accept the gift, but Eva, standing by her mother's side, seemed to increase in stature as she again refused it.

"You are too proud, young lady," said Lady Elizabeth, in an offended tone, as she placed the jewel on the table; "a princess might accept it."

"I can accept nothing from Lady Elizabeth Talbot," she answered, gently, though her words were stern; "but I will pray humbly that her son may be restored."

"How changed she has become," thought her mother, as with the dignity of a youthful queen, Eva passed from the second chamber.

THE VISION OF THE WOODCUTTER.

PART THE SIXTH.

ANY and great changes had taken place ere another Midsummer reminded Eva that she had added another year to her life. Cormac recovered slowly, and had sought, with his mother, the relief it is believed change of air and scene can, in certain cases, alone supply. Ard-Flesk was again left, like so many of the aristocratic 'homes' of Ireland, to the care of aged servitors; and rumour described the young heir as gathering strength rapidly when freed from the spells that hovered around 'the Lake country.' Randy wandered about more than usual; some thought he became wiser as he grew older; but, in truth, it was sadness, and not wisdom, that made him silent. Usually, when evening was drawing on, he would start suddenly from his musings, rush back to the Dovecote, and pass the night under the shelter of the old gable. Nothing could have more astonished a stranger, unacquainted with the woodcutter's habits, than to see him seated on the bank, looking into the deep waters of the Lake; his hands folded on his bosom, grasping a rugged and mis-shapen staff; his battered hat, garlanded with wild trailing plants, bent over his brows, and yet not concealing the fervent expression of his eyes, while he watched every ripple on the surface, every bubble that rose and floated, listening for voices only heard by him, and bending to the breeze, as if

in homage. But Eva perceived no alteration in the fidelity and attachment of her guardian, although he had more than once complained that 'a shadow was over him.' He seemed to have an instinctive knowledge of what she wished him to do; and with the zeal of true affection, his act followed her desire so rapidly, that she hardly needed words to tell her wants.

He comprehended the vacuum caused by the absence of Sidney; he brought her a young fawn, and by constant and judicious training, established so good an understanding between it and Keeldar, that the dog took Eva's new favourite under its protection; and if any one observed how watchfully he guarded it, he would skulk away, hiding

himself in the bushes, as if ashamed of being caught in so foolish and
undignified an act as protecting, or playing with, the fawn of a red-deer.

So well could Randy divine Eva's thoughts, that if the expected letter
had not arrived in due time, he would stride to meet 'the post,' and
without heeding the little lad's remonstrance, seize the post-bag, and
convey it forthwith to be plundered in the Dovecote; indeed, his eccen-
tricities and earnestness wiled away many a moment that had been
otherwise heavy with care.   Sweetly though her mother's voice sounded
in the duet, there was another wanted to perfect its harmony.   Geraldine
and Eva read from the same book, yet neither tale, poem, nor history,
were quite what they used to be, when one read and two listened; and
well as Geraldine walked, she could not mount the hills with Eva as she
had so often done : and her cheek became pale, not flushed, by exercise ;
sometimes Eva observed this; but her mother smiled away all anxieties
that had birth in herself.

Eva's beauty attracted as much attention, and was as much noised abroad as the fame of the lovely district in which she dwelt.   Many watchers waited her passing through the village, or her entrance to the village church, that they might be assured if she really were as fascinating as report represented her to be ; rude men gazed, yet turned away with reverence and respect, mingled with admiration ; youths and maidens alike followed her with affection ; in all things she comported herself as became one betrothed to an absent lover, and consequently bound to be circumspect in her most trivial ways ; not that Eva studied this ; she acted as she felt, not altogether because she reasoned thereupon, but because of the divine instinct of right that stirred within her.   She was devoid alike of prudery and affectation, and while she returned with cordial frankness the greetings of fair rich gentlemen, who would have perilled their lives to win her smile, they felt that not for them was the smallest particle of that pure heart's love—such love as lovers ask for. Everything that moved loved her ! and yet how sadly would her young life have passed, but for letters—not what are called 'love-letters,' and yet letters of earnest love—letters that told Sidney's history, brief as it had been.   He had found his father older by five counted years than when he had last seen him, but looking older by twenty—struggling through the ' fag-end of life,' with a proud spirit and impoverished means ; but, never having been either servile or insensible, still rich in the respect of all who knew him. So much Sidney said, but he did not add, that two days in the threadbare home of a half-pay officer with five children, of whom he was the eldest, convinced him he had nothing to expect from his parents but their love, advice, and blessing. His mother, with a heart sick from sorrow, saw him depart, with three letters of introduction and an ill-filled purse, while his father retreated into the privacy of a little room, to which a few bookshelves imparted the title of ' Library,' and there on his knees, offered up prayers, steeped in many tears, for the noble and brave, the eldest born of a late marriage. Upon the faded cloth of that table he found a letter from Sidney, recording the simple story of his love.   He could not speak of this deep passion ; but to conceal it was impossible.   The letter was refolded with a sigh, followed by a murmur—" Poor boy ! he has enough to encounter without this."

If Sidney's first letters were a little tinged by melancholy, Eva thought it was only natural they should be; then came the energies and breathings of hope; then wonder!—wonder that London should seem so altogether different now from what it did when he spent the holidays with Lady Elizabeth in Cavendish Square—wonder, but no mistrust! He had delivered his introductions, and been hospitably received, that is, he had been invited to dinner by all, and had good counsel from one, an old brother officer of his father's, and a brave man, still in the prime of life,

by whose side Eva's father fell. It was pleasant to visit the maimed, but handsome veteran, in his retirement near the picturesque bridge at Chelsea— where the trees that have been ' venerable ' for more than half a century, shadow ' CHEYNE WALK ' and its numberless associations of the olden time. Here, by the help of a stout crutch, he used to halt along beneath the shade of lime-trees, that lent a pleasing shelter and a delicious fragrance to the little damp plot of ground he was pleased to call his garden ; it was pleasant to see how he had turned his sword into a pruning knife, and trimmed the beautiful jasmine that would tangle over the windows, and amusing to hear him express displeasure at the invasion of his neighbours' chickens, who would step out of the ranks, and pick up his seeds; and above all, it delighted Sidney to hear the praises of Eva's father and his own father—the praises of the Raymond and the Talbot mingled.

There are few things so gratifying to age as the attention paid by youth to their 'thrice-told tales ;' sympathy evinced by the young in the few amusements of the old, is certain to double the remaining pulsations of life within their rigid veins; it is the most delightful revival of their own early days—it brings back the hilarity and cheerfulness of bygone times without their attendant bitterness—for every personal pleasure has its pain! And many a twilight hour did the young man gratify the maimed officer by listening to his stories of past repulse and victory. He was a charming study in every respect for the young painter : there was a breezy freshness in his voice—an intelligent sparkle in his eyes—a firmness on his lips—a dignity in his broad and lofty brow—a spirit-moving energy in his thoughts, given with so much genuine kindness, as if they were mounting guard over his young friend ; and, while they feared urging him forward too much, dreaded still more to hold him back in the glorious race he was self-appointed to run. Eva knew all about the old soldier, and about Sidney's fellow students, and about the themes he originated, and the subjects he copied ; she wondered in her own mind why he had 'fellow students,' or what he went to the Royal Academy to learn ; she thought all he did perfection, and could not understand why he copied anything ; she thought nothing but his natural modesty prevented his repeating to her the fine compliments he must ere then have received ; and she built his castle so high, that at last it became cloud-capt, and losing it altogether, she would descend to earth, and wonder, if surrounded by bright lords and beautiful ladies, as he must be, would he keep true to the village maiden of Cloghreen ! Poor Eva ! she little knew that Sidney's 'studio' was indeed a lofty chamber, for the time being, and for the sake of cheapness, near the bridge at Battersea, in a tall, red brick, quaint house, such as we now see in pictures;

that there he laboured with the unabated enthusiasm of one who has a noble end in view. He had shown his drawings to judges, who regarded them with astonishment, and told him he only needed study to set his name on high ; but that study must be continued—must be persisted in—and his right spirit shrunk from appealing to his father for aid to continue in the course he had chosen; he laboured, day by day, to achieve the knowledge he knew he needed ; and at night, his candle wasted long past midnight, to complete the drawing which, disposed of for a tithe of its value, was to provide him food and raiment; so much he was able to accomplish, and experience had already taught him he was far more fortunate than scores of others who were climbing the same hill ; his noble mind never contrasted this life of labour and privation with that of the luxury and ease he had hitherto led ; the independence of his nature strengthened it ; and when he heard of distinctions conferred upon some prosperous Academician, and the prices he received for his pictures, it sent a thrill of hope and pleasure through his frame ; he remembered that the great person had once toiled as he was toiling, perhaps more severely, and under even greater disadvantages, and believed the REWARD would come to him, as it had to others ; thus, his nature was saved by the elements of its own generosity, from the wasting and baneful poison of envy; and, of himself, he created nothing to distract his course; sometimes, indeed, when the body would faint beneath the fatigue and pressure of actual labour and anxiety, or he was stricken down by some unexpected disappointment, he would rest his head upon his hands, and recall the vision of her he loved, to revive his fainting spirits. Happy, happy, was it for Sidney that his trials came to him in the strength and spring-tide of youth.

Time had flown upon its swiftest wings, and Sidney still toiled on; his genius had attracted the notice of the masters of our only school, and he had been rewarded; Eva joyed because he joyed at this; but she could hardly conceive it a distinction proportionate to his desert.

Eva had passed another birth-day, her mother spoke less frequently than she had done about leaving Dovecote; and yet there was a perpetual restlessness about her that perplexed and grieved her daughter, who, nevertheless, rejoiced at whatever assured her a lengthened sojourn at Killarney. The year was rushing on with its usual velocity, when the stillness of the country was somewhat moved by the account of Lady Elizabeth Talbot's death; there were no tears shed to her memory at Ard-Flesk; no 'Ullagawn!' raised its appealing sorrows to the mountains; no prayers wafted petitions for her repose to the bourne from whence no traveller returns. In due time, a stately monument recorded her many 'virtues,' and when they were read over to Randy, he turned away, saying, "It's the first we ever heard of them!" In the solitude of his studio, Sidney earnestly and bitterly wept her loss.

Eva's birth-days were not as troubled as of yore; yet they were times of contending feelings and emotions; she had grown to an age when the past had its retrospect, the future its anxieties; the worldly and unworldly, it might be, sometimes contended even in her bosom. The Kelpie's power was enchained—the strength in virtue gained by Eva would almost have effected that, without the interposition of other influences; yet, what she could not destroy she troubled; and Honeybell and Nightstar entertained such opposite opinions, that Eva sometimes found it difficult for a few moments to decide between the whispers of their invisible agencies; but Nightstar always triumphed in the end, and soothed by dreams what had been disturbed by day; often did the bright Queen shadow forth to the sleeping girl the anxieties and toils of her lover; but her truth was always lighted by hope; look as you would into the dark

pit, the STAR was at the bottom; the great attribute of the most royal fairy was her *faith* in *futurity;* however she might sorrow with, and for, the present, she looked beyond it; and while Eva inspired others with love, the Fairy failed not to mingle nope with the love of Sidney and the deepest pity for Cormac; a woman is seldom at ease in the society of a rejected lover; but his memory is a perpetual sacrifice to the self-love which is never absent from our nature, and he has always an interest in her good wishes; thus, she thought with generous tenderness of the loss of his mother, which, in her simplicity, she believed Cormac could not fail to deplore—and wondered how he endured it.

The evening that Randy had repeated the words that were graven on the fine monument, that looked, as he said, so "unnatural in the ancient ould abbey, where the O's of ould Ireland lived and reigned—grey and grand — and could not feel kindly towards interlopers in white marble," Eva was pondering on Lady Elizabeth's death, and all the uncertainties of life. Her eyes were fixed upon her mother; the light of their evening lamp was shining full on her head; and as she looked, she thought her changed, grown thin, her eyes large—much larger than usual — and her cheeks sunk. Geraldine was copying music, singing now and then the note she wrote; but after she had lent it sound, she would sigh, as if breathing the melody gave her pain. Eva watched her for some time, and as she did so, the idea grew upon her, to perfect agony, that her mother was very ill; she felt the blood rush to and from her heart with suffocating rapidity, and at last, unable to endure it longer, she sought Kitty, and startled her from her wheel, by asking suddenly if she thought anything was the matter with her mother.

"Is it with the mistress?" inquired the maid; adding, "there's something the matter with yourself, angel dear! it's the fault of that half-wild crayther the woodcutter; he's been crooning over his sooperstitions, as he always does when Midsummer is drawing on—that's it!"

Eva repeated her question—Kitty turned away her head; but Eva was not to be beguiled from her inquiry, and finding that Kitty still averted her face, she turned it gently round with her hands, and looking steadfastly upon her, saw that the faithful creature's eyes were filled with tears.

"It's only the wakeness that's in them, dear!" she exclaimed, removing the tears with her apron; "it's nothing but the wakeness!"

She was not a good actress, and Eva felt assured that her mother was ill, that Kitty knew it, and that efforts had been made to keep the sad knowledge from her; for some time she was bewildered, her brain reeled, she could hardly stand, and the nurse, with an exclamation of terror, placed her on a chair. "Your heart's not beating the way hers do be, I hope, darling?" she inquired. "Oh, sure the life would lave me, without a warning, if both of ye got that way. Oh, a cushla machree! what would I give to put the remains of life that's in me into her. Oh, if we could only strengthen the strong in heart, with the strength that goes astray in many a bad body, the times would mend, jewel! with the world, and all in it!"

That night, unable to repose, Eva roused Kitty from her slumbers, to learn, as she said, the worst, and listened with breathless anxiety for her words: all that Kitty had to tell was, that the mistress slept badly; that she had wasted to a skeleton, and never seemed quiet or contented, as she used to be; that old Doctor Magrath—but to be sure there was no good in him—no use in minding what he said! She knew that Miss Eva did not know he had been often to the Dovecote; the mistress always had him when Miss Eva was away for a few hours with her friends, or attending to the poor; and twice he brought a great doctor with him from Tralee, and Doctor Magrath said he thought Miss Eva ought to know it, but the mistress would not hear of it, and after all, maybe, it was only Doctor Magrath making much of his own opinion; but he said the other doctor thought what he thought.

"And what was that?" inquired Eva.

"Oh, then, how could I tell! who ever in the world found out what a doctor thought; they bid her take nourishment, and keep her mind asy, and not walk or fret; they always bid one not to fret. I've nothing more to tell you, miss, darling; I wish I had."

"And what do *you* think, Kitty?"

"Oh, then I don't know, dear!—she's young, not quite nineteen years older than yourself; and sure the Lord will spare her, for you are two birds alone in the wide world—I may say two birds quite alone—for Master Sidney's a long time away. Ah, Mister Cormac was a fine young gentleman: there, I see the colour changing in your face; I'm always saying what I ought not to say, dear; and the mistress will never forgive me for telling you how bad she is; I wonder you never saw it before; I used often to tremble for fear you'd ask me."

Eva pressed her hands on her heart to still its beating. She crept into her mother's room so noiselessly that, though Geraldine was awake, she would not have heard her, but that her shadow crossed the moonlight that rested on the floor.

"Why is this, my child—who told you I was waking?" she inquired.

"I came to see," was the reply, as she knelt beside her couch; "I fancied you looked ill last night, and I questioned Kitty. Oh, mother, mother, why did you deceive me!"

"I hoped to get better without distressing you by the knowledge of my illness; but, my child, I fear it may not be!—and we must think and speak of what you must do when—when we are not together. I would have taken you to Dublin long ago, but I feared leaving you alone in a city. And, dearest, it will come like a thief in the night; it often knocks so hardly at my heart—that I know not how soon it will give way. I would have told you to-morrow, Eva! for I cannot conceal from myself the fact, that I am worse—much worse. Nay, my darling child," she continued, "I will not have those passionate tears; I know there must be grief; ours have been the habits of sisters, hallowed by the affections of a dearer and more holy relationship. I had a dream when you were born, my beloved, in which I thought I chose for you, above all other gifts, the happiness of 'loving and being beloved.' Yet truly if it has its happiness, it has its misery and its danger. My very soul is wound so closely round you, my own sweet Eva! that I lack the courage to intrust you to the care of Him who has given me in you almost seventeen years of the purest happiness that ever a good child poured into a mother's heart! I see you cannot bear this yet; for me—often as I turned from it—I have been forced to think of it; to you it is all new; and yet," she added, after a pause, during which Eva's sobs were the more distressing from the suffocating efforts she made to repress them— "and yet you will be saved much pain by finding all things in order; for my transit may be brief, rapid as the extinction of a trembling light which, however carefully guarded, leaves the protecting hand in very sudden darkness!"

"Nay, mother," exclaimed Eva; "why is this: there must be hope! hope there must be; it is quite impossible! you, so full of life, the young life that gave me life! whose decay is so slight that I have hardly noticed it. Mother, there SHALL be hope!"

"Yes, dearest, so there shall."

"Well!" continued Eva, almost crushing her mother's slender hand, within the earnest pressure of her own. "Well, then, why will you talk so—it is cruel insanity to think of you—and IT together—there is hope!"

"Ay, truly, my child; hope—the right bright hope! hope that will flourish, that will mount and triumph, when all that we cling to here shall vanish, like the vapours before the sun, whose rising we have so often watched together; this is the best hope—the hope, my blessed child! which I have sought to nourish—even with your bright eyes upon me, Eva. Often, often! during the watches of the night, do I pray for you, and yet pray not to let my ever-living, ever-renewing, love for you, come between me and Him—the giver of our spirit's immortality. I am excited, Eva! I must strike a light and take the lulling poison that procures me the only feverish rest I have known for months." And when Eva saw her trembling hand, and noted how the beatings of her heart agitated her night-dress, and marked the clammy hair matting upon her forehead, she understood why it was that of late her mother had forbidden her entering her chamber at night. Faint and sick with sorrow, she left her, at her entreaty, to the stupor which followed the draught; and no pen could tell, no commonly afflicted heart conceive, the anguish she experienced in the solitude of her little chamber.

Death was almost as great a mystery to her then as when she knelt and prayed beside the stricken wood-pigeon. She thought she knew it :— she thought, because she ministered so often beside the deathbeds of the poor, that she could question the grave as to its victory, and remain firm to the faith that there was no sting in death! Oh! how she longed for morning; it was a positive relief to her when, with the greyest, earliest, light, she heard Randy's voice in reply to Keeldar's whine—speaking as though the poultry and pigeons — even the young lambs and calves — understood his words. She was determined in her purpose; and the rising sun saw her cantering her pony over the Flesk bridge, followed closely by Keeldar, who never turned his head towards the ivied chimneys of Ard-Flesk, as they towered above the distant wood. Surely the spirits of the morning hovered around her and invigorated the old pony to do its best, for the usually wilful animal needed no reminder, but went as joyously forward as though only five—not fifteen—years had dappled his coat with grey.

On she went. "The blessing of the morning, and every morning she rises, be about her," exclaimed an old woman, tottering beneath the creel of turf that was strapped across her shoulders; "but I can't tell what's

come over her, the darling! for she never cast a look at me, let alone
a word; it's the first time she ever passed me that way. Well, God
speed her!—the sight of her rises my heart off the day's trouble."

Eva never pulled bridle until she sprung from her saddle at the door
of Doctor Magrath. Well might the aged man salute her, with the
almost forgotten compliment of the old school, as a 'vision of beauty.'
She lost no time in stating the object of her visit, and urging her entreaty
to know the exact nature of her mother's peril, and what could be done
to save her. The doctor parried these questions with the habit of his
craft; but Eva pursued her object through every turning he made, and,
at last, with genuine sympathy, he confessed that he feared there was
no hope of her mother's recovery. He did not say this exactly in words,

but it was easy to imply as much. She could not trust herself to speak; and the doctor promised to see her mother on the following day. She urged her pony to its utmost swiftness: how could she now endure to be away from her whose very hours were numbered?

Doctor Magrath was punctual to his appointment. He brought with him the doctor who had previously visited Geraldine. He told Eva that the disease had been stealing on for years, and that he was only astonished how her mother could have borne up so long against it. "I saw," he said, "that her desire to spare you pain was keeping her up in a way impossible to all but woman's love: we can do nothing more, young lady; nothing, but recommend you to be patient, and trust in Him!"

"He can save her!" interrupted Eva. "He can save her. Oh, because of my importunity, she may be saved! May she not? Oh, say she may!"

"With Him, dear young lady, all things are possible; but I, as a physician, see no mortal path to permanent recovery."

Eva struggled for composure—for words—for breath; and when struggles for all these were vain, she would have fallen to the ground, but for the supporting arm of the physician.

"You have tried her too much," said old Doctor Magrath. "Nothing that I could have stated would have afflicted her thus; but in you she had great hope!"

"And therefore was I truthful," he replied. "Of all cruelties there is no cruelty equal to that of permitting death to rush unexpected into a sick chamber."

Randy had never passed such a Midsummer Eve as the one that rapidly followed the physician's visit—never since he was stricken by fever in the forest! If sympathy could have alleviated Eva's distress, she would have been comforted; but she was completely overwhelmed in spirit, though her natural strength of mind supported her, and amid this great *trial* she *trusted.*

The woodcutter, in whose mind and heart there was a strange mingling of piety and superstition, after having offered to Eva a few brief but earnest words of consolation, departed from the Dovecote to visit a well of peculiar sanctity—the Holy Well of Lochfort; and here he passed many hours in sad communion with his own thoughts. The few wayfarers who were bending there, glided noiselessly away when they noted the more than usually mournful countenance of the Fairy Man: and knew that no common event could have called him into that mountain solitude, and amid objects where the 'good people' were rarely or never found.

"It is your birthday, my own Eva," said Geraldine, as she rose on her pillow to embrace her; "and I am most grateful to the Great Power that I am spared to wish you the joy I shall not be here to wish you another year. I have always prayed to pass away when the earth was in its beauty—to mount heavenward with the incense of the teeming world—to leave you amid the consolations of summer, rather than among the cold winds or bitter snows. There are people all around us, dearest, who care for us, and will doubly care for you when I am gone I had angel whisperings during the night, and whatever of doubt or fear I felt for you, my own beloved, has passed quite—quite away! I know you will be protected! I know that your progress even through the thorns and briars, and beside the pitfalls, of the world, will be joyful. I know where you have rested your heart."

"On you, mother, on you!" interrupted Eva, as she covered her white, worn hand with kisses.

"God is good!" said Geraldine. "He never takes from us one stay without giving another. As the blossom falls the buds expand; I wish you to write and tell Sidney that I have prayed to see him once more; you will find a present home with the vicar's wife. Eva! Eva!" she continued, in a reproachful tone, "I had expected more firmness! you tend me day and night; you are as unwearied in your watchings as in your love; but your self-command would rejoice me more than all. My fair sweet child, we must call on FAITH to aid us in the trials of life. I will write Sidney myself. I suffer no pain. I feel as though I could rise from this bed—not with these remnants of earth around me!" she added, looking at her wasted arms; "but leaving them as the spirit leaves the tomb—up, up, and away. My own love, I feel I could do this, but for you—whose loving eyes, and plenteous tears, and earnest, fervent prayers, keep me from the home that waits me there! Oh, beauteous sun!" she exclaimed, clasping her hands in sudden ecstasy, while a deep flush of crimson burned beneath the intense brightness of her large dark eyes; and she looked through the open window upon the little paradise her taste had created, where every leaf bent beneath the refreshing dews,

of which the glowing orb already demanded tribute, and saw far off the peaceful glen between the mountains, over which the morning was breaking in mellowed glory: "Oh, beauteous sun! and thou sweet balmy air! birds who have dwelt with me in safety! the grass green

raths! the holy meditative woods, and deep blue lakes! I thank and
bless you all, for the beguilement that you gave my sorrows. You said,
' We are here! proofs of His goodness,' and I heard your voices all;
and now, Eva, I hear the tender questionings of the poor echoing around
me, and I thank them. Each time we ministered to their necessities,
they, by their grateful prayers, most richly ministered to ours; but most
of all for thee—for thee! I thank my God "—for a time her words
ceased, though she moved her lips in prayer; and then she suddenly
exclaimed, "Nay, I *will* write to Sidney! You must not thwart me, Eva.
I know my brain wanders, but not into mist and darkness—rather into
light. My eyes are not moist like yours, because my faith is strong."
And though she rambled in her words, all were spoken in consolation—
her departure might be compared rather to the triumphal entry of a
victorious spirit into heaven, than the timid lingering of one around the
home and haunts of its earthly tabernacle ; and if we do not enter fully
into details of the faith, which could alone inspire confidence like hers,
it is because such themes should not be treated of, save in a solemn place,
or in grave books set apart for holy purposes. Geraldine became more
composed after she had written, and Eva herself took the letter to Randy,
her trusty messenger. He asked no question, for Eva's swollen eyes too
truly told the tale.

   " To bid Master Sidney back, is it?" said the poor woodcutter; "it's
a long journey ; and them's on the watch that will harry the ship they
havn't the power to sink.   Oh, I'll take it to the post, miss, darling; it's
long since you sent him one from yourself—but your heart's too full of
trouble to mind him now.   Five days! aye, indeed, and no curtain drawn
on your eyes by day or night! I lie on the green grass bench hoping I'll
be wanted, and the stars wink at me as they pass in friendliness, and the
very moonbeams say I watch them out; and *themselves* are in it, darling—
only *she* frightens them."

   " Of whom speak you, Randy?" inquired Eva, for her own brain
began to reel beneath her sorrow ; and the self-command she had at last
acquired, caused her even greater suffering than grief.

   " Of her — the shadow-woman in the dark cloak—the BANSHEE!
She always *follows* the Raymonds though she *cries* none for them. She's

been about this long time. I fling sticks at her on the sly ; they pass right through her, but she moves on all the same. I don't like her, nor does Keeldar—he bays her as he would the moon ; but she steals on— the way death to be doing—stealing without word, and often without warning, the warm soft breath from the withered lips of age, or the rosy ones of youth—it's all one to her."

"Don't speak so loud, Randy, she is sleeping !"

"If she dreams by daylight," he continued, lowering his voice into a whisper—"if she dreams by daylight, she'll win brightness without waiting. Oh, avourneen deelish! don't take on so—sure it's all His doing ! The little golden-wren one day sat at her hall-door : 'and if I was the eagle," she said, 'nature would take better care of me, and I shouldn't have to toil the way I do, to provide for them little golden-bills within there;' and the eagle sat on his rock—'and if I was the sun,' he says, 'I'd have great divershun, hunting the clouds about the heavens, and not have the trouble of thinking how to feed my royal prince and princess, that want as much food as if they had not the king of the birds for a father; how I wish I was the sun!' 'Ah! ah,' laughs the sun, and he up bright and strong in his glory; 'you're all a thankless set of cratures, from the little wren up to your kingly self; *you* provide for your children! you are only the means,' says the sun ; 'they'd be all badly off if they were left to you; wrens, robins, and eagles, the huge king of the waters, princes, people, all, are fed by a greater than you; let Nature withdraw her care, and see where you'll be then! The nature that can exalt the lowly, feed the hungry, take care of the nestlings when the hunter's arrow has struck down the father; *that it is* that feeds, and cares, and clothes—a pretty set you are to talk of providing? Ah! ah!' And the sun rolled on, and the wren and the eagle both remembered his words. Look up, jewel!" added the woodcutter. "Look up, darling, yours is *heart trouble*—only believe this—it's for the best ! She'll meet him she loved before you were born ; and many a young fawn, and young lamb we've seen deserted on the hills, and yet somehow hands were always found to foster even them wild things; it's another angel in heaven will be watching you, dear ! Sure the prayers of the whole country will make soft her bed in that blessed place : the prayers of the poor, the fatherless and the widow; there's nothing but grace and glory before you, Miss Eva; them that knows best shows me as much. I'll go now, dear; but just take a turn in the summer air, and think of the happiness that's coming to her, and think of what an ancient ould woman I once knew was always saying, '*there's a silver lining to every cloud!*' "

The whole of that day Geraldine enjoyed life in the prospect of death, as she had never enjoyed life before. She spoke of, and prayed much for, Sidney; but did not repeat her wish to see him; the future was already with her; her hopes seemed perfected long previously; she had arranged, what only the weak-minded dread to think of. She was free from pain, even the violent beatings of her heart was stilled, and at her request Eva sung to her one of her favourite hymns, in which at intervals her own voice joined so clearly and strongly that hope swelled in her child's bosom.

She was so grateful that Eva's birthday had been such a day of happiness. Evening lowered its mantle over earth; but all was so serene, and calm, and clear, that the watchers within and without said there was no night. The earth slept beneath a grey, soft, twilight; no one thought of shutting out the warm sweet breeze that did not ruffle a rose-leaf; and the shadows on the grass told Randy it was past midnight. As he lay in his usual place he became sensible of the presence of the sister Queens, floating in a circle around the open window.

After moving round and about, Honeybell, and the few attendants who were with her, disappeared; and Nightstar, with a timid and crouching air, as if fearful of intruding, slipped into the chalice of a sleeping lily, that rested its stem against the trellise. Randy's thoughts questioned of Nightstar, if there was no spell to stay Geraldine's departure.

"We know our place," she answered, in a faint low tone ; "we seek to make life happy, but meddle not with death! Even I dare not enter the chamber; Honeybell's more worldly spirit could not linger here ; but I can comfort Eva, can again whisper what I have whispered long. The day of her birth has gone without being a day of death, and now her mother sleeps; I can see the breath passing sweetly from between those lips that shall utter words no more. Now, Eva holds her hand! Oh, how she looks into her face, hand still locked in hand! and now, assured of her slumbers, her worn-out head droops on her mother's pillow —now !" said Nightstar, not in the gentle tone that sounded like a silver joy-bell, but solemnly, as the wind that sighs through the spires of some ancient

cypress; and rising half out of the flower, she waved her wand, and created a soothing vision in the mind of her endowed child ; slowly the suggester of sweet dreams went round, shimmering in the darkness—an undulating ray of light; but suddenly its motion ceased, and she crouched into the flower, drawing her tresses around her like a mantle—and then a Presence, a dim and shadowy outline, not horrible, but dark and untransparent, came—who can tell from whence? All nature shrunk and shivered as it passed; it seemed to fill all space, yet entered the trellised window—the awful herald of the grave! silently it passed, without disturbing a dew-drop, though ushering a mortal to immortality! Such was the faith of the departing soul, that it left no sigh upon the lips, nor did hand press hand in token of farewell.

The stars were bright as ever in the deep blue sky, and still Eva slept —the living pillowed with the dead—a sweet, calm, dream-like sleep, and when the stars went out, the warm rays of the sun awoke her; she loosened her fingers from the still gentle clasp, and gazed upon the white face, smiling her old sweet loving smile; and then something terrible crept through her veins; she put her lips close, closer, to her mother's —there was no breath! Eva was indeed an orphan !

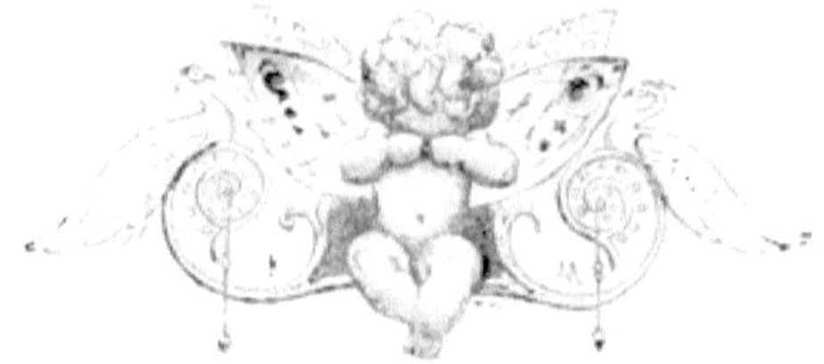

THE LIBRARY.

WELL might Nightstar triumph in her pupil; well might she exclaim to Honeybell, "See—behold! this is my work; could all your worldly wisdom have achieved an end so high? The maiden's influence has extended even below the waters of her native lakes; and, bowing to the power with which I endowed her, rather than to the justice that sought to wake him from his heavy slumbers, O'Donoghue has banished from his realm the Kelpie and her court. She has strength no longer to work Eva harm—so long as she treads the land of the Shamrock and the Harp."

"Go on," said Honeybell.

"In childhood, she was the idol of the poor; now those who pride themselves on the ten or twelve descents they number — sands that sparkle in their fleeting centuries—vie with each other to tempt the maiden of the cottage to their halls; they send gay equipages to wile her from her sadness; and speak of her beauty, and her song—as if no one had ever beauty or song like hers. These children of earth cannot appreciate the noble essence which, like the honey in the flower-cup, may be cherished beneath the humblest blossoms. The ruby lip—the polished brow—the swan-like form—the seraph eyes—the voice, which even we echo with rapture—have alone enslaved them; it is these alone that make her conquests."

"As long as they last," murmured Honeybell; "while we joy in perpetual youth, looking old only when we have a purpose to work out: how shocking to look old in reality!"

"The essence, mysterious in its birth as in its departure—for it knows no death," continued Nightstar, "is never old; and though they know it not, it is the purity of this immortal portion which commands more than the usual homage paid to woman. She exerts it, unconsciously, over all who look upon her —for their good, rather than her own glory."

"And yet," interrupted Honeybell, "what will it all end in ? Why all this rout about her, when you will not let her profit by it? I grant my once great interest in Sidney; but we cannot continue feeling interest in men we never see; they pass away from memory just like this—" and she blew the farina from the petals of a flower, while her courtiers endeavoured to avoid its contact.

"It is only trouble that tries strength; gold can be refined but by fire," said Nightstar.

"I am no alchemist," answered Honeybell; "but I know that if, after all the sympathy the orphan of the Dovecote has excited; if, after all the attention she has received, you send her forth to struggle through poverty with her first love—why, sister Nightstar, you are more cruel than I thought you!"

"Honeybell, you never will comprehend me."

"Nightstar, I never can!"

"Some evil is at hand: I foresee it and will avert it; I know it is at hand, for just as the moon rose upon the night that is now over us,

I saw the frightful Phooca, the enemy of all good, riding in triumph over the scenes we love so well; and which she, the mortal we protect, still

hallows by her presence. We must be astir, my fair sister, for danger threatens her this day—not her heart! not her mind!—they will be firm, amid all trials, all perils, all temptations; firmer than the cromleach that has stood for ages in Dunloe, which a touch can move, but an earthquake cannot shake from the base that props it. Knowing Eva, as you do," continued the Air-Queen, "I am astonished you could so completely misunderstand her nature, as to suppose her capable of change. I saw the renewal of her faith, as the grass grew green over her mother's grave, for though Sidney came not, yet there was no wavering in her love— no changing in her faith; that faith is her happiness; she values what you value, as I do—as nought. Honeybell, you are not listening."

"I am, indeed; only tell me something new," replied the heedless Fairy.

"Am I not telling you—here, beneath the moonbeams—of mortal constancy," quoth Nightstar. "Now, do attend my story for a moment. One who is good as well as great, suddenly sent Sidney to where, long ago, we flourished, till driven thence by superstition and its train of crimes —to fair and fervent Italy—to catch still more of the painter's inspiration;

a most noble art—for so men call it; lauding thus the NATURE in which we move, for Art is only perfect when it copies Nature most."

"Nightstar," quoth Honeybell, gravely; "can we not decoy one of these painters to our court?"

"May the moon shine on ye more brightly, my sweetest sister! Why, they know every nook of Fairy Land; they copy us on their canvas: it is by their genius the herd of common mortals know us so well. They sweep away the mists from history, and illumine truth; they give life, for all the purposes of life, to heroes of old times; they make the present of the past, and foredoom the future; they set high deeds on high— of freedom, virtue, charity, patriotism, loyalty; they preach great sermons without words; they are mighty teachers of the multitude—for the eye of man accepts what the ear rejects; they make the common rugged surface whereon they work, to discourse of powers that have moved the world; they bring gay foreign lands into the compass of a narrow room; they move a forest; the green verdant lawns—the flowery meads —the vistas—the blue hills and babbling brooks—they carry them into the very hearts of crowded cities, so that poor panting, care-worn mortals look upon them, and renew their youth."

"Do they build temples for these men?" inquired Honeybell, who was a great lover of justice.

"Neither *for* them, nor *to* them," replied Nightstar; "they seem to care but little how they live, knowing they prepare a noble mausoleum to their own names, to which, when they are dead, all men bow down in worship. Do you listen? Sidney departed suddenly—he, not receiving Geraldine's last letter, knew nothing of Eva's loss, until another letter followed him to Rome, in fond reply to one he wrote to her. In the brightness of her pure, unselfish love, she bade him not to think of her, but journey on—gathering health and knowledge in that bright-skyed country: that she was not alone, but would wait his return, remaining lady of the Dovecote until then."

"How many moons since?"

"Seven, or nine, I know not which; I cannot learn their count of time."

"And you say all the attention lavished upon her, by those who journey miles to pay it, has moved her to no new fantasy?"

"To nothing I could blame, were she the spirit of a star!"

"It is curious—very curious," mused the Queen; "and she not rich, yet with refinement, and a zeal for good."

"Good is ever done by rich and poor, if there be the will," replied Nightstar; "few things have ever joyed me more than the perfectness of this creature—so truly high, and yet so lowly-minded."

"Well, well," said Honeybell, "one wearies of perfection, as one does of moonshine. I am sometimes so glad when the broad-faced moon stares herself to death, and goes right out; the dancing, trembling, winking stars, that sparkle in heaven's high arch, delight me more. I hardly see the same two following nights; and if I do, I know them not. I love to watch them shooting to the earth, and fly to see where they have fallen. If a maiden catches a falling star, and keeps it, she is sure of her lover's faith! Know you that, sister?"

Nightstar smiled, but there was sadness in her smile.

"You were triumphing just now," observed Honeybell; "and now you do not heed our sportive elves. Look at yonder imps of mine; they are mimicking the loves of earth's poor children: wooing, where there is no heavier trouble than the dew-drop that weighs down the petals of the sheltering rose. Your favourite, Randy, is watching them from his old quarters in the garden, thinking himself asleep: how you have endowed that mortal! I suppose you will take him altogether to Fairy Land ere long; but you are not heeding; you are gazing into futurity—what see you there?"

"A trial—hard to endure for her I guard," replied Nightstar; "it approaches from a far-land—a speck, an atom, the veriest shadow! but it will gain strength and power as it comes on—still," she added, with an air of triumph, " I nothing fear; nothing can change her now, 'stablished, as she is, in virtue ! Our next great festival—our Midsummer—will be with us soon ; for the tender leaves, so lightly tinged with colour, as they burst through the pale-brown shelter of their parent twigs, are grown into a hardy green; the hawthorn buds are swelling ; the swallows of the old gable have come ; and the feathered choir are there in love and fullest tune ; there are nests in every bush and tree; and as I peeped at a greenfinch, I saw she had hatched her young ; the wheat grows

tall and strong, and the oat and the barley put forth their spiral leaves ; the blossom of the nut is dropping off, leaving the germ it sheltered to grow and ripen ; the insects stir in the long grass ; and——"

"Enough!" said Honeybell; "my bees have been busy gathering honey all day, and labour renders them lazy steeds by night. We must away, good sister, to *our* nests in the flowers and THE HOLLOW TREES, or to the disguises that perplex the minds of mortals. Where shall we meet again? When the weather was chill and the nights were dark we had light and music of our own in the halls of Ard-Flesk, and in many time-honoured but deserted mansions; but when summer is with us, I'm for the green-wood—the arched bays where the silver sands glisten, and the waters carry our songs to bards of other lands. We must away ; for the morning light is breaking over lofty Carran Tuel."

"Ay, look!" exclaimed Nightstar; "look at yon red streak, heralding the sun : we must indeed away ; my eyes ache with the rapid brightness that floods the sky. The busy hum of earth is beginning about us ; and as the earliest herald of evils that come with day, look at yonder wasp so soon astir for mischief—awake to disturb in others the repose he cannot himself enjoy. He will not be the only one, ere Midsummer passes, to use a sting—sharper than his."

" 'Twas as fine a sight as ever I saw," quoth Randy, as, waking, he stretched himself and looked towards the scene of fairy meeting. " 'Twas a mighty fine gathering intirely, as I could wish to see: people talk of having grate imagination and fancy, but they never could fancy those things, rushing like the four winds, from—who knows where!—aye, that's it. Where do they come from? Where do they go? If their home is in the stars, they'd be far too happy up there, sparkling in the deep blue sky, that has neither beginning nor end—to come down to this troublesome pilgrimage of a world, where smiles are finished with tears, and the dance ends in the coffin! Oh, wirah, wirah! the longer we live the more we see of it ; and yet we don't wish to lave it : that's just for want of faith in where we're to go to! I've hunted in ruins, and mosses, and in old trees, and deep caves—over and through the Holy Island of Inisfallen, down in the mines of Ross, high and low—in flower-bells and under broad leaves, in mountains, and beside the streams that make music on their way, but I never could make out one of the good people in the daylight—in the night they give me no rest; it is Randy here,

and Randy there, and Randy everywhere, with them; and sometime
or other they'll end by taking Randy altogether; and I don't care, for
if it wasn't for the child-stealing, there's no harm in the craythurs.
I thought awhile ago, how much I'd like to be with them, and go share
in their little innocent ways, drinking dew out of flowers, playing at
hide and seek with the moonbeams, and making love in roses! I see
it all! and yet there's some poor unenlightened creatures who would
as good as tell me I had not the sight of my own eyes; they would
swear all I saw and heard over there was only a drame, or think me
bewitched or crazy! They say if the good people were always about

Miss Eva she'd see them. Why, so she does, many a time. She looks
Nightstar full in the face, and does not know it!" and then he
walked carefully from one flower-pot to another, delighting in keeping
everything in order as it was when (to use his own expression) "the poor
misthress went away." "There's twice as many daffodils this spring as
there was last, miss, dear," he had said, when Eva was about to visit the
vicarage; "and the snowdrops are as thick as hail—a lucky sign, agra!

and I never saw the earth so tangled with violets—white and blue! You
could be lost in them, dear; and a wonderful promise of cherries and
roses.   I wish all them fine ladies and gentlemen would'nt keep you away
from the Dovecote: and though Keeldar's very civil when you're in it,
he's too proud to stay with the likes of me, when you're wanting; and,
jewel, you're not half as rosy or as happy-looking as you used to be. Ah,

avourneen deelish, you go too often to THE CHURCHYARD, mourning over
the one grave—where the sweetest herbs and flowers of spring and
summer always grow. Now, don't be angry with your poor Randy—
don't, dear! only where's the good of it ? She'd hear you just as ready
from this, as to sit there on the grass that's long now. Cry as loud as
we will, dear, there's no answer from the grave ; none that we can hear
with our ears, though there is a voice comes to our heart, after much
weeping, to comfort us!" and then, seeing Eva in tears, he would
reproach himself bitterly, and, to change the subject, speak of Sidney ;
that would produce almost as much emotion, until, in despair, he would
overwhelm her with accounts of a new brood of chickens, or amuse
her with stories of the wonderful sagacity of a calf Kitty was rearing,
or tell her of the steadiness with which every child in the village attended
school, 'because they knew she would like it.' Eva never considered

anything 'trivial' that proved how much she was beloved ; and when she left the cottage which she could not bear to resign, and yet could not endure to remain in—recalling, as it did, during the long solitary hours, all the happiness she had enjoyed therein—she told Randy she would return before her next birthday.

Midsummer was at hand—the woodcutter appeared to have forgotten all things connected with it—save that it was HER birth-day ; while Kitty wept unceasingly that the anniversary of her dear lady's death was so near. No one ever thought of calling Eva 'the young mistress ;' her authority was altogether of a different kind from that which the term implies : she was, in the poetic feeling and phraseology of the country, 'the world's darling,' the 'Flower of the Lakes,' 'the Rose of Mucross,'

'the heart's delight,' 'the pulse of the heart,' 'the world's cush la machree'—to all within her sphere ; and if they loved her before 'her trouble,'—with the warm instinct of Irish nature, they idolised her after it. 'Midsummer,' then, was at hand; Randy roused himself from his world of dreams, to gather Eva's favourite flowers, to garland the porch, to trim the roses, to DECK THE FAWN—now grown into a doe—with ribbands; until, at last, unable to shake off the heaviness that weighed upon his spirits, he sat down upon the old grass bench and sobbed like a child. "Get up!" exclaimed Kitty, "here's the world's darling in sight, and two ladies riding home with her; you ought to be ashamed of yourself, to meet her this way, and she coming from a real gentleman's house to stay with us. Make yourself up, like a proper servant; and when you open the hall door, don't begin blessing her, but stand straight, and bow—while I curtsey behind—and say—'Miss, here's the gardener! he would open the door for joy, miss! all the other servants would do the same.' We must keep up her consequence, Randy—we must keep up her consequence."

"She likes things as they are," replied Randy—nevertheless making an attempt to shake down his shaggy hair, and dry his eyes—"she likes things as they are, and no show, Kitty; she'd give me her hand friendly before the Queen, if she was to the fore; she has no half-lady pride in her—not she."

"But we must keep up her consequence, Randy," persisted Kitty, smoothing down her white apron over her black dress: "I have laid everything out to the best advantage; and, oh, Randy! if you had but a frill to your shirt, you'd look so nice."

"I'm very well to have a shirt, let alone a frill—as the plain sweet pea said to the feathered columbine; frill! enagh," repeated Randy, in a tone of contempt.

"Randy," whispered Kitty, "I shouldn't mind, for once, lending you one of my caps to pin inside; just to keep up her consequence."

Randy did not deign a reply to this considerate suggestion, but cast a look of reproach at Kitty.

"Do, Randy, be said and led—for once."

"I'm ashamed of ye, so I am, to think of her consequence. HER consequence," repeated the woodcutter, emphatically, "to be kept up by the ould frill of a yallow nightcap!"

"The ignorant nagur," muttered Kitty, as she rushed to the door, "the poor dark craythur!" Proud was Kitty of the fine horses, and the fine servants, and the beautiful young ladies who brought Miss Eva home, and were delighted with the Dovecote, and gave Kitty a golden guinea; and Kitty had sufficient bad taste to fancy, that if Miss Eva were dressed like them, she would look better than in the plain high robe of black silk, 'without a bit of anything on it but crape;' and though these young ladies were but new ac-

quaintances whom Eva had met at the Vicar's, they deeply regretted parting from her, and embraced her again and again, extorting a promise that she would soon permit them to withdraw her from her solitude once more.

"Paler every time she comes home," sighed Randy; "and a weight's about my heart, as if I was going to lose her altogether. I'm here, miss, darling," he said, gently putting his head into the window. "Your poor

Randy; Keeldar, the baste, came to me the minute he got home, and seems perplexed that the fawn's a doe: he sniffs at, and knows her, but he does not understand it. Won't you come to the flowers, miss? I never saw so many roses. Oh, murder, if it isn't crying she is, and not heeding me; crying, with her head resting on the misthress's Bible. Oh, then, no wonder my head's grey and my heart's greyer;" and Randy's tears were renewed from very sympathy. But when Eva came forth after a time, taking interest in everything that interested him, and smiling and talking—receiving thankfully the humble presents of her humble friends, as if they had been jewels of price, the woodcutter revived, as the perishing flowers under the beams of the sun, and thought she looked really happy, and longed to go forth and tell the villagers that though Miss Eva had been amongst great people, she loved her own people better than ever; and she rejoiced at his departure, with various little kindly gifts, such as she could afford from her scanty store; for she longed to be alone, to enjoy the loneliness—the perfect and entire loneliness—in which she could recall the past and ponder over the future. Yet Randy was far from easy in his mind; he felt that some event was coming; for on the night that preceded that morning, he had seen ARMED FAIRIES gathering above the trees that shadowed the Dovecote; and though they thus

supplied proof that they were on the watch for Eva's protection, he was anxious, if not apprehensive, for the result: something was approaching—the issue of which he could not guess.

As the evening advanced, she left the precincts of the cottage to visit her mother's grave; and there Randy had been before her; the grass around it was carefully trimmed; the whole mound was matted over with

the greenest clover; the head and foot-stones were garlanded with the
flowers Geraldine loved best; if there had been no other cause for tears,
Eva would have wept at this delicate mark of the woodcutter's tender
thoughtfulness. He had fed the robins there; and as she sat in silent
commune with the dead, the large-eyed birds came about her, looking
mutely into her face—not chirping, but gazing with their soft dark eyes
as if in sympathy. She could hear the murmurs of the Lake-waters,
as the currents rushed from one to the other, through the 'long range;'
and the full choir of distant birds filled the air with music. She could see
the proud tomb of Lady Elizabeth at the end of one of the long aisles;

perched upon the armorial blazonry that surmounted the stately pile, was
a raven—an ominous and unclean bird. She could not but contrast its
uncared-for loneliness and neglect, with the simple but endearing tokens of
affection that blossomed on her mother's humble grave. At last, she
wandered homeward and turned into the bower, which arose on a mound

above the Whitestone Well: it was only a seat, overshadowed by a luxuriant growth of bending trees, interlaced by wild roses and climbers of various kinds—a pretty rustic spot, the beauty of which no art could imitate.

The day had passed through its fainting hours—sighing for the cool of evening: it had been one of the most feverish days of a feverish summer. Randy's care had kept the flowers moist and the grass green; but the water had to be looked for in the Whitestone Well—so low had it fallen; the cattle lowed plaintively over the dried-up and scorched marshes; and the waters of the lakes seemed to recede farther and farther from their sedgy margins—now, indeed, no longer sedgy, for the green rush had become a brown, sapless, coarse-grained straw, and the broad leaves of the water-lily were drawn up by

the scorching heat into crumpled heaps, where nothing, not even a tiny snail, obtained food; the very woodpaths were thick with dust, and the bounding river reduced to a peevish brook—as if it were itself thirsty—crawled, where it had so often triumphed, amid huge stones and rocks. The day was, in truth, not only sultry but feverish; and Eva felt the enervating effects of such oppressive weather: it increased the weariness that weighed her spirits down. She knew she must use some exertion for her future maintenance, for her mother's store must, sooner or later, be exhausted. She was too proud, too right-minded, for a moment to endure dependence. She felt bewildered and sorrow-stricken; kind as were all to her, she had no heart-friend—no one to whom she could open her mind. She knew none who really sympathised with her spirit's yearning for activity. She felt as all feel, in a degree, who have been used to the companionship of *souls*. At last Keeldar, who had watched her, came and laid his head on her lap, and not receiving the attention he expected, placed himself at her feet. He had not rested long, however, when his flap ears moved; he arched them upwards, leaving more space for sound to enter; and then his tail stiffened, and he moved his nostrils, rose up, turned round, and stood in an attitude peculiar to his race, when expecting an intruder. A shadow rested on the grass—a lengthened shadow; and, before Eva could rise from her seat, a stranger, for she knew him not, stood before her. He removed his hat, and she saw at once that his hair was dark—it was not the nut-brown hair of Sidney.

"Do you not know me, Eva?—not know *me!* Am I either so changed or so forgotten that you do not remember Cormac Talbot?"

"Cormac!" repeated Eva, in a tone of the deepest disappointment; for she only thought of one, and though she had no reason to expect him, the very shadow on the grass suggested the possibility of his presence.

"Yes—Cormac! Will you not speak to me? I who have returned solely to see you; whose life has been cheered by the hope that you would hail my return as the return of a friend! Surely in nothing have I forfeited my right to that title, Eva!"

She extended her hand, and felt that his was chill and damp.

"Will you not speak to me, Eva?" he repeated.

"I am so astonished," she said, while endeavouring to withdraw the hand he still clasped; "I could not have thought of seeing you."

"And why not? Did you think I could forget you? Did you fancy my love was written as on sand? But I respected your sorrow, and would not suddenly intrude upon it."

"You have suffered also," she said, endeavouring to guide the conversation to another theme.

"My poor mother—yes—but that was long expected. She was never to me what your mother was to you, Eva."

"No!" she replied, shocked at the implied fault-finding; "there were

few like mine ; but she loved you. You should not efface such memories,
sir ; those who do so trample upon graves ! "

" It may be," he said, carelessly : " but I came not from the sunny
south to talk of sorrow, though I respected yours. I have journeyed
night and day to meet you here to-night. Why even *your dog* will hardly
give me welcome !" he added, in a tone of disappointment.

" We ought," said Eva, after the lapse of a few moments, " we
ought, indeed, to welcome back its gentry to this poor country. I am
sure that all the people will shout a welcome when they hear of your
return."

" I would rather you would whisper yours," he replied, attempting to
regain the hand she had withdrawn.

" I speak it without a whisper," answered Eva, her self-possession
fully restored : " it would be strange if I did not so welcome the
cousin of Sidney Talbot to his native land."

" On no such plea will I rest my welcome here," he replied. " Listen
Eva; not when I offered my young unpractised heart for your acceptance,
beneath the sanctuary of that roof, and with the entire approval of your
mother, did I love you with a tithe of the love with which I now woo you
to be mine. Eva, you shall hear me !"

She would have retired, but he stayed her.

" I am in nothing changed," she answered.

" Still you must hear me," he repeated. " Hear me once more ; you
have lately seen a shadowing forth of the power and luxury that wealth
supplies. You have seen every eye turn in admiration of your beauty,
and heard high-born lips sound your praises. You have witnessed the
strength of position, and looked upon the wide-spread tables that wealth
surrounds with grateful guests; but think, Eva—think ! When in addition
to your beauty—to the fascination which encompasses you, as with a
spell—think, if in addition to all these, you had the wealth—the station
—which Cormac Talbot's wife must have — think — think what you
would be !"

" A self-degraded, self-condemned woman, ashamed to look into my
own heart, lest it should rise in judgment against me ! "

" You cannot scorn such power for such good ! "

"I do not; I value it—would work for it—cherish it; but for it I would not *peril my soul!* Cormac, you know I never loved you."

"I know it! yet oh, Eva, you cannot withstand the deep devotion, the earnest loving sacrifice of my whole life!"

"You know," she said, and the sweet tones of her rich voice mellowed into still greater tenderness; "you also know I love another."

"I know you did; but he has been long absent; has failed in the career his ambition, not his talent, dictated."

"Who dares to say he failed?" interrupted Eva, indignantly; "who talks of his failing?"

"Now, do be patient; I repeat but his own words," said Cormac.

Eva grasped the chair from which she had risen. "Then you have seen him! Where and when?" she inquired, eagerly. "In his last letter from Rome he does not mention having seen you : where was it?"

"At Rome, not nine weeks past! I see you have not heard since then." Eva made no answer. "I thought he could not write to you under the circumstances," said Cormac in a sympathising tone. "Dearest Eva, compose yourself."

"Under what circumstances?" and the question almost stifled her.

"Driving in the neighbourhood of Rome, I recognised my cousin," replied Cormac, "though his dress and bearing were so changed, that a friend who was with me, laughed at my desiring such acquaintance." Cormac did not see the indignation that flashed upon him from Eva's eyes. "I entreated that the past should be forgotten, and hand pressed hand as in our days of boyhood. It grieved me to find his spirit broken; at times he abandoned himself to despair, lest he should never accomplish a mysterious task on which he had staked his fame. It was painful to witness it; I never saw one so changed; his temper ruffled at straws; his hands half paralysed, so that he could not guide his pencil. He worked— vainly for all great purposes—in his poor dwelling in the Eternal City; worked and failed! I say again—worked and failed! Eva, you tremble!"

"It is the moonbeam that trembles over me."

"He spoke of you; for his lone, and cheerless, and unhopeful heart opened with more than the old brotherly love; and he wished, in the bitterness of disappointment, that you had chosen otherwise."

"And bade *you* tell me so," said Eva, in a tone that made Cormac start. "Can you not add that to the false tale you have invented?"

"Now, by every sacred tie, in heaven and earth!" exclaimed Cormac, "you do me wrong; I have invented nothing. Every artist in Rome has been speaking of the failure of his task as a thing certain. Had he been less ambitious, he might have been more successful. He has no more chance of becoming a great artist, so to say, than yonder dog of becoming a lion." He turned to look at Kechlar, but he was gone.

"Or than you, his cousin, have of partaking his noble nature, you might add," said Eva, in the same tone which had before called forth such strange sensations. Cormac drew back and paused.

"I can endure anything from you, and nothing you can say shall move me from my purpose. I will endure all, to save you from yourself, from the deep and bitter poverty in which you would plunge—not alone, but with him whose love for you has cooled, though his honour may be firm, poor and feeble as he is ; with him, whom you would drag still more deeply into a fathomless abyss of want and misery! Ask yourself if this be just? Ask yourself if any woman has a right to immolate that which she professes to love?"

"I have heard you patiently, sir," said Eva, "and will hear you to the end: have you finished?"

"No," he replied; "not finished, until, on my knees, I again offer you the passionate love of a passionate nature. Eva, you love your country; I will minister to its prosperity, and never leave its shores; you love the people—you shall remain their guardian angel. You shall realise the dream of your childhood, and pour consolation and bestow comfort upon the hundreds whose breath lingers, not lives, within their feeble frames! Does not the very fact of your not hearing from my cousin argue his change? Write and ask him if he will not gladly resign the contract that clogs, not clings, about his heart. Oh, Eva! does not my constancy deserve some word? fair forms and bright eyes crossed my path, and sought to win my love—but it was yours! Your image lay as an amulet upon my heart, and shielded me from sin. Still cold and silent? Eva, speak to me; have you no word for me? I offer you wealth, love, honour, faithfulness—all that the fairest and richest covet.

Even were Sidney not poor and discomfited, you cannot cling to the tattered fragment of a travelled artist's worn-out fondness, feeding upon voluptuous forms, conniving at impurities I dare not name to you, until his sense sickens, and his——"

"Now I have words!" interrupted Eva. "I heard you patiently, though my pulse quickened and my heart beat high; though I disbelieved in all but your tale of Sidney's poverty—still I heard you. What should I care for the love of one who could not penetrate the heavy shadows, that press upon the noblest natures like realities, even on their very eve of triumph? What should my heart, were it as free as the fleetest roe that bounds to meet the sun-beams on Glena, care for him whose mean soul makes poverty a reproach, and thinks a true and earnest woman's love could be aught but a shield and a staff for protection and support! What should I care for the patriotism that may be bought and paid by heartless smiles? You know the breath lingers, not lives, within the frames of those God sent you into the world to sustain; and yet you bargain, in your selfishness, for a heartless hand as a price for your return to those you never should have abandoned; and for whose souls and bodies, hereafter, if not here, you will be as surely called to account as you now stand before me—rich and powerful in this world's gifts, though unchanged in the nature which made me shrink even from your boyish kindness. Sir, were the grass as green over the grave of Sidney Talbot as it is where I have been to-day, and where I would I were even now, I would die above it rather than be your wife."

As she spoke, and before Cormac could give utterance to the violent words that twined like serpents round his tongue, even as he grasped her arm within his hand, Keeldar burst upon them with a loud cry of joy; there was a rustling among the trees, a parting of the branches, and in an instant Eva fell upon Sidney's bosom. Cormac stood unmoved; his lip curled in proud defiance; he saw that she had fainted, and it was not until Sidney bore her into the open air, that her face, upturned to her native heaven, astonished him by the high-souled expression that elevated its matchless beauty, as the moonlight shone upon it—inspiring him with reverence, as though he gazed upon the face of an angel.

"Do not go," exclaimed Sidney—"do not go—I too hastened to be here on Eva's birthday; I heard your protestations, and while you urged her not to sink me into poverty, I loathed myself for seeking her as my bride, when I had nothing but poverty to offer her. In bitter self-reproach and agony, I turned to leave this hallowed spot—when her priceless pleading, her knowledge of the shadow which wrestled with me, when weakened by imagination and excess of labour, I felt myself a doomed man, encoffined by my own trembling hand—the shadow which made me doubt the power—the immortal power—that *has* conquered! Look up and hear that, Eva, my own Eva; though poor and penniless, I achieved my purpose; and those of whom he truly spoke as doubting, have followed me with generous acclamation; your image, your faith, your hope, your love! by some mysterious spiriting, though far away,

infused themselves into my nature, and I became, though poorly lodged and poorly clad—I became the art-wonder of immortal Rome no letter could tell you this! I flew, proud of my triumph, to claim your promise; I was mad with joy; I saw not, knew not, thought not, of the poverty you, Cormac, too truly pictured! I thought of Love and Art, and nothing more; yet had she failed a jot, had she wavered, had this marble brow become less pure beneath the gorgeous light your golden alchemy flung upon its surface, I would never have sought to clasp her—as I do now—as my affianced love. Nay, Cormac, though much you said was true, you did mislead."

"No," whispered Eva, as she raised herself from Sidney's bosom, "no—he did not : he could not."

"It was not worthy," he persisted—"not worthy of you to take advantage of the doubts which racked my very soul, when all my poor heart's beatings were laid bare to you—to seek to rob me of the one ewe lamb; but I forgive you, I may well do so when I look here. I pardon you—and may God pardon you—the wrong you would have done!"

"Always conqueror," murmured Cormac, and his voice gained strength as he continued—"you have made your choice, Eva!—you have again chosen between us; the time may come when you will deplore it."

"You must not rush across that lawn with wrathful footsteps," exclaimed the generous Sidney. "Eva, he did not tell you all the truth—though he said more than truth; something there was still to say : and let it be said by me. He did not tell you that at Rome his purse was opened to me by a true brother's hand."

"But you touched it not!" she said.

"I did not ; yet his generosity shines no less bright for that. Oh, my own love !—when I look at you I cannot wonder that men forget themselves to worship at your feet, and yet," he added, drawing Eva back and gazing on her with more than the true reverence of holiest love, "think again !—that in a far city home, to which I woo your presence, the air is thick with damp unwholesome vapours; there are no hills to look upon, no woods to wander in, no freedom such as that you can love ; thousands of strange eyes will meet yours as you pass, without sympathy or common interest; there comes no music to my lofty windows, but the monotonous song of some caged bird, whose clear voice cracks amid the roll of carriages, or the shrill cries of those who hawk the food—that *I* have wanted means to purchase; where I have passed hours offering up thanksgiving that you were *here*, in your native home, loving and beloved, by nature and natural hearts."

"That was when the shadows of which we spoke so thickened round you," murmured Eva; "I do not tremble at such poverty! being passed, 'tis but another theme for thankfulness."

"It may return!" said Sidney; "I would not deceive you—not for the price of your own priceless self. The reputation I achieved in Rome, came like electricity on me and all beside; it *may* follow me to England; but compliments are tardy servitors to stern necessity; and success may never come."

Cormac fixed his eyes upon Eva while Sidney was speaking; but the expression of his features was that of perfect hopelessness; he turned away, but listened still.

"Think of nothing for my sake," she again murmured.

"But," he added, "even if the ringing music of silver and of gold chime in this city home, *I* still am doomed to toil all day. I cannot walk with you abroad, for every moment's light is precious wealth to the poor artist; the sun—his taskmaster—is too fitful in these climes to brook delay; and you will miss the service and devoir, which are of right your own; and, oh! you know not how hard it is to climb the prickly hills that lead by toilsome and extended paths—by pitfall and morass—to fortune. I often think my very nature changed. As he has truly said, I am dark and fitful."

"You are a slanderer, Sidney," she exclaimed timidly; but slightly veiling the deep, earnest, struggling love, which taught her eloquence and banished fear—"I am not a child to take fright at shadows that companion loneliness, yet fade, like our hill vapours, in the sun. I know your spirit hopeful, but easily depressed; and I mind the time when you said (the words are yours), that Eva's voice and Eva's look, could"—the woman triumphed over the heroine, and, unable to repress her tears, she sought to hide them within the cottage.

Cormac, affecting a spirit that was not in him, cast his light cloak over his shoulder, and, addressing Sidney, spoke,—as though he felt not: "In love and war they say all things are fair;" he could no more in that strain, and his voice changed; "I could not have believed that such fidelity dwelt in the heart of woman; this truth puts all the schools' philosophy to flight—had I won her, I would have borne her beauty in triumph through the world!—you, if steeped to the very lips in poverty, will know a happiness that I shall never taste. She is too high above the earth and earthly things for me; fare ye well, cousin—cousins are crosses in most families, and mine is no exception. I would have wronged you if I could; but you'll forgive me cousin—you'll forgive me."

He walked bravely across the lawn, and passed the bower of the Whitestone Well; then turned, and seeing that Sidney had entered the Dovecote, sought beneath the shadow of the weeping ash a rose which had fallen from Eva's hand, and, placing it in his bosom, separated the branches that shielded the seat from the east wind, and fled across the meadows, as if he thought that speed might relieve his heated and throbbing brain.

KILLARNEY LAKE.

"ANDY, good luck to ye, Randy," was the salutation of one of the Killarney strawberry girls to the woodcutter, as from the Lake shore he watched the progress of a boat towards the fair island of Innisfallen.

"Good luck to ye, kindly, Mary," he replied. "Good luck to you and all the sun and moon shine on, by day or night."

"Thank ye, Randy; will you have a noggin of sweet milk? or a leaf of strawberries? you're kindly welcome to any or all. It's heart-broken you look; sure you never would hear tell of any one thinking of the Rose of Kerry but Master Sidney; and now he's come for her, and she's going, you're not satisfied."

"Because she's going," sighed Randy; "that's just it. No, Mary, thank you all the same, I'll have nothing. And sure it's giving you strawberries and milk I ought to be, and you having no one belonging to ye."

"'Deed, I have," replied the girl, cheerfully; "I have plenty to care for me, and, though I hav'n't a shoe to my foot, I've a light heart, and pleasant times:" she added, with a sigh—"in summer, anyway."

A A

"Winter and summer will be all alike to me when she's gone," continued Randy, in a subdued voice; "as long as she was on the sod I was content; though I could not hear the voice, I knew it was somewhere on Ireland's breeze; and though I did not see her smile, I knew it was brightening some Irish sunbeam. Do ye think that's a safe boat they're pleasuring in, Mary?"

"To be sure it's safe—Randy, man, what ails ye intirely? Listen! that's Spillane's bugle. Why, that last blast of music ought to rouse your heart; and there's Keeldar's answer to it! Miss Eva visits every spot before the time comes for her to leave them."

"Isn't there rough water round the island?" interrupted Randy.

"It's as smooth as glass, Randy; the rough water's in your own eyes," replied the girl.

"The boat's empty now; and yet I don't see them on the beautiful island. Oh, may the blessed sod that was trod by hundreds of holy men in the days of Ireland's glory, send an incense into their young hearts!"

"They say, Miss Eva might have married the young Lord of Ard-Flesk."

"Or any one she chose," answered Randy; his faith in Sidney only wavering when he thought of Eva's leaving the Dovecote; "any one she chose—I hope he'll always think of it—to her."

"Do you think them islands as handsome as the strangers do?" inquired the strawberry girl.

"You've no knowledge, Mary; you'd see more beauty in a little dirty bonnet-shop above in the town, than in that—Paradise," replied the woodcutter, angry at their beauty being questioned. And well did the

broken mountain, and dark deep wood, and fair expanse of water, spangled with islands, deserve the term. The ruined castle of Ross, the smooth lawns and stately trees of INNISFALLEN — rich alike in the beauties

of nature, and memories of ancient learning; the tiny islets, varied by every tint of verdure and of foliage; the bold sharp rocky promontories, each having its own legend — well did they all merit the woodcutter's enthusiasm; and when the wild clear notes of the magic bugle poured forth one of the melodies identified with the scene, Randy

for the moment forgot his misery ; many tears, not hard and bitter tears
wrung from his heart, but soft gentle dews of the tender feelings that
clung to his nature—as flowers garland a rugged rock—moistened and
refreshed his burning cheeks.

"I don't know what we shall do without her, at all," resumed the strawberry girl, casting tufts of grass into the Lake; "but what ails you, Randy ?
Sure it isn't fearful of squalls you are, such a day as this !   Tell us when
she'll be home again, that's what we want to know ; for they say the landlord won't have Dovecote, and that Kitty and you are to be care-takers."

"The heavens help those that have no wit !" quoth the woodcutter,
circling his brow with his hands.   "I wish I was wise !   I that could see
so much once, see nothing now—nothing, only that boat—a strip of wood
upon the waters !   She told me when she was going, girl ; but I shut my
ears, not to hear it.   If I wasn't a fool, I should go mad intirely ; but
they say fools never do, and I'm a fool—a helpless fool !   The bells in
the old gable rang all night—the hare bell, the silver bells of cuckoo-
sorrel, and of the Indian Moss—I knew them all—the deep boom of the
blue bell, and the soft note of my lady's rocket—I heard them ringing
from moon-rise to moon-set, and yet I could not tell one word they said
—I only know the marriage bell will ring to-morrow ; and then she will
go, and I shall never see her more !   My eyes are blinded, and the whole
world grows dark.   I am cast off and forgotten by Earth and Air.   Poor
Randy's thrown by ; poor Randy's forgotten."   He repeated, "Poor
Randy's forgotten," seve-
ral times, in deep sorrow,
when a low sweet voice
murmured—

"Randy deserves to be
forgotten when he loses
FAITH !"

The woodcutter turned to Mary, but she
was gone—gone without a word or a sign.   He
rambled a few steps in search of her ; and paused
in one of those quiet nooks, where stood the
solitary heron, heedless of his approach ; close at

his side was a white butterfly, sitting with folded wings on the petals of a pale wild rose.

"Why is it?" resumed the voice which endowed the insect for a time; "why is it that the sound of the bells of the old gable were no more to you than to other mortals; that you, so long favoured, heard nothing but the tinkling?—only because faith fainted in your bosom; even now your eyes are sealed, and, though you see the boat upon the lake you see not that which guides and guards it. Unhappy mortals! the purest spiritings are clogged in the mire of your unrefined natures. Have I not, from her entering on this scene of mingled smiles and tears, been with her, and averted what she could not avoid? Why should you doubt me now, and chill the air with tears?"

"It's asy talking with you, my lady," thought the woodcutter; "you who can be with her whenever you like; and though only allowed your own form, from sunset to sunrise, can whip up any shape that's plasing to you to sport round the world in, and the owner never the worse or the wiser of it. If *I* could do it, it's not *murning* I'd be."

"Randy," replied the voice, "do not attempt to deceive me; I see the thoughts that wrestle with, and supplant, each other in your feeble heart; because Eva cannot go hence with gay and gaudy trappings you think she cannot be happy—you forget that she herself is happiness! Ordinary mortals derive their happiness from external objects: Eva is endowed to give, and by giving, to receive; but you do not understand me."

"I'm trying, madam."

"People are not satisfied to let their fellow-creatures be happy after their own fashion; they want them to be happy after *theirs*. If the hawk said to the woodpigeon, you shall share my prey; I will divide with you the singing lark and the blue titmouse, and you shall fare better than ever you did before, the woodpigeon would say, 'No—that is not my habit; I cannot live on such cruel fare; give me the full-eared grain and the water of the pure spring.'"

"True, for you, my lady; everything according to its kind."

"Exactly so; and if our love is to be a benefit, and not a curse, we must forget what would make us happy, and study to comprehend what will make happy those we love. Everything according to its kind."

" And will she be very happy, my lady?" questioned Randy.

" She will, indeed! for the cankers and cares that disturb the minds and destroy the happiness of so many mortals will but show her forth the brighter; she will suffer much—but unhappy she will not be."

" If it's plasing to you, my lady," thought the woodcutter; " I wish you'd be so good as put every spark of suffering away from her intirely. I heard once of a rich gentleman who paid a poor man to fret for him. Now, if there must be suffering, can't your majesty put it upon me— not upon her? and I'll bear it—better than ever I bore a load of wood up the highest mountain in Kerry. Oh, avourneen, lady dear! do put it on me. I'll wait content and asy for the grandeur to come to her, and never turn my tongue to so much as ask for it, if I can be sure she'll be without the suffering. How can she be happy and suffer?"

" Do you not say, foolish mortal, that you could be happy, suffering for her sake?"

" Oh, joyfully!" he exclaimed, so loudly that the butterfly's wings vibrated, and she fixed her feet firmly upon the rose.

" And do you not think the love she bears to Sidney will make her joyfully endure suffering for his sake?"

" Oh, my lady! can't you settle it so?" persisted Randy, " that they'd have no suffering at all; they're young now—but life is short; and when it gets cut and crushed in the bud, there's never much good in the blossom."

" There's a care over both bud and blossom, Randy," said the voice; " and surely the Power that has guarded the past may be trusted for the future: the bud shall not be crushed; and I think, Randy, when you see the blossom (and you shall see it) your race here will be pretty well run, and you'd better come to my country; you would meet many there you have heard of long ago, and have pleasant times."

" I wonder," thought the woodcutter, slowly, " is Oliver Crummel among them; for if he was in it I'd rather stay where I am."

A little laugh rung in his ears; but before there was a reply to his question his heart beat with sudden delight at the promise that he should see the ' blossom!' his faith returned; he felt his heart expand within his bosom as the blessed influence infused its essence into his nature; his interest in Eva continued undiminished, but his *anxiety* was gone; the petals of the rose fell in a perfumed shower on the grass, while a dove of snowy plumage, whose glancing wings shone like silver in the sun, flew so close to his cheek that its feathers almost touched him; he knew the butterfly had changed its seeming, and watched the dove as it crossed the lake, until it was no larger than the smallest swallow that skimmed the waters; he saw that it hovered around the boat, which soon diminished to a white speck, as it passed into the wilder scenery

of the UPPER LAKE, among the mountains, spanned by a beautiful and auspicious rainbow. Insensibly the woodcutter sank into a deep slumber upon the bank. He was awakened by Keeldar licking his face; and when he fairly opened his eyes, he saw those he dearly loved looking upon him; for a moment he fancied they were returned in what he would have called 'great glory,' to their own land; but a second glance told him the reality, and that he should see them no more, for a while, after 'to-morrow'—to-morrow, the goal and the grave of so much hope.

The woodcutter had, however, many resources within his mind; and

as he thought over the good Fairy's words—"everything according to
its kind," he told one of his fables to himself, in his own rambling way :—
" Fine feathers make fine birds," he said ; " and yet when the feathers
drop off, the body's the bird after all! there's a dale of sorrow and
misfortune born of deceit ; and before I had the mistress, and Miss Eva,
and Master Sidney, to look to me, and the clothes would get into rags,
until one by one they'd stray away to seek their own fortunes, I used
to comfort myself by saying that if they were all gone, Randy himself
was to the fore ; and another thing, I often think the unevenness of 'the

Rocks,' is nothing to the unevenness of people's minds.   There was Lady
Elizabeth ! she had bare-footed images in white marble in her hall, and
yet she couldn't abide the sight of a naked foot ; though sorra a shoe she'd
give to cover it ; quare things come into my head, and that's why some
say I'm not wise, because I speak my own thoughts, and not other people's.
I've had grate lessons in my time, though I can't read a word out of a
printed book !   But I know the value of learning ; and 'tis that makes
me be SENDING THE YOUNG THINGS TO THE SCHOOL, when I meet them

by the road-side loitering among the blackberries. I was resting one morning close by where the wall of the ould gable creeps down and crumbles away under the long grass that towers about the ancient stones that, in their pride, had often said to the world, 'Behold my strength!' and the wall-flower sent about its sweet breath on every breeze, and the violets, with half-closed eyes, were nodding in the heat; and the stalks of the wild blue bells were bending over the sly cowslips and matted cuckoo-sorrel; and the great dragon flies (the tyrants of the earth they are! devouring every little helpless thing they can lay hould of!—beautiful devils painted up, they are), they were shaking their tails, and closing their wings, and rattling their teeth—then darting off like swallows, a thousand colours glancing on their long lean bodies; it was altogether a lazy time of day—the water was too lazy to ripple—the cattle too lazy to eat—the birds too lazy to sing; and yet the hum was with the heat of summer—a hum of silence, over earth, air, and water. And as I lay, two young hive bees lit on a tuft of thyme; one set to work rifling the flowers, bagging the honey, and stowing away the wax. 'Stop,' says the bee that had been dusting its wings; 'stop,' it says to its comrade; 'did you ever see anything so beautiful as that wasp? Look at the broad gold bands round his body, and the bright armour on his head; how I should like to have been a wasp, instead of a plain brown hard-working hive bee!' 'You are a fool,' says the other; 'the gardeners never object to our going among the peach-trees; they sow whole beds of mignionette for us, and the fairest rose in Ireland will yield honey to the brown bee. Many a time has Miss Eva watched us, and in the hard winters mixed up for us plates of moist sugar; the bean blossoms welcome us as old friends, and Queen Lily gives us the brightest colour for our wax; but every snare is placed for the destruction of the handsome wasp—man, woman, and child, hunt it to its death, its beauty only serving to point out its vices. We do not injure a blossom; but the idle and useless wasp devours and destroys; and its character is so detested that it is pursued and slain without mercy.' 'But it is so handsome, with its broad gold bands, and its armed head,' persisted the foolish bee. 'Handsome is that handsome does,' replied the wiser bee, as it boomed away; and presently I saw the foolish bee gathering the lily flower dust, and instead of stowing it away about its legs, it striped it in bands round its body, singing all the time how it was making itself as gay-looking as a wasp ; and if the creature had taken half the pains to gather honey, it would have carried home a rare store ; but it nothing heeded but to paint itself in a way that nature never intended ; and how it marched up and down the pointed leaf of a sweet lily, and flew to the Whitestone Well, balancing its body over the water in foolish admiration of the falsehood it was putting on the world, and the insult it was offering to the great Nature that made it!   Well, after a little, it boomed here, and it boomed there, whizzing and fuzzing, until at last it lit upon a fruit-tree, thinking to rest itself. 'Ah, ah!' said the gardener, 'there is a wasp—I must kill it!' 'Father,' answered the gardener's son ; 'Father, it has the head of a bee.' 'No, child; it is a wasp,' persisted the gardener ; 'look at the yellow bars about its body. If it was a bee it should suffer no harm. It is a wasp, and must die.' And the vain bee was crushed in a moment."

"Ay, ay," he repeated; "everything according to its kind!"

Eva leaned fondly on Sidney's arm ; her new-made friends had met her on her landing, resolved to be her bridemaids, and render their last homage, for a time, to her worth and beauty. "It is only for a time we shall lose her," they said to each other; young, guileless girls, knowing nothing of the world and its trials, and believing all the anxieties their parents expressed for Eva's future prospects were little more than tales to fright away love, could not look upon them both without admiration and affection—both so glorious in their beauty ; so high-souled, so richly endowed with the exact talents that best befit the man and woman. They had adorned THE DOVECOTE during her absence, so that it seemed an entire bower, clustered and crowned with flowers ; and had placed their varied gifts within her room, which glittered like the enchanted chambers of old romance. They wished to surprise her on her return from her farewell visit to the lakes, and playfully insisted she should be led blindfold into the Dovecote. Keeldar did not like his mistress to be thus treated, and showed his teeth more than once to the sportive bridemaids ; while Randy carefully laid a crossed stick on the threshold, which Eva stept over without disturbing—a sure sign, thought Randy, she will overcome the crosses of the world.

Eva had enough of the superstition of her country to beautify, but not encrust, her nature; and she knew it would give pain to those who loved her if she knelt beside her mother's grave after sunrise on the morning of her bridal; she arose, therefore, while the mists lingered on the

mountains, just as the grey dawn was stealing into the valleys, and passed beneath the arched entrance to the abbey, resolved to regain her chamber before her bridemaids awoke. Early as it was there were pilgrims there who had preceded her; but with natural delicacy they quitted its precincts at her approach, and left her to the solitude of the time-honoured ruin. She knelt beside her mother's grave, on the spot consecrated by much loving service. Her hands were clasped in prayer. "Oh, my mother!" she exclaimed; "look down and bless your child, with the full earnest blessing which you and you only, of all who have lived on earth, know how to bestow. Oh, mother mine! mine in heaven as well as upon earth, counsel me for good—so that I may not be unworthy to meet your pure spirit in heaven!—Oh, that I could have but a sign, a token that you hear me; that you are near me—happy I know you are—Oh, that you had but lived to bless me on this morning!" She bent her head until her long hair falling upon the violets whereon she knelt, was gemmed with dew; there was something ineffably sweet and harmonious in the scene, the deep grey shadows of THE ABBEY, the funeral pyramids of ivy, the

hardly-heard moaning of the old trees, felt rather than heard—the balmy air—the solemn silence, as yet unbroken by the song of the earliest bird; the hares, as they returned to their forms in the undisturbed pastures, hardly paused to listen to Eva's murmured words, falling as gently as her tears, while she repeated, "Oh, mother!—my mother!—be with me on my entrance into this new existence; teach me, counsel me, that I may be to him I have chosen, all that you were to my father; my mother! could you but hear me, you would give me a sign; I ask it not from the cold grave, the chill, dark cell that holds the shrine from which the spirit has departed; I ask it not from you, green-coated mound! but from on high—where the emancipated live in infinite variety of holiest love, and purest joy, and in the everlasting brightness which dazzles not their eyes—mother,—oh, mother! is there no sign?"

Like all high-hearted creatures, Eva never questioned in her most secret mind, the lightness, or abiding, of her lover's faith; if he could have been harsh or false, she would have thought she had given him cause; her only fear was of her own unworthiness—nothing but that! She had made ready all of value in money she possessed, and which, in her want of knowledge, she considered a large store—more than two hundred pounds—and her mother's jewels, the rather valuable for that they had been hers; these she had placed in a small casket, as a gift to Sidney, all she supposed she had to bestow. She had not told him of this store, but left it ready to place within his hands, an hour before they commenced their journey; she thought how astonished he would be at its

magnitude, and had it been thousands it would have been all the same; her hand was as generous as her heart was pure; she remembered how her mother had given all she had to her father, and that they had but one heart and mind between them; and as she knelt by that green grave, she recalled all that mother's love and tenderness, and her tears flowed, as she repeated, "Mother—oh, mother! must the sun arise without a sign from thee?"

She was not long alone—stimulated by the same spirit, Sidney sought

the same grave, and seeing his beloved there, he sank on his knees beside
her, and replied, " Oh, let me give the sign—the sign from her to thee;
would that she were here to listen and hear my vow recorded in this holy
temple, framed by human hands in the pious ages long gone past, and
now canopied only by the everlasting heavens; would that she blessed
us as we kneel together, while I pray that I may be forgotten and a cast-
away, when I forget thee, my best, my beautiful! whose generous heart
clung to my uncertain fortunes; and who, trusting all to my love and
faithfulness, goes forth with me to battle with the unknown world. My
own Eva!—I could have yielded you to Cormac in that hour when he
pictured my lone state; but now I see no danger, fear no trial; strong in
your love, I am strengthened; this fragile form is my shield against the
troubles and trials of the world!—I could not yield you now, Eva!" he
continued, as he pressed her to his heart; " with this amulet upon my
bosom, what can I feel of harm? Here, beneath the canopy of heaven,
upon a sacred grave I kneel! FATHER ALMIGHTY, teach Thou me to
evidence my gratitude to Thee and to her! by righteous dealing, and true
faith towards all mankind; by using the great gift, which, if it ripen, will
stamp an immortality upon the name we both shall bear; grant, that my
Art which, next to THEE, and HER, I honour, may be used for purposes
both high and holy; that nothing poor, or mean, or sordid defile the
pencil Thou hast taught me to guide; that it may show forth great acts
and noble deeds to emulate the young, and revive men aged in honour;
may we walk in Thy ways and shine in Thy light!" Eva, kneeling
meekly beside him, uttered some broken sentences of prayer as fervent
as ever passed from human lips; but still she entreated her mother's
spirit for a 'sign,' repeating, "Oh, mother! must the sun arise without
a sign from thee?"

"The sun will arise in a moment, dearest," said Sidney, "and its
beams must not find us kneeling beside a grave – you know the old saying
about the ' fears' that come from ' bride-tears,' and would not, I know,
grieve those who love, and yet must soon be parted from, you; the
dew is still heavy on your path; arise, my own Eva, and return!" She
arose from the grave, and as she passed from beneath the arch into the
meadow, the first beam of the sun came over her brow, like a heaven-sent

messenger, and then the god of day stood on the mountain-tops, flooding
the land with glory. They paused to look upon a scene so beautiful,
and the painter's heart palpitated, and his cheek flushed at its tranquil
magnificence.

"See, my beloved!" he exclaimed, "the wondrous beauty with which
the Creator enshrines the earth—the matins of light that paint its rejoicing
on the universe! is not this a sign? Oh! to catch those effects and stamp
them upon canvas—to show the heavy-lidded world what they lose by the
indolent sleep of morning. One dissolving view succeeds another and
surpasses the last! look at that creeping cloud, whose pale rose-tint
mingles with the deep-hued arbutus, while yonder saffron-coloured vapour,
pierced by the grey pinnacle of the mountain, passes into air even while
I am speaking."

"And now the birds begin," said Eva, "answering each other from
the trees and boughs wherein they shelter; but the insects are tardy risers
—they do not love the dew."

"How, dearest, could you ask for a particular sign," continued Sidney,
gazing around him, "when the broad world gives ready tokens of love,
and mercy, and angel-winged hope, to its inhabitants? What is its change
of seasons, but a renewing of the beauty our parents ever have in
paradise? We are too little with the actual and creative beauties of the

world, my own Eva; we do not look enough upon nature, either human
or divine; we keep too much within the darkness of our cells—unlike the
bees, who, though they work and store at home, go forth into the natural
world, among its hills, and heaths, and sunlight, to procure their honey—
singing while they are learning what is best and wisest! Are these strange
bridal thoughts?" he added, looking doatingly upon her.

"No," she replied; "I love to hear you, Sidney, for your soul is
neither limited nor confined, but fresh, and full of the pure freedom, which
is one of man's best birthrights; it will joy me so much hereafter to know
that all the homage you receive will not clog your high thoughts, nor
damp your love of nature, nor your veneration for its holy cause."

"The homage I receive!" he repeated, fondly pressing her hand to
his heart; "nothing can I tell you, dearest, of the battle we must fight;
nothing of coldness, or wrong, or unrequited labour, or jealousy, or strife;
nothing seems to stand between you and the vision you have created of
the—homage I receive!"

"Which proves my faith as true as the reality," she answered. "Oh
Sidney! in what should we have faith, next to our creed, if not in a spirit,
like yours, that can WILL—in genius, like yours, that inspires———"

"And in love and trust like yours!" he added; "the torch of the
modern Hymen is lit amid the bakes and broils, the savoury stews and
fumes of the kitchen fire! ours has been kindled in Arcadia!"

Eva laughed. "He does not dream," she thought—"he does not
dream of my golden store—of the surprise of my rich casket;" so little
was her earnest bright nature accustomed to concealment, that she had
watched her words, so that she might not betray her secret; it had at one
time appeared to her a mine of wealth; but even the little she had learned
of the world at the vicar's, combined with the memory of her mother's
estimate of household expenses, pruned the wings of her imagination; still,
she was not quite portionless, and the casket—the richly carved and inlaid
casket—the jewel box of some ancestor—Sidney, she was certain, would
put it in a picture some day, it was so beautiful! Thought of the
surprise she intended for her bridegroom, restored her mind to its
elasticity; and when Sidney bade her adieu for a brief space at the
garden-gate, she entered the Dovecote without one feeling of fear for

the future; her whole being was trust and love; she wondered why her bridemaids had risen so early, and arranged her simple tiring with so much taste, and placed the pearl chain ready—which surely she had never told them she should wear, although she had resolved to do so only the night before. And whence came the perfumes that enriched her chamber; and whence the flowers! Such flowers as never grew within the compass of her garden; and what multitudes of bees were booming about her window, fuzzing in and out, some lighting on her very lips, as if to gather honey, and then away again; she feared them not, for from her childhood the bees had been her friends, and seldom suffered wasp or hornet to

remain near the Dovecote. Surely, never was bridal chamber so magically decked, and a bouquet of real fragrant orange blossoms seemed powdered with diamonds; she sat like the lady in the enchanted chair; her casket— Sidney's casket—was covered with flowers, and the bees kept such a buzzing about it, that Eva fancied they danced and shook their wings to some wild minstrelsy. No fear of the future clouded her happiness; hope shone forth in her eyes; and still the fervent womanly prayer, 'to make her worthy of his love,' if it did not find words, arose again and again from her heart to the high throne of Heaven.

When her bridemaids entered to deck her for the altar, they were so full of words—of joy—of sorrow; so full of the contradictions of

affection—so devoted to the tiring and adorning of the fair bride, and
yet so loth to part from her, that she neglected to solve the mystery of
the pearl chain, and passed to the little stone-roofed church amid the
blessings of the people—without even thinking of her perplexity.

Before the ceremony began, she had turned to look for Randy
amid the crowd; and when exchanging her snowy robes for a plain
travelling dress, she inquired of the weeping Kitty if she had seen him.

"Just one sight I got of him, miss—oh, then it's ma'am I mane—at
the brake of day, and he not a morsel like himself—only clane, and shaved,
and dacent, looking out of the tower windy, and a bran new shillela in
his hand, stiff and tidy, as if he was going a journey. 'Come down,
you unnatural wild baste,' I says to him, quite mannerly; 'come down
and wish her joy;' and he made no answer, only pointing with his stick
over the mountains towards the sea.   I shouldn't wonder, darlin', if THEY
gave him the shape of a gull, or a heron, or a phillipaweeken, or something of that sort, and sent him over the wide ocean with you ; not that

I'm shooperstitious, as you well know, dear—only they're quare things, so they are, and ever and always had a hand in you, darlin'—some pulling one way, some another, as is the way through life with the whole of us, from first to last, as that poor natural, Randy, says; says he—but sure I am, he'll tell you himself, only the crayture is so foolish and tender, he could not bear the way the people were crying for the joy, and his heart bating for the sorrow. He should have waited till you were going,

darling, and then he'd have heard the 'keen' that will rise over the hills; why the very paths you've walked on in the fields, they call after you; and wasn't your meadow of hay always cut unknownst, by the neighbours, and the little field of potatoes planted and dug without your knowledge, all out of gratitude, avourneen deelish! You will never forget *that* to the poor Irish, will you? And sure your cow gave as much milk as an Alderney, and she only a Kerry! Oh, then, maybe you'd cast a thought to the poor cow, also, when you're away, and how everything about you, dear, was doubled by a blessing, fresh and fasting; but oh, to think of you laving us now—and Master Sidney! Oh, the dear life! what will the country do, at all at all, without you, let alone your poor Kitty; but don't look sorrowful, dear jewel of my heart! Darling! here I kneel on my bended knees, and if I fail in a promise to you, may I suffer here and hereafter. I am your own, to do your bidding, and keep your place till you come to it again; I'll not ask you *when*, jewel, for I know *your* heart's in it, as well as my own; and yet that's not so! for it's my heart that's with you, and its shadow that will wander here like a ghost when you're away; and, sure, if earnest prayers find their way up to the coorts above, mine and those of the people will be in the heavens this blessed day, gaining strength long before you, for your honour and glory—standing between you and harm, now and for evermore." The faithful creature prostrated herself in continued and earnest prayer; and the crowd without, actuated by the same feeling, waiting to catch a last sight of her they had loved since her birth, knelt as by one common impulse, to invoke blessings upon her as she passed—now totally unable to control her tears—to the carriage that waited to convey Sidney and his bride to the place of embarkation.

"Oh, lanna machree! won't you take this blessed cross, that my mother prayed to all her life?" said one; while another exclaimed, "Here's a root of the hare's-foot fern, and the house has never burned that gave it shelter;" another, "Here's a raal four-leaved shamrock, lady dear;

my brother was on the seas with it all his life, and never got hurt or harm : it's the raal thing, jewel, and you'll never be sunk in the waters, if you wear it on your heart." Those who had nothing else to give flung heather and flowers at her feet, exclaiming, " From the wild Gap of Dunloe "—

" From the top of the Toomies "—" The sweet strawberries from Glenn,
lady "—" The real arbutus, lady, that grows nowhere out of Killarney"—
" This handkerchief, dear, was steeped in May-dew, maybe you'd keep it
for Mary Maley's sake "—" along with a sprig of the real witch elm,"
said another. Keeldar never had been so caressed ; the children hung
about his neck ; and seeing how completely Eva was overcome, Sidney
entreated the people to spare her further leave-taking.

" The sun has not shone since she has been a bride, nor the rain
rained," suggested a woman.

" But it won't be so ! " said another.

" The shower is hanging in the clouds, and when that is over, see
if we don't have the sun," quoth the beggarman, as he waved his tattered

hat to the carriage, and turned to his more serious companions ; while
one more serious than the rest looked upwards, and murmured something
about a storm gathering in the sky, adding, that the ' Fairy man ' had
seen the good people " last night, hiding themselves behind rose-leaves, a
sure sign that the fierce wind was coming."

"The blessing and the prayer are both with her, now and for ever-more," murmured the people.

"With them both," said poor Kitty, wringing her hands.

"To be sure; and that's quare; this morning they were two—a few holy words, and they are one—for time and for eternity," he added, lifting his hat—"to live together, to rise together, at the last day, no matter where they're buried, they'll rise together at the last!"

Kitty continued to talk disjointedly, for her sobs prevented her finishing a sentence; and long after the crowd had dispersed, and she was alone, she fancied she heard the chiming of bells and whispers among the trees, and voices repeating,—"The Dovecote will be blooming then;"—while others murmured, "When?" Kitty would have closed out the sounds by drawing the curtain of the lonely room; but she saw there was a '*braugh*' about the moon; and again the chimes struck up in the old gable, and the weathercock creaked and moaned in the changing wind.

Drawn by C. Stanfield, R.A.Engraved by W. T. Green.

THE WRECK OF THE SWIFT.

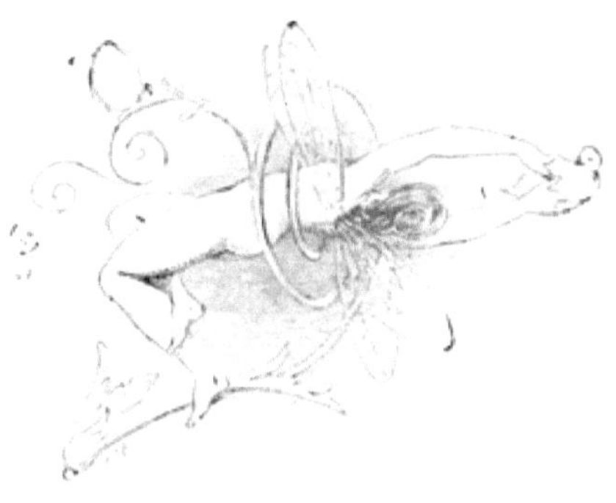

PART THE NINTH.

OW lovely was the morning—the early morning! the vessels that found shelter and repose in one of the loveliest of the many rivers—the river Lee—that, content with the mere manifestation of beauty, wander through the most fertile and most inactive island of the world—gave no signs of being freighted with life, or endowed with the power of motion. The ships at the quays were scarcely moved by the barely perceptible heaving of the waters; while others nearer ocean, rose and fell gently under its influence: the villas, that lined the banks, or crowned the heights, peeping from amid thick foliage, sent forth no curling smoke; the cattle were half slumbering in the pastures: no flies danced on the surface of the pools; no rising lark sung out to the corn-fields or the waving grass.

There was a total absence of movement, where, in an hour or two, there would be so much. The vapours seemed to linger over the lonely scene as if with feelings of affection for the objects they had enwreathed at night—imparting even a fantastic character to the shipping, twining round the rigging and capping the masts, rising and descending, until, like the memory of a dream, they vanished altogether, leaving clear vistas, with "the blue above and the blue below," while beyond, in the dim distance, were mingled tall vessels and green lawns, the shores at one point seeming to touch each other, at another melting away into the softest haze.   In the opposite direction, far from ships and their traffic, the lovely Lee wandered "at its own sweet will" through green meadows of the richest grass; passing beside rugged ruins, with their records of past feuds and legends of departed grandeur—ancient

abbeys converted into broken tombs—rising upon the placid and flowery banks, a cottage or two clinging to the base, like barnacles on some mighty rock; then away again, a clear, strong, fertilizing river, singing to the heavens or murmuring to the earth—seldom spanned by a bridge, never disturbed by a water-wheel—and at that early hour, when all things are undefined, reflecting nothing but the soft grey tone of the morning atmosphere, or repeating the outline of an ivy-cumbered tower, or over-hanging tree. Within about three miles of Cork, in the silent time, 'when night and morning meet' upon the hills, and as one descends into the valleys, the other separates from the advancing light, and leaves the world to the activity that succeeds repose,—at that placid hour, a man, fatigued by much walking, stood for some time gazing into the water, and then seated himself on a projecting bank of the Lee, and, after resting, plunged his swollen feet into the refreshing stream. He looked as if he had been led astray by one of those seductive and perilous night-fires that so often precede destruction ; he seemed bewildered, and had evidently 'missed his road,' for he peered from right to left, and from left to right, in a state of uncertainty as to the course he was to adopt: he was certainly a stranger to the paths among which he

had been wandering—a stranger with no guide to consult. A few of the late sitting-up stars lingered in the heavens—just here and there—dimly sparkling, as though wearied with their night-watch, and yet unwilling to relinquish it: the traveller directed his gaze to them, and looked round and round the firmament, seeking those whom he could recognise as old acquaintances—friends—patrons of his wanderings; he thought, as all who think about them must think, that the heavens are more companionable by night than by day; we feel the heat, and see the glory of the sun, yet we calculate his services rather than take him to our love; it may be that his magnitude and power place too large a barrier between him and us; and that his fiery heat inspires occasional dread; or, again, it may be, that he is too great a benefactor to enter our hearts on the footing of a friend; but the stars are dear to us from childhood;

" ———— in the deep blue sky they keep,"

they are familiars; we have known them from the earliest dawn of life: we look at them from our infant beds, at home as well as in a far-off

land; it is BENEATH THEIR LIGHT WE HEAR THE FIRST TALE OF LOVE; what
lover has not evoked the stars! what sailor has not hailed them as men
hail their brethren! bright tell-tales of home, sparkling to eyes that note
their rising, so that two, far apart, may gaze upon them at the same
instant; what watcher by the sick one's couch has not felt relieved when
looking at the galaxy of heaven? what poet not speculated as to which
of the 'starry orbs' might be his home hereafter? what traveller not

tarried for their coming out? when the crackling frost tells of the approach of the lightest footstep, we hope for their advent; and in the
long sultry evenings of summer we pant for their issuing forth—heralds
of a cooler atmosphere; we count them in the deep waters of the
lake, or the ripples of the multiplying river; or in speculative mood
vaguely seek to calculate their numbers—bright unknown worlds! aged
—yet never dim!

The worn-out wayfarer looked for them, as, chased by the morning, they were gradually disappearing from his gaze.

"They are all going to their homes!" he exclaimed, in his simplicity, "and she that was my home will be on the seas before the next sun goes down." And wildly he talked, while the generous Lee rippled soothingly over his feet, until at last his bushy head sank upon his chest, and he half slumbered—starting at intervals; for though his rest was brief, it was troubled by 'thick-coming fancies,' and he could hardly be said to sleep—speaking, as he did, his visions—"I tell you," he murmured, as if addressing some one in the air, "they are passing under the waters this very minute: don't I know their dark forms and faces, rushing on, rushing here—and there? yes, and I hear their voices; they are passing to the sea; they will rouse its waves—yet you thought them banished—oh, my grief!—they *were* banished from the lake to the rivers! Sure, I see one of the worst of them floating this

very minute out to sea—evil be to him that evil brings! Oh! can't you keep her with us," he continued, clasping his hands in wild entreaty; then after musing a few moments, he added, "shine the brighter! Oh, isn't she the brightness of the country? what need of more than that! they are rushing on still, some to get before, others behind, the ship; but they can't get ABOVE it, you say; yes—I know that; you are great in your own land; but when I look at ye, how can I think you'd ride over a sea tempest! I'm struck with blindness!" he exclaimed, suddenly and loudly,

starting up from the bank ; " I'm blind !" and the echoes caught up the
sound—there was a long pause, during which he groped idly about in the
darkness—" I'm blind and lone, is there no one to hear me !" he continued,
frantically ; " Is it day or night?—am I Randy, the woodcutter, or am I
another? hush ! I hear the noise of streams and laughing sounds, such
as I once heard through the rushing of the Tore waterfall.   Oh, had
I too small FAITH again ! and is this my bitter punishment? is the little
light I had, taken, because I had not the great light ? why not give me
more, if I had not enough !—is that justice ?   But well I know I was to
blame ; that there was no right faith in me ! but there was ! at times there
was, only it comes and goes, like everything good ! Who is never hasty ?
who never infirm ? whose heart, mighty power ! goes always in the right
without stumbling ?   Oh, and sure if the good was always with us, we'd
need no other guide ; am I blind—or is it the wakeness that's over me,
or some sudden darkness come on the world ?   I'll strive to gather my
thoughts and humble myself, and take a turn at the prayers, if I can ; and
after all maybe I'm only in a dream.   Many's the strong trials I've had
in dreams !" and so he muttered, and groped about, his half-audible words

expressing contrition at his constantly failing FAITH, which, as he said truly,
was the one thing above all others that ought to gain strength as he grew
older.   Why should he have dared to suppose that SHE who had cared for
Eva since her birth would not ride safely over any storm by sea or land ?
And AT LAST HE SANK DOWN, APPARENTLY ASLEEP; if, indeed, it had not

all been a dream; and after a time he fancied something—it might be the light of morning—passed over his eyes, and sitting up, he saw the blue and green dragon-fly darting hither and thither in the morning light, and heard the buzzing of bees, and the distant croaking of the ill-omened frog, and the lowing of kine, mingled with the bleating of lambs, and the

trumpet-like neigh of the free-limbed horse, as he joyed in the invigorating air, and with flowing mane and distended nostril bounded round and round the enclosure, which he could have cleared without an effort; then arched his neck, and stood a model of strength and beauty, gazing with gentle, yet fearless eye, upon the landscape—every fence of which he had taken when a-field with his companions. Yet, early as it was—for no human foot-print had marked the sappy dew that clustered the luscious clover into a matted carpet—early as it was, an aged woman stood beside the woodcutter, and questioned him as to where he was going.

With pleasure as intense as had been his agony, Randy looked upon her withered features; even in his boyhood days, when, like all of his country, he evinced the most extraordinary aptitude to 'fall in love' with every pretty face—never, even in those days, had he felt greater delight in the fresh beauty of seventeen, than in the clearness of vision which enabled him to count the wrinkles in the crone's face!

"I'm not blind!" he exclaimed, exultingly.

"Many a one's *dark*, good man, that has the sight of his eyes; but what ails ye to be here, like an eel in the grass?"

"Tell me this?" quoth Randy, looking at her; "why is a sarpint treated with all manner of respect, when an eel, his own blood relation, is considered only fit to be skinned?"

"Because," replied the woman, "the one has power and the other none; power to defend itself—power to punish an aggressor."

"I see now you have understanding," said the woodcutter, "and so, maybe you'll tell me the road to Cork."

"I'll guide ye that far, and welcome," she answered.

Randy looked perplexed. "I'd not like to be troubling an ancient lady like yourself."

"You're fearful I can't walk as fast as you, maybe; but if I can't, why, leave me behind, that's all." The little old woman trudged on towards THE CITY DIMLY VISIBLE IN THE DISTANCE; and, though the wood-cutter plied his stick as a help to his speed, yet she, without any assistance, kept before him, leading him, not by the high road, but over hedges and through bog and morass, stopping at nothing—not even a park wall, which Randy scrambled at, but could not conquer.

"Where are ye?" she screamed from the other side.

"I'll go no farther in your track," he replied; "you're something not right! I'll go back to the high road."

"Then you won't reach Cork in time," she answered, "and the ship will have sailed, for the wind is changing and the tide is fair; but take hold of this—

"'Shred of flax that ne'er was spun.'

There, now—you're over; but walking is weary work," she continued.

"It's not much trouble to you," muttered the panting woodcutter.

"Oh, yes, it is a great deal of trouble.   When I travel, I generally manage differently."

"You can't go faster, I'll go bail," hinted Randy.

"But my horses can, and my *will* can."

"Oh, never a doubt have I of the will, ma'am, whatever I might have of the horses.   By all accounts a woman's will would beat the Kerry coach with four."

"The Kerry coach," she repeated, contemptuously; "why, look at it there, crawling like a snail on a sunny wall! while we—keep the line of flax in your hand, and see how we go!"

Then Randy knew how it was, but thought it more prudent to ask no more questions; he had even an idea of making an apology, touching his want of faith ; but he could not.

"The mind is a wonderful thing, Randy, and when you see HER—as you will very soon, for there are the steeples—Saint Barry's—and Peter's —and Shandon, that one of our own poets tells you

> "' —shines so grand on
> The river Lee!'

and now you can hear the hum of far-off voices, and the turmoil and din of a city—which I hate."

"I believe it's a wicked place, sure enough," suggested Randy. "The Lord be praised, it's little I know of it."

"Wicked, only because wherever there are many, there must be much bad, as well as much good," she answered ; "but the one draws out the other, and though they work one against the other, still it steadies the balance—it steadies the balance," she repeated.   "The world is not so bad a world, after all, if one knew how to use it— and to be useful in it ; those who serve it the least complain of it the most."

"There's a terrible deal of poverty in it," said Randy, shuddering ; for the interiors of the suburban huts they passed, however rapidly, were now exposed to view, and there, squalor and misery, starvation and disease, contended and struggled with one wretched human frame after another, prostrating the strong and crushing the weak ; and that within ear-shot of traffic and its wealth, and while car and carriage rolled on in comfort and luxury. "It's happier on Glena—brighter among the Toomies—oh, if the breath of this pestilence should reach HER!" thought the woodcutter; and the little old woman turned back and scowled on

him. Randy jostled against one person and ran against another, yet nobody seemed to notice him. At last, he began to think he was invisible, and then remembered that he still held in his hand the

"Shred of flax that ne'er was spun;"

the identical shred of fairy flax with which he had been drawn over the wall. This, of course, he regarded as a great treasure, knowing that by its power he could see all things—yet not be seen. If his mind had not been so full of Eva, it would have delighted him to prove this power; but his guide hurried on so as to give him no moment to indulge even a fleeting propensity to see the wonders of the 'beautiful city,' as mortal

eyes had never seen them before : and he found himself on the quay, now
bustling with life, and opposite the ship in which Eva and Sidney were
about to sail, standing beside the fleet-footed old woman who, not in
the least wearied, was folded in her cloak, while he, from fatigue,
could hardly stand. Earnestly he gazed on the ship whose pennon floated
gaily on the wind, and earnestly also on another that was moving slowly
out to permit the one in which Eva was to embark to near the quay ; this
ship was newly painted, and prepared for a long voyage—*an emigrant
ship*—and a man close to Randy was extolling her fleetness and safety, to
a group of those who were about to seek in a far-off country the advantages denied them in their own ; for what can the emigrant find—or
rather seek—but the land !—waste, yet craving labour for cultivation—
which he leaves idle and useless by his own cabin door at home ! What,
indeed, is Ireland—and what are its people—but lands wanting hands,
and hands wanting lands ?

"Fleet and safe !" repeated the woodcutter, in a loud voice, as he
looked upon the vessel ; "why she is riddled by rats ; there is not a
sound timber in her ; she is patched and painted like an ould beauty to
hide decay ! Never set foot in her, if you value your lives. Oh, the
wickedness of risking life in such a thing as that ! "

No one could tell who spoke, for Randy still held the shred of flax, and
the iniquitous man who was deluding the poor people stood chafing and
trembling with rage and terror at the unknown voice that had proclaimed
the truth, while each asked another who had told it—who had spoken ?

The woodcutter felt relieved when he saw how sound the English
packet was, and how nobly she sat the waters, like a thing of life—steady
and willing to obey her helmsman ; he rejoiced at this, and only regretted
that she was so soon to set her sails for the other land. He stood gazing
at her, forgetful of all things else, until his eyes filled with tears ; he
neither heeded the rushing to and fro of the people who had nothing to do
but to impede those who had work to accomplish, nor the cries of the
sailors as they heaved in the luggage or tugged at the ropes ; nor the
quarrelling of the car-boys ; nor the importunity of the beggars ; neither
did he think of the presence or absence of his guide, nor remember, when
he brushed away his tears, the stem of fairy flax which he must have

dropped—for more than one began to ask him where he came from, and where he was going; and moreover, when he chanced to look again at the emigrant ship—in consequence of the great outcry that had been raised against her, the people threatening to destroy her if not permitted to examine her for themselves, he thought he must have been mistaken—she seemed so fair and strong; but the boaster of her merits had disappeared; conscience-stricken—knowing that, if they did examine her, the mysterious words would be found a true prophecy.

Presently the packet was ready, and there was a movement in the crowd, for a lady and gentleman were coming; and the beggars closed them in by their importunities, entreating alms, and passing jests on their own wretchedness; passengers and sailors had to fight their path through the mob, which at length opened, as if of its own accord, to make way—no one said for whom, except Randy, who muttered, "At last!" as Eva and Sidney passed along, followed by blessings—"A look and a smile, lady dear—it's all we'll ask, whoever you are, from you, just to keep our hearts warm till we see you again!" "Oh, it's worth a walk of twenty miles to see her face." "There's charity enough in her eyes to keep the poor from starving." "May they never taste sorrow, either of them." "May the holy saints make soft their bed in heaven, and grant them a long life and a happy death." "Well, the sight will leave my eyes after looking at the brightness of hers." "Lady, let the blind man hear your voice, and then its sweetness will tell him of the beauty he can never see." And eager as were all to gaze upon her, they held back, one the other, from involuntary respect. Keeldar, who, had he followed any one else, would have attracted much attention, slouched after his mistress, and was absolutely obliged to snarl the town curs out of the way. Suddenly, the face of Eva was illumined by joy—she saw her childhood's friend; she had anxiously watched for him, for she had felt dispirited at leaving her country without bidding him adieu.

In a moment he was almost at her feet. "I am here, lady dear; I am here, watching and waiting to see you off—where I'll be again, if I'm alive, to see you come back."

"Can he not go with us?" said she to her husband; "with Randy and Keeldar, we should hardly miss the Dovecote and the Lakes."

"If you wish it, dearest," was Sidney's answer.

"No, lady darling," exclaimed the unselfish creature. "I know what I am, and I know something of where you are going; and I love you too well, bright jewel of the world, to be a hindrance to you, or a burden on you; it isn't fond hearts that have no power you'll want—no, no; it wasn't for that I came here, but to tell you that I'll do everything that's plasing to you, and tend the flowers, and the *churchyard*, darling, and not let the rough nettle, or the dandelion, or broad-leaved dock, go near her bed—only violets and cowslips; and I'll feed the robins by her side; and I'll drive all the girls and boys to school, and live on the thoughts of you till you come back. And, Master Sidney, sir, I'll take many a turn round Ard-flesk. I dreamt many happy dreams there of you and yours; and, sure enough, the dreaming was the most of the happiness that was in it."

Both Eva and Sidney were greatly moved by this proof of poor Randy's affection. He looked so travel-worn and anxious; his manner was more than usually collected, and yet it had lost nothing of its intensity; his eyes wandered from Eva to the ship; he followed her on board; he thought he recognised his old guide, and peered so perseveringly under every blue hood, that more than one vender of fruit and eggs reproved him sharply for his impertinence. He asked every sailor if the wind was fair, and watched each movement of the ship with tremulous anxiety.

At last, those who were not outward bound hurried on shore; the various stowages that had crowded the deck were put away in dark holes; there were sundry warnings given to parents who would linger beside their children, and friends who were loth to part from those they loved; planks were rattled previous to their withdrawal. "They're putting me back, Master Sidney, sir!" said Randy, in a voice stifled by emotion, while every muscle of his face was agitated; "and one thing I wanted, dear, only I don't like to tell her, sir, because ladies don't understand; I've bound it round with three strips of a hazel wand, the bark, you know, peeled from left to right last Midsummer Eve under the moon's own beam, and steeped three nights in the water of Whitestone Well; I've no use for it, for every one gives me the bit and the sup, and I've my ould shelter at the back of the Dovecote; and, if I hadn't, no one but would let Randy the woodcutter under the shadow of his roof. And as to clothes, Master Sidney, sure you set me up for ever with the clothes. I've so much of them that it's a throuble to count them; so take it sir—my little gatherings ever since she was born, sir; odd bits of money—I hid them for her in a hole in the ould gable. I never thought them mine to use—sure I haven't the sense to know what to do with money. Oh, Master Sidney, it isn't the pride that makes you turn from poor Randy's offering! Sure, when I'd get a tester or a tenpenny, all the joy I'd have would be, like an ould magpie, letting it drop into the hole and hearing it chink—thinking that as she grew oulder she'd have the sense to use it. Och, machree! when the earth is dry, it drinks the drop of dew as eagerly as the shower! Look, if ye won't have it I'll fling it into the sea—I'll never carry it back to its ould place. Oh, if I have been true and faithful, lighten my heart, avourneen, and don't kill it with cowldness!"

Randy's plainness and earnestness wrung Sidney's heart; he took the extraordinary-looking receptacle of his wealth, determining to appropriate it for his benefit, for he knew the tenderness and generosity of the poor fellow's nature. The woodcutter little thought, that out of her small store, Eva had left a provision for him, in case of his illness or destitution, to the almonry of the parish priest.

And now the packet left the quay, amid the smiles and tears of those on shore and those on board, threading her way, amid the pathless windings of the glorious Lee, that by a royal lavishing of Nature's bounties, perplexes the stranger-ships that seek her harbour as to which of her many beauties is to be admired the most; while those whose sails are set for foreign ports, go forth with the knowledge that, steer where they may, they can see nothing in the world to surpass in loveliness the loveliness they leave behind. Randy still stood upon the deck, for the captain had said, " Let him go as far as Cove, young lady; the poor fellow looks like a follower of the family, and can as quickly find his way back from Cove as from Cork."

Randy could not speak his thanks, only again and again entreated Eva to tell him what he could do for her. Being near her, hearing her voice, and crouching in her shadow, had dispelled all the fancies that

had haunted his journey: he would have forgotten where he was but for
the motion of 'The Swift,' and when obliged to go on shore at Cove,
he appeared transfixed to the spot where he stood, tears flowing down
his rugged face, while Eva could not restrain hers.   Accustomed

to the world, and having visited many lands, Sidney felt not a little
triumph in the earnest and deep respect his beloved excited; the
charm was certainly working; the few words she spoke always told
of her loving and earnest nature; and drawn towards her as much by
the invisible and certain agency of her goodness as by her beauty, all,
even to the silent man at the helm, whose homage beamed in his eyes,
were ready to speed to do her service; Keehdar looked a proud dog by
her side, neither knowing, nor if he had known, caring at the prospect
of city life and close confinement. He was advancing in years, and
could better do without the forest glades than he could have done three

years before; he looked and moved a dog of rank, vouchsafing to notice nothing except his mistress, save, indeed, the glancing flight of a pigeon that hovered about the rigging; the sailors, too, pointed it out, and said it was the sign of a good passage; Keeldar watched it closely, and even rose up to look for it, when it vanished, and then re-appeared again; and once it descended, so that Eva saw the sweetness that beamed in its beautiful eyes, as it hovered over the sea.

The moments were angel-winged to those who had long loved each other, and they little noted the passing scene. How wonderfully

glorious was the setting sun when they were far at sea :— " Too beautiful," the captain said, as 'The Swift' bowed gracefully to the warm strong breeze that filled her full-bosomed sails : " too glowing," he repeated ; and slight scorn at his non-appreciation of such beauty curled the artist's

lip, as he watched the light feathery clouds, tinged with the deepest
rose colour, that scudded over the heavens, until the whole expanse was
flooded with vapour, which, as the hues faded, seemed to cling together
closely and more close. How Sidney joyed in the effects—the light and
shade — the gorgeous colouring—canopying the deep-toned waters —
sketching with a clear eye and truthful hand the outlines of the clouds,
rapidly changing as they were, comparing them to sights he had . seen
abroad, and pouring, with enthusiasm, into the ears of his fair bride
tales of the wonders that Nature shows her true worshippers. She
heard not the wind that followed fast, nor noted how the ship's speed
increased, nor how the captain stood as if the sea world was his home,
triumphing in the ease with which his vessel rose and glided into the
deeps of waters now heaving themselves into waves. Nothing in sea-
craft could be more perfect than the graceful motion of the ship; every
portion worked together in the stiffening breeze, as if courtesy, not
necessity, bowed her over the billows.

"It is magnificent!" said Eva, as she turned once more to gaze
upon the heavens.

"And you fear nothing?" inquired the captain.

"Nothing."

"By Jove!" said the good sailor, when he returned from the cabin,
"that lady's smile would quell a tempest." As the night advanced, the
storm gathered down upon the waters, but not so fiercely as to cause any
alarm for the safety of the ship, while the good seamanship of her commander, and the steadiness of his crew, convinced Sidney, that, despite
the increasing gale, they could weather it bravely—if they kept the open
sea; and when he assured Eva ' all would be right,' she but smiled at his
supposing she entertained a doubt. Her fellow-passengers already looked
to her for hope; at first, whenever the ship laboured in the trough of a
heavy sea, they screamed violently; but Eva's self-possession by degrees
communicated itself to them, and they were tranquillized—talking in
whispers; but when, at intervals, the pale lightning flickered through
the cabin, they crowded closely together, like affrighted sheep, while
Keeldar vented his apprehensions in low moanings. Sometimes a lull
would come, and it was hoped the storm was passing off; but after one

of those 'lulls' it increased so as to make stout hearts quake with fear. The impending clouds were so highly charged with electricity, that wreaths of fire sported around the gallant ship, which, nothing daunted, rode upon the waves like a war-horse over a field of battle. The scene became too awful to excite so tranquil a feeling as admiration; but, at the moment when the captain exulted on the strength and bearing of his vessel, and congratulated himself on the good seamanship that had so ably and quickly prepared for the gale, the lightning struck the main-top-mast, and thence rushed like a fiery serpent down the body of the mast, which it crushed and shivered into splinters, shattering the stout iron hoops into small pieces, which, driven fore and aft, sprang into the foaming surge.

The scene was awful beyond description; nothing pictured or imagined could equal its reality; amid the elemental strife the stricken ship, heaving in its agony, showed like a pyramid of fire, as though some bright volcano had been cast forth from the dark yawning waves to affright the ocean and the heavens. Every object, every straining cord and madly flapping sail, the very features of the terror-stricken crew, transfixed in various attitudes, were visible each to the other; the thunder rolled away in triumph; the darkness that succeeded, awful at it was, was a positive relief; men could not breathe till then; the vessel reeled violently, then shivered like a living thing in a paroxysm of ague. There was a lull—a pause—a fearful moment of silent horror; so long—it seemed an eternity concentrated into an instant.

" Now, God protect us, we are struck by lightning! struck—but not crushed!" That was whispered in the terrible moment.

Who but Eva thought of consolation then?

" We are lost!" exclaimed a voice, loud and distinct in its terror.

" He who said so, deserves to be so," shouted the captain. " Cut away the wreck of the mast; there is life in the good ship yet."

" The fireball has gone right through her, sir!" exclaimed the mate, as another flash of lightning showed his ghastly face to his officer.

" Well, sir," was the cool reply, " and what of that? I have had a ball through my body, and yet I am here."

" Brave heart!" exclaimed Sidney; " we shall be saved!"

" I will not cling to you or impede your movements," said Eva to her husband ; "but will go anywhere, or do anything you tell me."

The pitching and rolling of the ship prevented her words from being heard ; but Sidney saw her face, pale yet calm, and could trust her then, when death with life was struggling for mastery. No time was lost ; each hand was ready, each heart true ; what men could do was done ; the deck was cleared, the pumps were rigged and got to work, and several of the people were left between decks, to hoist up and heave overboard whatever they could manage. Had 'The Swift' not been struck, she would have had little difficulty in weathering the gale ; but her main-mast gone, the water gaining in the hold, despite all efforts at the pumps—one of which had become disabled—she was left completely at the mercy of a heavy sea ; and though the thunder had ceased, and the lightning no longer, with bitter mockery, exhibited their danger in its varied and lurid lights, they looked in vain for a break in the black and stormy clouds that poured upon them, and seemed to some as if collected to hide their perils from the compassionate eye of Providence. Sidney was prompt to assist and prudent to advise. Eva's influence increased with peril ; "God," she said, "was with them," and so great was her command over the feelings usually inseparable from woman's nature, that the captain did not hesitate to tell her their only chance now was to run for land.

" We shall lose our all," said Sidney, " but we may save our lives—your casket, dearest ? "

" It is gone," she answered, calmly ; "I heard them say the passengers' luggage was overboard."

Sidney could be of little further service ; he twined his arms round Eva, and felt that her heart did not beat more quickly than usual ; half an hour of intense anxiety succeeded. "It cannot be," he said, "that God will cut off our young lives thus in the summer of the year and of our age ! "

"And if it were, dear heart ! " she answered, "what do we fear ? a plunge into that gulf to wake in heaven ! But, Sidney, trust me, we shall have a far longer struggle with life, nor know the perfecting of immortal love so soon ! " It seemed, as she spoke, that there was a lessening of the storm ; but in the distance they saw the fatal foam wreath, telling of rocks and shoals that guard the land. The captain ordered the boats to be lowered, and said how thankful they ought to be that the drenching rain had extinguished the fire, which otherwise must have destroyed them in their sudden terror; the jolly boat was hoisted on the lee side, and afterwards the other boats on the booms were got into the water; but the sea ran so high that it was with difficulty they were prevented from being stove alongside, and one was instantly drawn under and sunk; this, too, with the water gaining fearfully and the ship tumbling on towards the shore. The captain gazed on the fearful breakers and endeavoured to change the course of the doomed ship, so as to turn a point and run her for a bay where there might be comparatively still water, and safety obtained on a rock, which was never covered even at high tides; breathless anxiety stilled every lip; while the breakers foamed and frothed around the spiral rocks that stood up dark and frightful in the grey light, which a dense haze prevented from brightening into morning; the faithful vessel worked strongly in the current, as if zealous to obey her commander to the last. How the poor thing laboured! a wreck of the noble craft that had queened it over the sunny waters of the previous morning; how heavily she rose and fell, now drifting helpless, then, by an effort, still struggling in obedience to the helm that creaked and groaned like the weathercock in the old gable. "One more such plunge," muttered Sidney, "and we are in still water." What a moment it was; men laboured for their lives; others seemed transfixed, paralysed, as they shrunk from the fierce dark crags that overhung their course. On a sudden, a sunk rock that projected under water, considerably below the limits of the visible point, struck the bow of the ship; instantly, she swung round—her head cleared, but her stern coming on the rock, struck repeatedly, and the sea being very heavy, her rudder broke away, and all her works aloft were shivered; for a moment, helpless as she was, she forged off, but at the same instant ran upon another rock, the sea breaking over her; a half-suffocated cry of despair arose from the deck; several persons were washed overboard; the confusion of a death-struggle succeeded; but the captain never for an instant lost his presence of mind; some cried, "The boats—the boats!" and seemed about to rush into them, as they tossed about half-full of water, knowing that the ship could not

long hold together; if there were any means of getting on the reef, the
captain knew there was still water on the other side; but the breakers
lashed the ship furiously, and dashed in a fearful gully between it and the
reef; it was impossible, the most daring thought, to attempt, short as it
was, to cross it; no one for an instant supposed they who had been
washed overboard could climb the precipice; the fog was evidently
clearing off, the light increasing, and the ship did not pitch unceasingly,
shaking rather when the surge dashed over her; at last, they heard a hail

from the reef, and, much to their astonishment, they saw the figure of one
of their crew—he was saved! he made signs to them to throw him a rope
lower down, and descended with an ease which proved him unhurt to
a point where a rope might be secured; every moment increased the
danger of those who clung to the ship; if she got off the ‘spike,’ upon
which she was as it were impaled, she must instantly settle and sink:
every effort was made to fling a rope across, but in vain—one bold-hearted
fellow offered to carry it through the surge. A plunge, and he struggled

bravely, but a spar struck him, and he sunk. That made the bravest shudder—Sidney and Eva clung together, not venturing to look into the abyss. Keeldar, as if understanding the peril and the resource, eyed the distance with his deep blood-shot eye, and whined.

"He is not a water-dog, unfortunately," said the captain.

Eva bent down and kissed the creature's head. He looked up in her face, and licked her hand. "He will try, if I tell him," she observed to the captain. "You will go, Keeldar!" The dog shook himself, advanced his fore paws to the edge of the vessel, and looked steadily forward. The sailor on the reef comprehended what was going forward, and let himself down, so that he stood hip-high in the water.

Eva ungloved her hand and attempted to fasten the glove to the rope; this was done for her; she showed it to the dog, told him he was to carry it there—pointing across. It was flung off, and the gallant brute sprang after it with such high courage, that at the shout raised by the sailors the white pigeon, which must have been sheltered somewhere in the rigging through the storm, fluttered towards the reef.

"Do not look, Eva; I will tell you what occurs," said Sidney, as he turned her face to his bosom. "I do not see him yet, my love; all is one mass of foam; the rope floats idly—no! he has it—he has it, good dog! No! it is loose again! No! he has it, I see his head."

"Let it go, let it go; he is uncoiling it; steady!" cried the captain. "Lady," he added, "call loudly to the dog; he will hear your voice."

Eva was at once herself. She advanced —nothing heeding her dripping garments, nor the deaths which gaped around her. Beneath her feet a thousand demons were tugging at the yet firm-set planks—reeving them one from the other, and yelling, half in mockery, half in triumph! Some of the passengers lay on the shelving deck, so ill as to be indifferent whether life or death were at hand. Each wave shook the shattered bark, as it hissed and spattered over the timbers; but Eva stood like Hope, steady to the anchor, on the spot from which Keeldar had plunged. "Forward, good Keeldar; forward, brave dog—forward!" she exclaimed, clapping her hands. He turned his head once towards his mistress, but swam on. All knew their lives depended on his strength and sagacity. They grouped together, watching with panting hearts and straining eyes the movements of his head, as he struggled onwards.   Again Eva encouraged him, and all knew the influence of her voice.   Eagerly at last the sailor grasped the rope, and waved his arm in triumph; but the dog would not yield up his charge.

"It is the glove he wants!" exclaimed Eva, in agony.

The captain put his trumpet to his mouth.   "Give him the glove!" There had been a fierce and determined wrestling between the man and

the dog; but it ceased at once.   The sailor clambered to the nearest ledge, the rope coiled round his arm, while Keeldar, unable to shake the water from his coat, shut his teeth firmly on the glove.   Still the waves rolled on, though the gale abated.   The sailor on the reef made fast his rope; but it had been injured in its progress, and was unequal to much weight.   Doing as he was ordered, the little cabin boy coiled one of great strength round his slim body, and grappled the other foot by foot across the abyss. Oh, if his mother had been there to see him! That secured, two strong men went over to provide for the safety of those who were to follow, and, valuable as time was, there was no confusion.

Nothing could keep the trembling Keeldar tranquil during the minute that his mistress was wafted across; but when she was lifted to the rock, he pressed the glove into her hand. Each, as he arrived, greeted the dog as a preserver; but he responded to no caress of a stranger hand.

Sidney wished to remain to the last with the captain, but he would not permit him; and Eva watched with her husband his every movement with intense anxiety, as he stood alone upon the reeling deck, taking a last farewell of the timbers he had regarded with fidelity and affection. He had hardly swung himself off, when a heavy sea struck the ship, and so completely unseated her, that the ropes were cast from their holdings, and the gallant officer was immersed in the waves; the men pulled as if their lives were still in his keeping—even Eva put her frail strength to the rescue; all shouted to him, as with one voice, to 'hold on,' and so great was their anxiety to preserve his life, that they hardly noticed the utter destruction of the vessel, which, before he was landed on the reef, had gone to pieces so completely, that nothing could be seen but the spars and bulk heads, jostling each other in the trough of the sea, which had lifted her up, and then dashed her into fragments.

One or two old sailors declared there must have been 'a reason' for all this—in the summer time; something not right going on, for they had heard sounds such as thunder never uttered, and seen shadows on the deck never cast from mortal form; they whispered to each other, 'looking out' for the white pigeon, which seemed to have passed from the reef as mysteriously as from the ship.

Keeldar might have been a popular dog, if he had had popular manners; but he never courted 'the people,' and when each had patted him on the head, and all admired his courage and sagacity, there seemed to arise a tacit understanding that he only desired the approbation of his mistress. A warm and beautiful sunrise saw the subsiding of the raging waters, and the arrival of several landsmen on the beach, some to plunder —some to save. Within a short period after the shipwreck they were safely lodged in the few cabins that skirted the coast, Eva, still the guardian angel of those whose weakness required encouragement and aid, and Sidney active everywhere to remedy in part the misfortunes of the night.

"You have not lost your sketch-book," said Eva; "some day you will immortalise the clouds that last night beguiled us by their beauty!"

"My own dearest," he replied, looking mournfully upon her; "that and poor Randy's purse are all our wealth."

"Sidney, the mine is not exhausted so long as the ore is there!"

"But the means may be wanted to work it."

"Never, while the will and health remain! I could chide you, dearest, for a distrustful word or look, living as we are, memorials of God's mercy. I did hope to have eased your toil by the contents of that casket, which now, perhaps, the fishes look upon with wondering eyes: but it was not to be; it is I who should grieve, seeing that I come a burden to you; and yet I do not! This is indeed a new world, but none the less to be desired. I have still some few jewels, and one above them all, that never tines—Hope! Faith in the future—born of the past!"

THE STRUGGLE FOR LIFE.

PART THE TENTH.

"ALL like a dream, it is," said Eva to her husband, as, 'the daylight done,' in London, they sat at the open window of their apartment, looking to where they knew the sun had set, without discovering a lingering tint of colour on the dense atmosphere — thick and grey from the vapours of congregated multitudes: "all like a dream, it is," she repeated; "the brief, yet eventful, past of our young lives—the fearful wreck—the most merciful preservation—the loss of our little store; and yet this later darkness serves but to render still more bright the tender help, the affectionate interest, shown and expressed towards us. What is so dear as human sympathy!"

"True," answered Sidney; but the word came coldly from his lips.

"And," she added, "the prosperity that will be sure to follow!"

Sidney neither spoke nor sighed, but he shuddered, or made some movement, which caused Eva to pause; and while pushing back the abundant hair that clustered on her husband's brow, she whispered, "Dearest, you are fevered with over-work."

"I am not working now, sweet Eva."

" Nay, but you are ; it is not only while you hold the pencil, giving palpable existence to the creations of your mind—it is not only then you labour. I know you better, my own dear one ! You look, even at me, with a vacant eye ! Seeing beyond, or turning in your gaze to what is spread so richly on the broad table-land of your great heart."

" It is the only table I have to spread," he answered, smiling bitterly.

" That table will supply others in good time," was the bright reply ; " and even if it did not—if the furnishing of our earthly feastings and trappings be as scanty as—as—it must be—for awhile—I could welcome its continuance, with you, for the immortality you *must* win— hereafter ! I could not have knit my heart to a reputation that could have crept into its grave—nothing doing—nothing done ! Had you inherited a fortune, your course, as well as your duties, would have been different ; then, as now, having the great power to will—which is, indeed, the right to conquer. But, Sidney," she continued, in a voice of reproving tenderness, " all my eloquence is thrown away upon you. Come, we will go on a voyage of discovery, and meet our old companions—air and freedom—amid trees which the late showers have enriched with verdure."

" No, not this evening," he answered ; " there is something I want to sketch, and you have been out to-day."

" But not Keeldar—Keeldar has not been out ; not had his walk— poor Keeldar ! " And the dog aroused himself with a shake from beside the easel, looking more wearied than he would have done after a day's hunting on Glena ; the deep-toned grey about his muzzle and ears had become lighter ; he seemed dusty, and his eyes were heavy. " Keeldar wants a walk," continued his mistress ; and the dog again shook himself, and gave a low hollow bark ; then standing on his hind legs, sniffed out of the open window, gazing with a haughty air at the chimney-pots.

" They are not trees, old friend. Do come, Sidney ! "

The artist answered only by a kiss, and prepared to do as Eva requested. It was a very delight to see how quickly she prepared for the purposed walk. How, with playful earnestness, she smoothed with her soft hand the ruffled silk of her husband's hat, and drew forth the fingers of his gloves. " There never was a better valet ! " she observed, pulling down a wrinkle in the carefully kept coat—" this temporary discomfort,

Sidney, has increased my knowledge; our single room is as well ordered as though attended by a dozen Kittys. I can clean a palette! mix a salad! pleat a frill! my hands are all the stronger for the exercise; and when I get a harp, I shall ring out right bravely those chords, which, if you remember, baffled my fingers so provokingly once."

"Nothing baffles you," replied Sidney; but his voice was sad— "nothing! you look poverty in the face, and bid it welcome with a smile."

"And did it ever vanish at a frown? Is there not a scripture—I read it this very morning—which says—I forget the exact words, but their spirit ran, 'Shall we receive good from his hand, and shall we not receive evil also?' Hope is the birthright of immortality. Surely, even the murky world wherein we now exist was never made for misery; if we *think* it so, we *make* it so! the harder the struggle, the greater the given strength. One moment more—I will set our little supper ready against our return; the radishes look so bright in this glass of sparkling water; and you praised my choice of this cheese a week ago; now, Master Sidney, am I not worthy to be an artist's wife? does not that little round table, with its snow-white cloth, relieved by the green leaves and glowing red, make a charming foreground to that lovely picture on the easel, and the deep back-ground of two old chairs, and the worm-eaten cabinet—which Kitty would call a kitchen press!—the poor lay figure looks sulky in the corner, ever since I took its place; but it adds to the picturesque of our little scene; and so does your dusky painting-gown, and that maroon curtain—not to catalogue the odds and ends of armour, and much pictorial rubbish! Now, let us go, dearest, or Keeldar will begin to bay; he has been up and down stairs already, and may disturb that sick lady on the second floor below us, whom no one ever sees."

"I saw her once," replied Sidney—"I forgot to tell you; it was while you were repeating poetry—(for, as yet, your memory is our only book, save one)—when you sat to me yesterday. She came up the stairs, opened the sliding window just outside the door, and then half-entered, listening while you spoke, shaking her finger at me, to keep me silent."

"How strange!" said Eva, rejoicing within herself, as they descended the tedious stairs, that his mind was somewhat diverted from its melancholy.

Keeldar followed slowly behind Eva; touching her hand occasionally with his nose; the shops in Oxford Street were still open, and the white slaves of commerce toiled about the counters and beneath the hot gas lamps; twelve only of their sixteen hours of labour gone! The pavement was thronged by noisy stall-keepers, pressing their fruits and hot potatoes, and tins, and toys, wooden ware, and baskets, upon the passers-by, who sought nothing but a path-way through the market; yet here the poor room keeper, or more prosperous tradesman's wife, was sure to find what *she* considered good and cheap; crushed and mangled lettuces which had

been so often 'damped down,' that their very hearts were macerating— apples, spotted 'like the pard,' hand-polished oranges, and half-blind nuts; while more than half-dirty children, clinging to their mothers' skirts, clamoured for striped sticks of fingered sweetmeats.

" Give me a penny to buy a bit of bread," exclaimed a fierce-looking man to the artist and his wife. The beggar was buttoned up close to the throat, and his eyes glared beneath his knitted brows—" Give me the penny," he repeated, " I am starving !"

"Are you sure you want it for food?" inquired Sidney, as his fingers wandered amongst the few 'halfpence' that were in his pocket—hard to find! The man muttered no thanks, but pointing to where the spirit Pest-house displayed its coloured poisons through panes of costly glass, waved the coin in exultation as he dashed into the door, exclaiming, "Now I shall have gin!" A young fragile woman, lingering on the threshold, staggered to Eva, and gazing in her face, whispered—"You give to bold beggars like him, while you, lady, and such as you shrink from such as I; and yet a kind world would have saved me once. God bless you!" she continued, following a little behind, and not heeding Keeldar's growl; "I think you would help me now, if you could—I am not drunk, nor am I starving; but I am heart-broken." Eva gave her the smallest of silver coins, and while she clung more closely to Sidney's protecting arm, she spoke a few words of mingled counsel and kindness, which left the unfortunate flooded in tears. "It's long since I heard such music as that voice," she muttered to herself, as they passed on; "and I'll keep this for a token; it may do me good."

"If our natures were such that we could distil happiness from the comparative misery of our fellow creatures," said Sidney, as they enjoyed the twilight beneath the noble trees of Hyde Park, "we ought to be happy, for we see many to whom our position would be positive prosperity; and yet we do not know all their trials."

"Nor their consolations," added Eva; "when we lost all except poor Randy's treasure, and were shivering among the rocks of a stranger land, how deserted and desolate must we have appeared; and yet what a world of happiness existed within ourselves!"

"That is quite true," replied Sidney; "we did enjoy a world of happiness; we were so full of hope; but ever since our arrival here, one disappointment has followed another; I do not know that circumstances are worse than before I went to Rome, but I had just cause to expect they would be better; and then I suffered alone, and did not feel it so bitterly—my greatest trial, dearest, is knowing what you endure."

"You exaggerate that endurance; truly, I suffer nothing, except from the shadows of those clouds that pass at intervals over your spirit, and which time will soon dispel; you have lost your best friend by death, not desertion: and though one or two dealers have refused to purchase until what they have are sold, that will soon be, when the town fills."

"If I could stoop to manufacture old masters, or imitate the style of those who are popular, I should make, instead of want, money!"

"I would rather see you perish than paint a lie!" exclaimed Eva. "Let us," she continued, after a pause, as they stood beneath one of

the stateliest trees of the beautiful park, "let us, now that we are refreshed by the cool air, and while the murmurs of the leaves whisper of Nature, sit here and think of means to anticipate the future, and rob it of all bitterness. I could not prevail on our usual chapman to take those drawings on any terms."

"I did not like to ask you about them, though I have thought of little else," was Sidney's reply.

"To-morrow evening I will go where money may be raised upon them; indeed, Sidney, it is our only resource."

The young man turned his head away, for his cheek was crimson.

"Nay, my own love," she added, "it is an honest means: better than borrowing, even if we had friends to lend; I would have gone this evening, but—the streets were so light, that—I shame to say, I was ashamed."

Sidney said, in a voice suppressed by emotion, that when nothing else could be done he would so manage that she should not be subjected to such degradation.

They wandered about the noble 'garden' of Kensington, and stood upon the graceful bridge that spans the small lake which divides it from the Park, until wearied, but wearied pleasantly, they sought their homeward path. Sidney had determined to concentrate his energies upon a great picture for the May Exhibition; there was abundant time; but, in addition to the want of means for the necessaries of life, his health had become unsettled; the earnestness and anxiousness of his mind engendered an irritability which, kept in check as it was by his loving and generous nature, found vent, not upon others, but himself. His spirits, when in health, were not buoyant; his feelings were more intense than those of Eva—more concentrated; and at times he reproached himself bitterly for marrying upon a prospect, not a reality; deeming he had committed a pardonless sin by bringing her into much sorrow. Her reflections were the very opposite, as though, mentally, she breathed another atmosphere; as if in a morning dream, she saw the broad-bosomed lake, or heard the rush of the Tore waterfall, or smiled at Randy and his fairy lore; as if accompanied by sweet and solemn music, the picture of Mucross and its sainted grave arose before her; and the mountain breeze kissed the ringlets that played upon her cheek; while the Dovecote, with its flowers, and birds, and pretty spotted doe, and her old servant, appeared and disappeared; she awoke, day after day, to the confined air, and dim discoloured light, and narrow room, and the bewildering din of city life; yet she awoke with a bright smile of joy upon her lips, and tender words springing from her thoughts to cheer and cherish him she loved—loved far, far better than lakes, or woods, or rank, or wealth. Her love was rich as inexhaustible—a love to be perilled neither by poverty nor prosperity; if Sidney could have been happy in a desert, she could have been happy with him—he was her universe. Faith, which is the stronghold of hope, never forsook her, not even when she thought that Sidney grew thin and worn, and—worse than both—restless and uncommunicative. She spoke to him of this, during their homeward walk, and chid so gently, that reproof struck upon his ear like praise; and he promised to amend, and cast his moodiness away; and his spirits were refreshed, simply by the communion of her gladsome nature. They agreed they would endure patiently, and labour together hopefully—she, with the ready thought and willing hands that work with circumstances, not against them—he, in his noble calling, promising her again and again, that never more would he lock up his feelings from her inspection. Nothing during their walk had changed their condition, and yet his sorrows were half gone; he sprang up the attic stairs, feeling a load removed from his crushed heart, simply by her words and sweet companionship. Silence is the canker of sorrow, and once the proscribed subject had been entered on, he wondered why he had not poured forth his thoughts long before; he could hardly account for his revived spirits. "After all," said Eva, when they had returned, "there *is* a magic in the *name* of home; if the room were half its size, I should cling to it as a sanctuary; it has a fine clear north light—the painter's delight."

"And see, Eva," added Sidney, while she sought the materials for striking a light; "there is a veritable moonbeam; it seems astray here, not knowing where to rest; and at this moment there is a fine effect of shadow."

. "Yes," she answered, smiling, though in darkness, "cast by that tall chimney-pot; fancy it our dear old gable; and that cat, whose eyes are glittering upon us from those tiles, the ancient owl—— Down, Keeldar; did you never see a cat before, that you set your bristles at it."

The candle was lit, and its inmates formed a strange contrast to the odd, yet picturesque, appearance of the chamber; the light gave an unearthly, yet most angelic, effect to Eva's beauty. "I wish I could fasten that expression on your picture, dearest," he said, turning to the easel, where he had placed a small portrait he had taken a fancy to paint; the easel was there—the portrait gone! Sidney uttered a loud exclamation of astonishment: it had rested against the outline of his large picture: it was not even finished. They looked everywhere, removed the easel and the pictures, the chairs, the cabinet, all in vain; it was gone. Eva descended the creaking stairs, and asked the landlady if any one had called during their absence. "No; no one that she had seen." Perplexed and grieved, she returned, and fancied that as she passed the old lady's room, she heard the sound of light young laughter. They sat silently down to supper.

Upon Sidney's plate was a purse. He raised it; it contained gold—not much—but more than he had looked upon for a long, long time.

"Is it true—is it real?" inquired Eva; "there is no doubt it is intended as payment for the picture—much more than you would have considered its worth; is it not so?"

"It was not painted to sell," he answered, in a tone of mingled perplexity and disappointment; and again and again he looked at the gold suspiciously. The mystery connected with this incident prevented the money being as highly valued as it otherwise would have been, and caused them some anxious conjecture. The purse was evidently of foreign manufacture, but there was nothing about it that could lead to a guess as to whence it came. The feeling of dislike which Sidney entertained towards using its contents passed away, and for a time he laboured at his great work with a mind relieved from the immediate pressure of necessity. Eva believed their destiny was guarded by some mysterious but powerful friend, who had taken the picture as an excuse for leaving gold; and she strongly suspected the old lady knew who the visitor was.

As the winter advanced, Randy wrote her various accounts, by the hand of the schoolmaster, of the progress of things in her old neighbourhood; and at the termination of each letter the schoolmaster apologised for the diction, saying that Randy insisted on all things being written exactly as spoken by him. Among these came a fable. "I heard it," he wrote, "from the King of the Crickets, and he sitting beside the fire, at which I was looking, while the turf sparkled and blazed; and the grate ould grey cricket, whose fine hearty 'chirrup' I'd know among a thousand, came out of his kingdom at the back of the hob, and riddled the

story out of him. 'Send that,' he says, when he was straggling back again ;
'send that little history to the darlint in London, who fed me and mine
many a day ; send her that,' says he, ' to rise her heart!' and these were
his words :—' Some of the flowers of the trees thought they'd petition the
snow not to fall upon them in winter, but come in the summer, when it
would melt while falling. " You keep us back," said the flowers, " wrap-
ping the earth in your cold shroud ; come in the summer, and you will
then refresh, and not blight, us." "Foolish things!" answered a snow-flake
that trembled like a feather on the impatient bud of a white-thorn tree.
" It is I who protect you from the bitter cold of winter, and give you
strength to enjoy the beautiful summer : all things in season are best."
So when the weeks danced into the months, and the sun sent his heat into
the flowers, and the shadows fainted upon the grass, the blossom of the
white-thorn tree reproached a sunbeam that trembled on its leaves.
" Where were you in the keen cold weather, when you were wanted ?" it
questioned ; "where ?"   " What matters that to you," answered the sunbeam ; "if I told you where I was you would be none the wiser.   I am
here now.   Was not the tree, you grow out of, once a small seed ; and has
it not increased and prospered, been heated and cooled by the Power that
sends me, in due season, a messenger of heat and brightness into your
very heart ?   The snow told me of your murmurings last winter, and now
I shall have to tell the snow of your murmurings this summer : a pretty
world we should have of it if every flower chose its own season ?"   " I
shall drop before my time," sighed the blossom.   " That is impossible,"
answered the sunbeam ; "poor silly thing! can't you understand that the
snow and I could not meet together.   I should destroy its usefulness,
and it would destroy mine ; each in its turn ; and that's the way of
Nature !—each in its turn, and all for good!' ' "

    " Each in its turn," repeated Eva in her own mind : "each in its
turn—joy and sorrow—and sorrow and joy ; I had a vision of them once,
chasing each other round the globe, as it turned, while the stars twinkled
in the firmament ; first the one and then the other paused for a moment
before me, and methought the tears of sorrow expanded my heart more
than the smiles of joy. Beautiful both—and wisdom-giving ! The cricket
sung a true song : each in its season—and all for good!"

Well and earnestly did Sidney labour; and some of the very happiest hours of Eva's life were spent in watching how his mind enriched the canvas—calling into existence the noblest forms, and adding to their development, by each touch of his vigorous pencil, some new beauty or stronger character. It was wonderful how every creature in that house of many inhabitants loved her: the lame child of the widow, to whom it belonged, would climb up the stairs, and, knocking against the door with lean fingers, entreat to be allowed to do something for her. Careful she was, even of a flower, tending the fading plants of her poor landlady so diligently, that the old leaves regained their colour, and the young ones sprouted forth all fresh and green beneath her charge. The lark, whose dingy cage had cracked beneath the sun, renewed its life under the shadow of the leaves she spread around it: and enjoying, poor thing! the freshness of the sod her charity bestowed, sung until tears quivered upon Eva's cheek. She sought out misery, and prayed within walls that had never before heard the voice of prayer. Her step was the music of many a sick-room; and never was her birth-gift more palpable than during this time of bitter trial. She was still 'loving and being beloved.' Sometimes (but that must have been pure fancy) she heard the murmur of bees, and scented the perfume of flowers, as if borne by a passing breeze across her brow; and in her absence small household duties would be performed, as if by invisible hands; and, in winter, when flowers become the luxuries of the wealthy, who would hardly notice them in the time of their abundance, she would find some beside her work; and Sidney often perceived his palette set and his brushes washed when Eva declared she had neither touched the one nor the other. How did these things come about? Perhaps Randy could have told.

But Eva had stern realities to deal with. Like all persons of great talent, Sidney was discontented with his own labours. He had 'looked' at the old mighty ones—not to imitate, but to *emulate;* and it might be, that their strength was beyond his grasp, though not beyond his aim. This frequently dispirited the artist; and so intent was he on bringing up his picture to the ideal of his conception that he would destroy the labour of a week, if any new thought—or a thought fresh set—suggested a better working out of his subject. As the spring advanced, Sidney became more abstracted—more nervous, lest his great labour should not be completed in time. He ceased to concern himself about the necessaries of life, and then Eva rejoiced at being able to labour unobserved. She gloried in the great privilege of shielding him she loved from petty anxieties—the frets of life. She endured all things patiently, save the terror which arose from an idea that his mind was at times confused—overwrought, overburdened : he could not endure noise; the very gentlest tap of the lame boy's finger at the door would make him start and render his hand unsteady. As THE TIME approached when, finished or unfinished, his picture must claim admission, he could neither sleep nor eat. In the dead hour of night she would awake, and hear him pacing in the darkness, or see him through the gloom, leaning his head, at intervals, upon the frosted glass of the window to cool its burning. It was at these times—in these dark thinking hours —that Sidney struggled bravely—as great men do, not only with the hard and knotted world, but with themselves—against apprehensions, which Eva never felt; but for her, the picture he laboured at would never have left the easel : he thought it unworthy of his better genius : he had neither space nor light for his great conception ; commencing his figures on so large a scale, he had worked upon too small a canvas; the praise Eva bestowed upon it, at times sounded like reproach, while at others it reconciled him to all contingencies. *She* looked upon his talent as certain of triumph ; and, secure in *that*, was able to combat what, after all was achieved, would serve but as shadows to the great brightness of the future. He knew that such were her thoughts, and, despite his promise, he loved her too tenderly to tell her how much he mistrusted the fruits of his toil —how he believed they must fail to produce aught but disappointment. He looked through the darkness, and could discover no hope to replace the one he ought to take from her. There was high heroism in this silent suffering : and, truly, the spirit of a hero, in this our age of facts, finds refuge only in poet or painter ; it has no other dwelling-place. Sidney's imagination was vivid as fire in a dark night, and yet he sought to crush it in a mould—to compress a volume into a page! He curled his lip in bitter disdain at the anxiety that was eating into his heart. Although, at times, he had worked doubtingly, yet the intensity of his labour had been as though the colours on his palette were mingled with his life blood;

and while he moved noiselessly in the darkness, fearing to awake her who
watched his motions through the dim, dim twilight of the little chamber,
filling the atmosphere with the most earnest prayer-breathings that ever
passed from the depths of woman's love to the throne of HIM who
hears unspoken emotions, as though a trumpet told them to the heavens,
the devotional feeling, inseparable from truly great minds, by degrees
softened and soothed his disturbed nature, until unconsciously they prayed
together—each for the other—in silence and in darkness ; and Eva would
hear him listening lest she might be disturbed by half-breathed prayers.
A little longer, and their necessities had grown so urgent that every
trinket—every small luxury—had disappeared ; but Eva did not murmur,
for Sidney never missed them. Sometimes he would talk wildly about
his hopes; at others, sink down beside his easel in a sleep so unre-
freshing and disturbed that his wife would abridge it. The picture was
his great stimulus, and he revived to fresh exertion. At length it was
sent to the Academy—not finished as he intended it should have been, for
painting in and painting out retarded his great purpose. But Eva thought,
notwithstanding, that it would attract the world. Poverty in England was
then denied all access to high works of art ; but she would look at the
pictures in the shop-windows, and return with increased faith in the
greatness of her husband's conceptions. A long period of uncertainty
and suspense elapses between the reception of the works at the Academy
and their exhibition, during which the painters have no means of knowing
their fate—whether they will be received or rejected it is not in their
power to ascertain. The sufferings of the artist at this period can better
be imagined than described. His struggle was great and unconquerable ;
he had resolved what to do if this effort failed, and if his health were not
shattered in the contest ; a fear, too, would sometimes come with others
that trooped through the throbbings of his brain—a fear that his thoughts
too often did battle with circumstances rather than with himself; for he
was a just man—just and true, or Eva could not have loved him. When
we consider these things, and how his frame was worn by sickness, there
was a noble greatness in his silence. Things of love and tenderness
grow tenfold in the imagination ; and so do things of terror. Sidney would
have given much to recall the picture, to satisfy himself upon particular

points, but it was gone! and its faults, its want of finish, assumed a monstrous and malignant vitality, and mocked him; he could tell Eva that even if it were admitted, it might be so hung as to destroy its effects, and so form a target for shallow-brained and heartless critics to fly their shafts at; but she, so high-souled and simple—judging from her own pure and generous nature, of the nature of others, told him he was all wrong; that critics were generous souls, appointed to show the world true excellence.

The days had length, the light came early, and continued late within their chamber: Keeldar had learned to remain outstretched and silent upon the floor, rising only to follow his mistress; Sidney tried to paint— he used every effort his wasted body and shattered mind could devise to avoid sinking; but the power of action was netted in by poverty; Eva's cheerfulness came with an effort and departed in tears; they had not told even the old officer of their whereabouts; at first they waited for better times, and then, when the times grew worse and worse, they were ashamed to let him know of the blight that withers up existence; even at the last they agreed it was better to wait until the Exhibition opened. Sidney would care little for his threadbare coat when Fame heralded him to the world, and wealth followed in her footsteps; and so they went on from one long day to another—the poor painter and his wife: he fancying that she paled daily; she knowing that he was gradually wasting—until at last they divided crusts with Keeldar!

It was strange, and painful as strange, that she could not bear to see her husband's eyes turned upon her. He would make a few rough sketches—then muse—those long, long, wordless musings, in which neither heart nor mind take part—his eyes fixed upon her—silently, with an intensity of expression which deepened them beyond all power of description, taking no note of aught, nor replying to her words, until driven to agony, she would arouse him by an effort that ended in the mingling of mutual tears. Anything could she endure, but those hours of silent gazing. Well she knew that his noble spirit was racked by a combination of sufferings, of which he could not trust himself to speak, lest he should add to her distress. She saw him become hourly worse; the day had long advanced upon a night of increased but awfully silent restlessness— more distressing than the most continuous complaining. Once only he suddenly folded her in his arms, exclaiming, "Eva! Eva! what is to become of you!" She soothed him with the gentlest words and holiest hopes; and at last he slept. When assured of this, she propped up a box upon their two remaining chairs, and commenced writing to one whose sympathy with suffering was known to her. A terrible feeling urged her

to this. *If her husband died from false pride, should she not be his murderer?* She wrote on rapidly, until the last, and then she questioned how she could sign their name—*his* name to such a document. *His name,* which in less than two short weeks (so ran her thoughts) would be blazoned to the world as that of the 'Great Artist.' She paused—would not a feigned name answer? "I cannot write a lie nor shame his name," she murmured. She gazed hopelessly round the room—she knew there was nothing disposable within the box, yet she raised its cover; it fell from her fingers—the hollow sound told of its emptiness, and with a shudder she looked towards the mattrass on which Sidney lay, fearing he had awoke; not so; he slept soundly. She pressed her head within her hands, tightly—and sinking gradually on her knees, her long hair covering her, as with a shroud, she prayed, though no sound escaped from her heaving bosom, no sighs accompanied her abundant tears;—she prayed the strengthening and refreshing prayer of an earnest and pure heart ; then rising, she tore the note into the smallest fragments, which fell like snow upon the dark boards. Again she wrote—necessity conquering pride, but not stooping to beggary. It was to the old officer—a little—a very little she required for the present, just to give them food, and procure him medical advice—that was all. The first day's exhibition over, and immortality was sure to follow. This was finished, and she thought she would take it to the post and return before Sidney awoke. As she descended—outside the old woman's door a glittering guinea, dropped on the stairs, arrested her attention. Never before had gold shone so brightly in her eyes ; never before had such a grim host of skeletons floated around her ; never before had such whisperings—tales of those who had died of hunger—not in the wilderness, but amid the busy traffic of city life—suggested the duties owed by self to self, to her throbbing ears. She pushed the coin away with her foot ; it rang out—what awful music to the famishing is the sound of gold! She picked it up ; it felt like molten lead. What was it that quivered in her bosom—that made her shut her hand close, close upon it, when the lame child's footstep sounded in the passage, three stories down? She knocked at the old woman's door, it was instantly opened ; there was a brightness about the very aged face, almost unnatural; her eyes shone like stars beneath her wrinkled brows. "Is this yours?" inquired Eva. The old creature pointed, with averted face and quivering finger, to a table on which there were several of the same glowing coin. Eva laid it down mechanically, and turned away with a relieved heart, and yet hungry and penniless. That had been a heavy day! Keeldar—the noble brute—disdained to ask for food, but laid apart, rugged and scraggy, with half-shut eyes. As the evening advanced, Sidney became much worse. Passing down the stairs, Eva asked the old woman to watch for a little by his side. She walked rapidly from street to street, until she arrived at the door of a well-known physician. She knocked—he was not at home. She said she must see him, and would wait. The servant showed her in as if she were a duchess, and a lovely child, who had seen her cross the hall, immediately entered, creepingly, and, climbing upon her lap, insisted on sharing its cake with its new friend. The physician soon followed—a man of few words and grave; and when the door was closed —" Sir," said Eva, " I am come to ask you to visit my husband, who is, I fear, very ill,—but stay, sir; we are too poor to pay you now; will you trust a stranger's honesty to do so hereafter?"

The good man rang the bell, ordered back the carriage he had just quitted, and drove her home.

The old woman had been faithful to her trust; more than faithful, for a judicious supply of refreshment was on the table. Eva turned to thank her; she had disappeared.

The physician said but little—" Quiet of mind and body, perfect repose—nothing to agitate or disturb."

" You hear, dearest," whispered Eva, as she bent over his pillow.

" I will try," he replied; and the tone of his voice was greatly calmed; he looked into her eyes with his old look of tranquil love.

" He is already better," she murmured.

" I will come again to-morrow," said the doctor; "and you must not be too proud to borrow more than advice from your physician." He inquired his patient's name.

" Sidney Herbert."

" Herbert!" repeated the good doctor. "Herbert! the Herberts are curious in christian names. I wrote a prescription for one poor fellow to-day—a hopeless case. How unequally the world's goods are divided!"

Eva was, indeed, the physician's debtor for more than advice; and though, for some time, a low wasting fever had ascendancy over Sidney, yet his energies revived. While the last days of the month of April were passing, his physician encouraged his artistic hopes, and his old military friend, who came to him with as much joy as if he had been the denizen of a palace, was ready to vouch, though he had not seen it, that Sidney's was the finest picture ever painted in England. The pressure of immediate want removed, each day improved his health. Keeldar's appearance improved also; and he never failed to receive the physician with an air of polite gravity, a very slight movement of his tail duly indicating his satisfaction. "I will not come," said the good doctor to Eva, "if you so overwhelm me with thanks. I have looked too closely into life not to distinguish truth and virtue—ay, at first sight. I have perfect faith in the existence of both. Large faith in human virtue is great happiness; and you have increased that faith a hundred-fold. It is I who am your debtor. You have enlarged my interest in humanity; you have shown me that the most adverse circumstances establish and strengthen love."

Eva's hopes were, as usual, sanguine. She was happy in Sidney's improving health, happy in the bright benevolence of her new friend—more than happy in the prospect of the 'golden fleece' that should be acquired to manifest gratitude. The day of the private view had arrived; Sidney's strength was to be husbanded for the first hour of the public exhibition; such, however, was Eva's anxiety to witness the entrance of the company who were to see the produce of her husband's genius, that she braved the crowd alone, and returned overflowing with joy and hope. The weather was fine, the people looked pleased; some one said that royalty (and when was royal judgment ever doubted) had declared there never had been such an exhibition. That evening she sat at her husband's feet, and rested her head on his lap, while they told—the one the other—how they would apportion the wealth the sale of the picture would certainly realize.

"There is but a little longer patience necessary," said Eva; "and so I told our landlady and the good-natured baker; and I tapped at our old lady's room, and gave her some bright words, which truly she needed, for I heard her sobbing as I closed the door; perhaps, dearest, the gold I told you of is gone, but we shall be able to lend her what she requires."

"And perhaps get you a harp," suggested Sidney, obeying the suggestion of his taste rather than his judgment.

"And our dear physician; only see all the good we have learned of human nature in our poverty. But you must sleep now, my own dear one," and kneeling devoutly, side by side, they prayed together, the same thoughts, the same words, and slept. Only once when Eva awoke she fancied she heard her aged neighbour again sobbing bitterly.

"Did any one ever see a lady so beautiful as our lady, mother?" inquired the lame boy, as he gazed after Eva the next morning. Sidney fancied she was leaning on his arm, but truly she managed to support him, as pale, and bent, and feeble, he, notwithstanding, walked rapidly on.

Eva and Sidney walked quickly along Oxford Street, but were obliged to pause at the crossing to let a pompous funeral go past. It moved slowly; the hearse heavy with plumes; the mourners in trappings of the deepest woe—all, except their features! they expressed no sadness! the eloquence of death made no impression on them; they kept time to the horses' tread, and that was all. Some private and mourning carriages followed.

" We shall not be among the first," exclaimed the impatient Sidney; they crossed; another mourning carriage was passing; they were recognised by one of its inmates—it was the physician; he thrust his arm out of the window. " God bless you," he said, and every feature of his kind face was lit up with pleasure ; " I give you joy, with all my heart."

" I daresay," whispered Eva to her husband—" I daresay he has heard the picture is well hung."

" You speak, dearest, as if you were certain it was admitted."

A light, light laugh, such a one as had often echoed through the Dove-cote, followed this observation. On they went.

" You are looking pale, dearest," said Eva; " shall we call a coach ? "

"You require it more than I do, my own kind love," he answered; "but I fear we cannot spare so much."

"I have three shillings."

"The admission two, and the catalogue one."

"But you will get in free—have your card for the season, Sidney."

He beckoned to a passing carriage, and the manner in which he threw his wearied frame upon the cushions proved how much he needed rest.

They alighted in the Strand; crowds of persons were hurrying forward; the joy-bells of the churches were ringing merrily; every person seemed to them in holiday dress. Together they passed beneath the portal of the once palace of the proud Somerset; pausing for a moment and looking at each other. Eva fancied Sidney became paler than usual; but she could not be certain; her head swam round, and motes—strange tiny forms—floated between her and him. She could not have defined her feelings; they were already of mingled hope and despair. She saw clearly enough that the 'elect' walked confidently in, knowing they were 'well hung'—they had touched upon their pictures, a grace only accorded to those whose station and knowledge in art ought not to require such a privilege. She rejoiced in the happiness of others, but she wished that Sidney had the same certainty! she pressed his arm more closely to her side; he did not tremble, but she felt that he breathed earnestly, as if nerved for trial, and she dared not look at him again. Numbers who pressed forward were haggard and care-worn; brows of noble mould, wrinkled by anxiety, not age, contracted over eyes filled with fire—blazing it out in discontent; some, again, with compressed mouth, so rarely defeated—men who shape their own fortunes; others whose frank features were changed into recklessness by disappointment; a few, bitter thinkers, who mistook a desire to paint for the power to do so; all these mingled with the visitors, some loving art for its holy self, others for its fashion; others, again, because the exhibition passed away time—that grand raw material of the skilful workman!

Sidney asked for a catalogue; the good-natured porter (one who was a truer friend and worthier patron of artists than many a high-born lord) expressed his regret that all he had were sold; he would have a fresh supply in a few minutes. Eva suggested they should not wait—they would be sure to see it.   They ascended the steep stairs, Sidney paler than ever, and suffering much fatigue from the ascent.   Some persons he had known met him; but so changed did he seem to them that they did not speak, wondering if it really were Sidney, and where he had found that lovely wife, who seemed unconscious of the admiration she excited.

At any other moment Sidney and Eva would have hung over the beauties that were illumined by the matchless pencil of Lawrence; they would have appreciated the natural sympathies of Wilkie; the magnificence—Nature's true magnificence—of Turner; but, to Eva, all appeared a mass of gilding and colour, with no more distinctness than a child's hand may give to the transient forms of the kaleidoscope; the one picture was stamped upon her mind: it was not there!

Few could imagine her feelings—more vivid, but hardly so intense as those of her husband: his bitter disappointment burned into her brain; insult offered, as she at that moment believed—premeditatedly—roused her indignation.   She then remembered the promises she had made to those who had entreated for the little she owed them; they struck upon her heart, with the dull monotonous clamour of a funeral bell.   Sidney, in whose name she had promised, would be considered an untrue man! Could he survive such an imputation!   Sidney!   Sidney to be deemed faithless to his word.   She felt that her powers of sustaining such a trial were passing away.   In a whirlwind of conflicting emotions, she talked, hardly knowing what she said.   She sprang to the next flight of stairs after her husband; but, eager as she was, she could not equal the rapidity of his movements.   "You see, you see; it is not here—nor here!" he repeated.   Then in a hoarse voice he added, "let us go down for a catalogue."   Eva followed him breathlessly, but she felt as if her heart was breaking.   When they were opposite the principal rooms he paused, drew her hand beneath his arm, and bending down whispered, "Do not sink now, my own heroic wife; you have sustained me through much worse than this—when all earthly friendship was far from us; it is not so now.   I am, you see, calm—calm! there may be some mistake,—bear up, Eva.   He who gave me such a treasure, will give me strength to keep it!—bear up, my darling—you always hoped more from this picture than I did!—bear up!"

Gaining strength from his, Eva muffled her face in her veil, and, clinging to his arm, they descended.

"A shilling," said the porter, as he handed the catalogue.

Sidney could not say he had it not; but he turned away.

"Pay me next time," added the man—whose generous heart was in his kindly countenance. How their fingers trembled among the leaves, as a bird rustles amid the foliage that surrounds its rifled nest; eagerly they glanced over it.

"H—H—H—No Sidney Herbert!"

"Sad want of room, sir; some of the very finest pictures rejected for want of room. A fine exhibition could be made of the rejected pictures," explained the kind porter, who comprehended the scene at once.

Sidney returned the catalogue.

"The gentleman looks tired," persisted the man; "better go and sit down in the sculpture-room."

Neither replied; but Eva's look thanked him.

"There it is again," he muttered, looking after them. "I often wonder how I have stood it so long—poor things!"

"You hear, Sidney; some of the finest pictures have been rejected for want of room," said Eva.

Oh, what agony was in the answering smile; what power—what eloquence—what anguish! too earnest, too intense for words. Heart understood heart. Never—never—never! in their long course of love, had each loved the other with such entireness of devotion as at that moment.

"My Eva!" he said. She felt him tremble; she hurried him to the open door. There, rushing forward, came the physician. Although the mourning crape was still on his hat, his face was charged with tidings of great good. He was too full of it to impute *their* changed looks to more than ordinary fatigue. "I am delighted to have found you," he exclaimed; "such true homage as you have received!" Before the sentence was concluded Sidney fell on his shoulder—to all appearance lifeless.

"I knew it would kill him," said Eva, as she wildly flung herself beside her husband. "And you knew it also, doctor; you have met him dressed for the funeral—dressed for the funeral," she repeated, utterly unconscious of her words and actions, or of the people who gathered round her.

"It has struck her more deeply than it has him," said the kind man; "and that at such a time!"

There was solemn music, that night, in the woods of Ard-Flesk; sometimes a hollow rushing sound would pass above and around the castle; the mightiest trees of the forest bowed to it, and the young saplings trembled; but the sky was clear, and the stars were bright—the meekest daisy could look up to them without closing a petal—there was something so sweet and full of charity in their gentle aspect. Sometimes, the music assumed a tone of tender melody, trembling amid the leaves, and issuing from the flowers; but never once was there a strain that could be called mirthful; the waters of the beautiful river Flesk were troubled, but not disturbed, and moaning sounds arose therefrom, as though they repeated, "She was ours—she was ours."—If there had been any to look into the deeps of the rapid river, they might have seen creatures shrouded in the long green weeds that tangle the limbs of the drowning, and net them to their fate! In what was called 'My lady's flower-garden,' beneath the great drawing-room of Ard-Flesk, and the window where, together, Eva and her mother once stood, during Cormac's illness, there is a lawn of exceeding beauty and verdure; and reposing as it does in a valley, old Doctor Magrath (who was accounted a philosopher as well as a physician) had said the lights that danced on it were phosphoric—how Randy tossed his arms and laughed aloud at his wisdom! Randy knew that on that same night the Fairy courts held solemn meeting on the very spot. They were there now —when the fair valley, as well as the crowded city, was shrouded in darkness—all were there—all, but Queen Nightstar; the light, the purity, the chief grace of the Fairy courts was wanting. Honeybell, as usual, pouted, and declared that two kingdoms were more than she could manage; that she should rejoice when Nightstar's caprice for mortal life was ended. "She had reasons," she added, with the increased dignity of mystery, "to declare it might be possible for the Queen of Air to appear before them very soon." This announcement was received with so much movement and acclamation by the Fairy troops, that if old Doctor Magrath had been near them, he would have been blinded by 'phosphoric light.'

The compliment paid to their favourite Queen, Honeybell received as a tribute to herself, and bowed and smiled graciously. At that moment the hollow rushing sound increased; as it approached, it changed into a universal wail. Sighs seemed heaved from the very bowels of the earth; the old halls sent forth groans piteous to hear; the affrighted spirits of the woods

and flowers sought refuge amid the leaves and blossoms of the earth—as THE BANSHEE floated onwards to Mucross! How the deep mysterious spirit lingered about the Old Abbey—how its transparent outline mingled with the shadows of the material world! the owl ceased to hoot, and the bat to flap its heavy path through the murky air; the beetle folded his armour over his filmy wings, and the death's-head moth trembled on the broad-leaved ivy. What had called her forth, and why did she circle round one particular spot? Why, descending slowly upon earth, did she clap her hands at intervals, and, though she cried not loudly, sob and moan that one so young should mate with the red earth-worm, and be closed up—until THE APPOINTED TIME—in the damp and lonely grave!

Those who watched—if any had been brave enough to do so—might have seen the awful shadow pausing, for a brief moment, upon one of the two mounds—of earth and stone—raised above the other graves in gloomy Mucross!

Drawn by Sir J. Noel Paton, R.S.A.
Engraved by H. Linton.

URELY and beautifully the moon had set; but her departure from among the stars had not diminished the brightness of the heavens. Midsummer eve was passing into Midsummer morning; they had saluted upon the mountains, and would soon meet in the valleys. And yet it seemed that twilight lingered longer than usual; or was it the countless multitude of spirit-beings floating in the atmosphere, and crowding the vale of the Flesk, that stayed the progress of day? Myriads hovered in the mist; every leaf and flower beneath was freighted with life; detachments were constantly arriving, as if some great event were waited for; and in the midst of all, Queen Honeybell held special court, upon the summit of a Rath, which commanded the most interesting spots in the Lake country—Ard-Flesk, and its towers and woods; the cleft-crown of Mangerton, the Long Range, and Eagle's Nest; the village of Cloghreen; the grey arches and green ivy of Mucross; Ross Castle, and the stately trees of Inisfallen; the trembling towers of Aghadoe, the Purple Mountain, and Macgillicudy's Reeks—all these objects, so varied and so apart, seemed concentrated by some magic power; while the Dovecote, crouching amid trees, sparkled like one huge diamond, illumined from within and without—every pane of its latticed windows, every moss and stone of the old gable, distinctly visible; the very Doe appeared transfixed and motionless, as if listening for some expected sound; at intervals, the crags of the Recks, touched by light, shone out against the soft grey sky; suddenly, stars of all colours sparkled among the foliage, then glittered upon the long grass, and vanished; THE BELLS OF THE OLD GABLE chimed the sweetest and wildest music

that ever floated through Cloghreen; every flower poured forth a melody, so calm and soft—the very echo of a sound; and still the fairy hosts augmented—those of the earth and air mingling in sweetest amity. There was much state in Queen Honeybell's court; all her officers, and ladies, and knights, and pages, were cognizant of some great ceremony, at the nature of which the attendant troops could only guess: her bees were in perpetual motion; while she herself was decked more gaudily than is warranted by good taste, and, more than once, she chid her husband's mirthful laughter.

"Our sister, Nightstar," she said, "has been sojourning in the land of state-form, and has, no doubt, made herself mistress of court etiquette! I would be in no way behind her in knowledge. Our poor sister is full of theories for mortals' purification; and, therefore, will the more rejoice that

the banishment of the Kelpies to the wild waters of the black North
is fixed and irrevocable."

A sudden illumination floating around the principal tower of Glen-
Flesk, attracted Queen Honeybell's attention. The Air-fairies landed
their Queen in single chant and chorus; bursting forth on the instant,
they sung her brightness—her tenderness—her purity—her self-sacrifice.

"She crossed the stormy waters," they said, "of the deep and
angry sea."

"She mingled with and tasted the wretchedness of human life, with
its weariness and sufferings."

"She hid her beauty under the wrinkles of age."

"She knew that the child of her adoption must quaff the cup of life:
but she was by, to sweeten its bitterness."

"Seeing and knowing all things, she passed from the artist's attic
to the gorgeous chamber of the dying Cormac; and when the life-beatings
of his earthly nature became feeble, she whispered thoughts of the good
he had power to work for the hereafter of his kindred and his people
—this as a foretaste of his happiness in that lofty world, of which it was
not HERS to speak!"

Again and again they waved their banners, shouting joy and honour
to their Queen!—their Queen who had triumphed; for Cormac, unstable
in purpose, but fervent in spirit, had passed to the tomb of his ancestors,
having bequeathed to SIDNEY the lordship and domain of ARD-FLESK!
And again, and again, their green banners fanned the air, perfumed by
the dews of night.

"She comes!" echoed through the trees; and, swift as a shooting
star, the expected Queen, more radiant than ever, stood beside her sister.

"She is safe! she is here!" resounded from rank to rank. Nightstar
returned the greetings of the multitudes, with folded wings, her arms crossed
over her transparent bosom, and every eye that drank in the power of her
purity and beauty, saw how her spirit rejoiced—that her task had been
accomplished; her frame quivered with emotion; her eyes beamed with
love and tenderness. When the bursts of welcome were somewhat
calmed, and the banners ceased to wave, and the music sunk amid the
echoes of the Eagle's Nest, she advanced to address the denizens of Fairy

Land; but as she turned towards the east, she espied the heralds of MORNING, proclaiming its presence on the hills.

"Behold!" she exclaimed, pointing to the fast-coming influences; "the hour is at hand: but to-night, friends, true and faithful—to-night! we will again make populous these glades and halls—to-night!—and for a purpose."

Where went they?—fanning the air with unseen wings, leaving the trail of their brightness above the dark morass—while in a moment, oblivious of the past, the cleft-crown of Mangerton and the crags of 'the Reeks'—mingled in dim obscurity with lingering clouds. The time-honoured arch of Mucross cast its shadow lightly over Cormac's new-made grave, spanning it as with a blessing! It swelled beside his mother's stately tomb, marked by a simple urn—recording, in compliance with his

latest wish, the plain inscription that preserves his name. The Castle
of Ross and the Island of Inisfallen, faded in the vapours of the Lake,
and the Eagle's Nest mingled with the Toomies and Glena! In brief time,
they would resume their proper characters; for morning moved noiselessly
and joyfully onward; it had not yet darted a single beam into the thickets

that shaded the Dovecote from the
summer's sun and the winter's wind;
but when it entered the long avenue of 'Patrician trees,' that led
to the stately mansion, it shone upon many scattered groups that were
waiting, joyfully and hopefully, to welcome home the lord of Ard-Flesk.

Against the green bench of the cottage, known to all who have thus
far watched Eva's footsteps in the pathways of life, reclined the form
of an aged man; his arm was so placed that his head rested upon it,
and his long white hair fell around his throat; his limbs were rather
shrouded than clothed, so loosely did his garments hang upon them.
Suddenly a bright light flashed upon his face—a lark, rising from the
grass, warbled forth her matin song, beating the air in time to her own
wild melody. Before this song commenced, the man's countenance had

been troubled; the features disturbed; the lines of age and suffering broken by the tremulousness of a wandering yet tender nature. So aged, within a score of months, had he become, that twenty tranquil years would not have left such records on the lofty brow—a very tower of dreams—that rose above his closed lips! The peasants—his near neighbours and dear friends, had said—"the woodcutter's heart was breaking ever since Miss Eva went:" and Kitty, putting in for a word of sympathy on her own account, declared "that hers was the same, only she did not show it so much."

On the Midsummer morning, when Sidney was to return as Lord of Ard-Flesk—on that morning, when the cup of Randy's happiness was full to overflowing, no one who had not seen him for a time could have recognised the guardian of Eva Raymond. He had changed into an almost spirit-likeness of his former self: the earthiness of his nature had

gradually disappeared; the once stalwart woodcutter was but the shadow of a manly frame; he wandered around his early haunts almost unconsciously, gathering herbs, caressing children, succouring the unfledged birds if they tumbled from their nests, visiting Geraldine's grave, and forgetting how minutes passed into hours when he folded his arms, and mused upon some passage in Eva's simple life, beside the Whitestone Well, or in the depths of the forest glades; he prayed much, but not where the peasants of the vale and mountain prayed together—not by carved cross or in consecrated aisle; he would climb the mountain to meet the rising sun, and offer his matins on its highest peak, his face turned towards England—kneeling alone, with outstretched arms and floating hair; the shepherd boys beneath, among the crags, crouching together—in awe not fear—wondering if, in his dreariness, he sought that spot to be the nearer God! That wild prayer finished, he would hood his eyes with his hand, and bend a never-satisfied gaze towards the English coast, fancying he saw the sea and ships, created by his own imaginings; his thoughts— no matter what he did—*were there*. His kind friend, even in her darkest

hours, wrote to him regularly a few kindly words; and he would ponder over the letters he could not read, with eyes full of unshed tears!

When Cormac's funeral passed to its resting-place, anticipated by the intelligence which the good doctor had so earnestly desired to communicate in the Hall of the Royal Academy, on his return from conducting the hearse on its journey—and when the land was ringing with joy, because those the people loved were coming to dwell among them, Randy, in reply to the warm congratulations of those who watched his footsteps, even more eagerly than usual, whenever he took his daily walk through the pretty VILLAGE OF CLOGHKEEN, to visit the one grave at Mucross—had said—"I knew it all! I see it; great glory and prosperity—a long reign —a flourishing land; the mountains will clap their hands, and the rivers sing for joy; blessings will shower down on them; the poor man's fire will burn brightly, and the young child dip white bread in the rich milk of the Kerry cow! Much learning will trouble the people, but they'll put up with it for the sake of the teacher. I'll see it, at times, though I'll not be in it; so best! I'd have nothing to do, when everything's going right. It troubles me a little that when THE HEIR is born—she who left her pleasant kingdom in the pure air to watch and ward my bright lady in her sorrow, will have no more call to her or hers; but she'll not be wanting, any more than poor Randy. What call has she to smooth calm water? to lay smiles upon smiles, or to scent sweet roses? She's done her duty to her god-child; she's turned evil into good. I could walk under the water, from one lake to the other, and not meet a single Kelpie—nothing worse than the sporting worm or the fisher king's followers!"

"But you're proud, Randy, that they're coming back," one would say.

"Proud's not the word," he would answer; "though the likes of you can't find a better. My heart's bothering the life out of me, till I see her. I'm gone then."

"You'll speak a good word for me, Randy, about the bit of land," hinted a cotter.

"You'll all speak your own words to them, boys, without any middle-man. My word won't be needed; their ears will be opened by their hearts, and their hands never be closed. No call for ' good words' when a just landlord's to the fore."

The woodcutter was far more calm, more self-possessed, when he heard they were really on their way, than he had been since Eva's departure; but he was also more melancholy: there were none of those wild bursts of excitement in which he had formerly indulged. Kitty said she could not bear to look at him, he was so unlike himself.

The lark had finished her song and disappeared before Randy woke; and he might have slept longer but for Kitty, who had been sitting, dressed in ' her best,' in the kitchen of the Dovecote; the old cat—old, although a daughter of our ancient friend—purring at her feet. After

enjoying awhile, in silence, the luxury of coming dignity—as housekeeper at Ard-Flesk—she rose and paced slowly forth to join the woodcutter.

"Are you going to stay there all day, Randy, astore!" she said, touching him with the black oak staff she had found, of late, a wonderful aid in the collecting of stray chickens, and a needful support to tottering footsteps. "Are you going to stay till the strength of the day pours down upon you, and every living creature in the whole town land gone up to Ard-Flesk to meet the young master and mistress?"

Randy rose, smiling like a child—a child that had tasted sorrow.

"I'll go by'n-by, maybe, Kitty, thank you, kindly."

"Just wait to break your fast, and come," she continued; "of all living, you have the best right to the first sight of them, even before myself and Doctor Magrath—I'll own to it."

"Thank ye kindly, Kitty."

"Come along, then: I'm younger than I was twenty years agone."

"Not yet, Kitty; I'll not go to Ard-Flesk yet."

"The whole univarse will be in it!" exclaimed Kitty, in a tone of paramount exultation; "and I don't know what's over you to think you'd not be to the fore among the foremost. You've been at your drames again, I see; but it's time they were over."

"It is—quite time. You're a wise woman, Kitty Kelly."

"And you won't come?"

"God be with you, Kitty; not yet."

"The bands are up from Killarney, and there's loads of highborn ladies and gentlemen from all parts: and knowing you're such a favourite, every one would be hand and glove with you; and it's many a present you'd get."

"Of what?"

"Of money; and scarce enough it's been."

"Money!" repeated the woodcutter, and a flush strangely brightened his features. "Money!—the dirty dross! Money! oh, then, the lowness of people's hearts is a grate trouble to me! And you, so honest and true, to be letting such mane thoughts into your mind at such a time! It's little call I'll have for money!" This was said in so melancholy a tone that Kitty was not angry at the reproof, but hobbled through the garden, not pausing to wonder why there was so little water in the Tore Fall, nor lingering longer than was needed to cross herself at the Whitestone Well. Relieved by the absence of every human being, Randy was not as insensible to the caresses of the tame Doe as he had been to Kitty's request; the creature entered the gate she left unfastened, and commenced licking his hands, pausing occasionally to look into his face, with its deep, soft, hazel eyes. Randy enfolded her neck with his arm, and pressed her head to his bosom, and talked to her as though she understood his words. "She's coming, avourneen deelish; she's coming! as a grand lady, they say. They think she'll roll down the grate avenue to the shouts of the people and the noise of loud music, and bow to many a high head that will bend low to her for the first time; but they're wrong, bright eyes! they don't know her as we do. She'll come first to the Dovecote. She'll enter it, as she always did, like a sunbame. She'll press the ould Bible to her heart, and bend her knees beside her mother's bed—don't I know her! The devotion is in her; but not for what the world worships. She'll rise as pure out of prosperity as she did out of the black trouble. I'll not forget it to poor Kitty, that she said I had a right to the first look; and you, my dappled darling, you'll miss your Randy soon; but I'll have my turn with the rest, and spend many a moonlight in the ould places: pleasant times we'll have of it! And yet I'd rather stay as I am a little longer, only for the weight of clay that's round me!" And so he continued until the afternoon, talking incoherently to every familiar bush and flower, apostrophising the old gable, and reproving the weathercock for creaking at such a time; taking no note of the sounds of music and laughter with which every breeze was freighted: nor heeding the boat-race, nor contributing a single stick to the bonfires which that night were to blaze a welcome upon every hill. "All is decked in Mucross," he muttered to himself; "I did that yesterday."

The intense heat of the day was passed, and Randy, becoming more and more restless, stood on the mound above the Whitestone Well; he commanded a view of the avenue of Ard-Flesk; he saw the flags floating, and the noisy music jarred upon his ear. Suddenly there was a heaving of the multitude; the great gates, heavy with garlands, were thrown open; the servants marshalled on the steps and along the hall, under the able direction of the late Lady Elizabeth's old butler; a carriage and four entered; the echoes of the Eagle's nest took up the shouts, and sent them round the lakes. The carriage proceeded slowly up the avenue. Randy covered his face with his hands as he descended, so that he could not see that the carriage only contained two gentlemen—the

London physician and the old officer; while others, who had been waiting at the entrance, turned away with an air of disappointment.

Randy sat on the grass bench, his fingers pressed upon his eyes, but not so closely that tears did not stream through them. Had he been mistaken! Had she really gone first to Ard-Flesk? No, no—two rough paws were on his shoulders, and Keeldar's hot tongue and panting breath upon his cheek. Clutching the dog to his heart, he looked in at the window—there was Eva! her lips upon her mother's Bible, kneeling beside her mother's bed! Sidney, too, was there; pale, almost as a spectre, but with promise of health in his bright eye and erect carriage. A few moments more, and the woodcutter had his reward.

"Why Randy—*dear* Randy—is it you; can it be possible—is it you?"

"As much as there's left of me, darling," was the plaintive reply; and then quite unable to control his feelings, he bent his head over Keeldar, and wept aloud.

"You will soon be quite well again, now we are returned, dear old friend," said Sidney; "and we shall have gay times at Ard-Flesk. You shall be my prime minister, and take the same care of——" and Sidney whispered some words into the old man's ear. They failed to produce a smile.

"She's under God's care, and needs no care of mine now, sir," he said, conquering his tears. "I knew she'd come first to the Dovecote. I did not tell them, and if I had, they would not have believed me." And then he advanced, and with his fingers traced Eva's features. "It can't be a wholesome place that England," he said, shaking his head; "and there's been heaviness on that brow, and tears in those eyes—often; but it's over—it's ended; prosperity and peace are met, and will remain with them!"

Keeldar's bloodshot eyes rolled with sullen distaste upon the Doe; he did not like her to share his lady's caresses; but he treated her rather with contempt than with ill-temper, and she did not seem inclined to renew the acquaintance.

As the little party quitted the cottage to proceed by the woodpath to Ard-Flesk, Eva paused to gaze upon it again. "Shall I be as happy in that lordly place," she said, "as I have been here?"

" To the full, dear lady, because you're the same still; your nature's not changed; your bed is made ABOVE, by the blessings of the poor, and you won't spoil it, avourneen ! "

Her heart was too full to reply, and she leaned on the arm of Sidney for support.

" In adversity," whispered her husband, " you were my staff—my shield; and now, in prosperity, you cling to me as feebly as a child."

The woodcutter followed, and more than once Eva turned and smiled upon him, Sidney asking various questions, which Randy answered briefly, shrinking from the wild huzzas of the excited people, when they perceived them, and twisting his fingers in the long ears of old Keeldar.

And so they entered the Halls of Ard-Flesk—their happy owners!

No sound is more magnificent than the swell of a multitude of voices sending a shout aloft, impregnating the air with the enthusiasms of earth, until the cry is echoed through the blue vault of heaven; the people shouted, but far more touching than the shouts were the sobs, and prayers, and blessings, of Eva's humble friends. She made grievous mistakes in her recognitions, speaking to the juniors as if they were the elders of a family, so that, at last, Kitty, "seeing," as she said, "there was no good in Randy," identified them with her staff. But Eva was quickly overpowered by the scene; Sidney supported her into the great oak-panelled dining-room; it was one of those rooms of sombre magnificence which are delightful to write about—to walk through—to paint—but not to live in. The panelling shone like a succession of darkened mirrors, with here and there a grim family portrait; the carvings were heavy, the enrichments of the ceiling faded, and the Turkey carpet seemed as if it had gathered itself up from the polished boards; but the windows looked into the woods—the deep, deep musical woods, with their eloquent leaves and waving boughs; and the atmosphere was cool and pleasant. Eva's eyes wandered from one to another of the paintings; no matter how poor, or dull, or quaint, a picture may be, it suggests something; but Sidney, whose eyes were fixed on her, could not help smiling, thinking, as he did, that though she looked she saw nothing. He was mistaken. "Sidney!" she exclaimed, springing forward, "Sidney—look!"

He was as much astonished as she was; for there, upon the walls, set in all the splendour of new gilding, hung his own picture—the picture concerning which he had never inquired since the day of his fearful disappointment in London; there it hung. He walked towards it, followed by the physician.

"Full of great faults," muttered the artist; "and yet for a rejected picture, not so *very* bad! How came it here?"

The woodcutter's wild laugh made Eva start.

"Poor Randy loses his wits at times, and finds them again. The daisy looks the sun in the face; a whisper came to me over the sea, and said—one told him—he's in the churchyard now; and were you to sit by his side the length of a summer day, he would tell you nothing."

"We must watch our old friend," said Eva, in a whisper to her husband; "it breaks my heart to see him thus—how wild and strange he seems." Again she looked at the picture. "How it joys me to see it."

Sidney and Eva gazed at each other for a moment—steadfastly. "What a monitor it will be!" he said. "While I was painting in that drapery——"

"Which is as light as though a full-drawn sigh would waft it from the canvas," exclaimed Eva, triumphantly.

"Well, while I was painting that, my arms aching from weakness, so that I could hardly hold the pencil, you sat beside me, converting the wire of an old bird-cage into chain-armour, which we were too poor to hire, to deck my hero in; you did your work, dearest, though your fingers bled!"

"And these plumes, these golden goblets—an artist's gold—all on his canvas; that boy holding up the grapes, so ripe and luscious—we never knew who sent us those ripe grapes!"

Another wild laugh from Randy again startled them both.

"We toiled to seek a fitting model for that boy among the active-earning faces of the city children; there was none whose brow was free from thought—not one who smiled unconsciously! What a record it is!" persisted Sidney. "What a lesson it must ever be to me! Where the brightest inspirations were shrivelled by the beggar's want; and you, bright angel, shining, as angels do, more brightly in the dark! companioned —counselled—bore with—prayed for—me! Of all the gifts that Cormac lavished on me, I ought to value that picture most. If pride—or arrogance —enter my bosom, *that* should drive them thence; if genius needs protection, *that* recalls to *me*, its sufferings, and my duty."

"Poor Randy!" whispered the woodcutter, "he will soon be going; but if the Lady Eva were to ask man with the bright star to let him stay another year, she would."

"You shall stay many years, dear old friend; do not look so wildly into the woods, Randy; you shall tell me all your dreams again, and how you did battle with the Kelpies for my sake."

"They're gone!" he exclaimed, eagerly; "gone—not one in the whole country! Sail away, Queen of the Lakes! there's nothing to trouble the.

waters now—Don't stay longer looking at a picture; they all wait, my lady, in the hall! Old Doctor Magrath has not had a word with you yet. It's all your own, dear—to work goodness with—that's it! If we don't work goodness, we turn the high gift into bad service. Master Sidney, sir, come away from the dead picture to the living people; the evening's closing fast, and I haven't long to be with you!"

They set these warnings down to his usual wanderings; Eva soothing him, as mothers soothe their children. As the night advanced, bonfires blazed on every hill, and it seemed as if the rejoicings were but commencing; the responsibility attendant upon the duties which followed their wealth, hallowed the joy of those whose love had been weighed in the balance, and not found wanting. They escaped from their friends, and set forth to a mound that commanded a view of the Dovecote; Eva longed to see it STEEPED IN THE MOONLIGHT. The little lame boy of their London lodging limped past them in the hall.

"The place is so large, madam," he said, "that I'll find my little room, and go to bed; I'm tired following the old lady who lodged under you. I called and cried to her, but she would not stop." Eva assured him that was merely his fancy; old women were all so like each other. But he said, "he knew better than that."

Eva felt relieved when the cool air fanned her brow. They walked together, enjoying the eloquent silence when heart only speaks to heart— thinking the same thoughts—framing the same prayers—creating the same hopes—neither quite realising the positive scene, as *their own*, and both longing to nestle in the Dovecote—thinking they should be more happy in a cottage, as people who are doomed to castle life sometimes do. It looked most lovely in its little valley, steeped in a moonlight as bright, as clear, as warm, as if sunshine bountifully mingled with it. It was very calm—calm even to holiness!

"If my mother had but lived to see this day!" whispered Eva. Sidney pressed her to his heart. A few yards in advance of where they stood, Randy crossed the wood-path. Sidney called to him. The old man came immediately, so pale and wild in his appearance that Eva entreated him to return to the castle; he should have a little room to himself, and be quite a king, she said. He did not seem to under-

stand her words, but kneeling before her, as a child kneels at its
mother's knee, entreated her pardon. "I might have minded better,

darling, and kept more trouble from you. Yet,
I'd have died, any hour of the day or night, to
serve you, or the mistress, or Master Sidney; and
grand as you are now, you'll not forget the pleasant
times of childhood; their innocence will come back to you, and light the
dark path you'll have to take one day or other—You'll think of the
pleasant times when I brought you the wood-strawberries, and the young
birds, and the flowers; and hunted the children to get their learning; and
nursed the fawn. You'll think of the good and forget the bad. Hush!"

he exclaimed, half-rising. "Hush! did you hear that? the first blast of the royal bugle! and now the trumpet! Hush! never did such a note as that rouse the old stag on Glena! there's not a lord about the place who dare ring out such a call as that!"

"Observe how he listens, as though the echoes were reverberating in the distance," said Sidney.

"Hush! don't speak—only look! It's no wonder I'm going blind with their brightness," he continued. "Ay, in with you to the Dovecote, and light it up; there's nothing to scare ye there! The first bit of the butter is on the doorpost, the crickets are fed, and the sweet mead is ready in the chiny bowl! Look, they are chaining the weathercock, and putting their spells round the old gable."

"His wits have quite left him," whispered Eva, as she clung to her husband. "Our good doctor must see to him. And now he bends low to the fancied multitude, peopling the scene with his imaginings."

"Salute them! salute them!" he exclaimed to Eva, who saw that his excitement was increasing. "It is their WELCOME to the lady of Ard-Flesk! From the four corners of the winds—from earth and air they gather—ah, ah! The great bee who punished the Kelpie page—isn't he grate! Whisht! how he booms! Hornet and wasp! hanging spider! leaf-rolling worm! sly field mouse! and matted mildew!—have at them all, my brave ones with the golden banners! Ay, ay, I forgot—it's love, not war, you're bent on now: bow to them, lady; bow when I do! It's grate honor they pay you, mavourneen deelish—grate honour intirely."

Eva, to humour him, did as he desired, and the old man's face became flushed with intense delight. He moved restlessly about, bowing and pushing back the hair from his fevered brow;—then, addressing the invisible world, he exclaimed—

"See, fair Nightstar, she bends to your goodness! bright Honeybell! there's a welcome for you, as well as for her; don't be jealous, sweet Honeybell! Look! there is a ring on the earth, and a ring in the air! they are above us—around us; the Queens bow to the lady—the lady to the Queens!" For an instant he looked into Eva's face. "What large pearls are on your cheek, darling. It isn't tears they'd be—what should tears do there now? What call have you to tears?" Eva could not control her emotion. Randy wandered again. "They are going! it was well done—it was well done! Yes—you see I must follow. If you had asked another year when she looked at you; but it's too late now—there's nothing for us to do when love is prosperous; nothing to do then!—you don't want prayer or blessing now from the poor woodcutter. Don't you hear them calling me? Not that—that's the wind! but now—Ay, ay;" and, bending reverently, he at first went slowly on, and then rushed into the thicket.

"Follow him, Sidney," said Eva. "Poor faithful creature! his mind is a ruin so thickly overgrown with such sweet fancies, that to restore the one you destroy the beauty of the others. He is out of sight."

"I might as easily follow the track of the red-deer," replied Sidney: "we will send after him. You are almost fainting, my own dear one; I should not have suffered this."

"We shall see him no more!" sobbed Eva. "The moment I saw him to-day, I felt that he had but tarried to welcome our return. We shall never see our faithful Randy more!"

The next day, and the next, witnessed troops of eager visitors crowding to Ard-Flesk; but they could not divert Eva from her anxiety respecting her old friend. He was sought for in wood, in river, on mountain, and in valley; but in vain; and evening after evening the sweet lady of Ard-Flesk wept as she said, "We shall see him no more!" and the echoes caught the sound, and repeated "no more," in saddest cadence, from the Eagle's nest to the Purple Mountain.

The Dovecote was preserved as a temple for repose and thoughtfulness—a place of self-questioning and sacred communion with all the memories of their lives—a place wherein to keep the heart's true jubilee—holding the feasts of childhood and of age upon its lawns—distributing alms within its porch; all living things therein tasting repose and liberty. Once in the deepening twilight of her birthday, Eva, her first-born sleeping on her bosom, fancied she saw the woodcutter pass and repass her window; and, once—on a Midsummer Eve—the child to whom Keeldar had transferred all the attention his extreme age permitted him to pay, told his mother that a very old man, with flowing white hair, had met him in the wood, and looked at him so long, that though he was not afraid, he was glad to return to her.

The peasants speak of Randy, even now, as present at times—not in the flesh, but in the spirit; a sort of moving shadow, yet shadowless; they tell the children going to the mountain, that, if they are good, the woodcutter will take care that no harm shall come to them, on hill or glen—by water or wild. They say he hides the tender fawns from the foxes, and saves the young trees from the fury of the east wind; they tell of his wondrous knowledge, of the dangers which surrounded Eva's childhood, and of his prophecies concerning her, whose nature, impressed by the Divinity, imbibed the great and useful knowledge, that woman's true happiness—the only happiness her pure soul can taste of, unalloyed—consists in

LOVING AND BEING BELOVED.

www.ingramcontent.com/pod-product-compliance
Lightning Source LLC
Chambersburg PA
CBHW020940120726
47905CB00008B/2604